I0593060

A CERTAIN KIND OF POWER

BY RYAN BUTTA

This book is for Carolina, for believing in the absurd, the impossible, the ridiculous; in other words, me.

"*The Argentine feels that the universe is nothing but a manifestation of chance, the fortuitous concourse of Democritus' atoms; philosophy does not interest him. Nor does ethics: the social realm, for him, is reduced to a conflict of individuals or classes or nations, in which everything is licit, save being ridiculed or defeated.*"

Jorge Luis Borges 'Nota sobre (hacia) Bernard Shaw',
Otras Inquisiciones, 1952.

CHAPTER 1

Mike Costello looked skywards. The sun was a pale-yellow orb stamped on an uncorrupted blue. Below his feet the detritus of humanity that accumulated in the gutters swirled about him. Inside his sock, under the ball of his foot, Mike could feel the two folded twenty-peso notes that he had hidden there for insurance against robbery. The notes represented a cab ride home or at least to the nearest hospital.

His body pulsed to the pounding of a bass drum that beat the air like an external heart. He could feel it deep inside his ears, a baseline to the swarming clamor that cascaded from the walls of the Fortress, an audio crush that mixed with the fevered chanting, police boot-steps and the thud and whir of a chopper that flew low overhead. And above it all the screams of street hawkers vying for the business of this alcohol-soaked, ragtag army.

To Mike's left, two policemen shoved a young man against a wall. The youth's hands were clasped behind his ahead in submission. It didn't save him from two practiced blows from a wooden truncheon to the back of his legs. He crumbled to a kneel. Mike turned away. It wasn't his fight and he had his own legs to think about.

Either side of him, groups of men swarmed the footpaths and spilled onto roads that had been closed to vehicle traffic. Some chanted songs, keeping time with fists punching the air. Others twirled shirts around their heads until they became a blur, bare torsos already glistening with sweat despite the low, winter temperatures.

The smell of smoke and beer and cooking meats drew Mike to a makeshift stall where a man dressed in the dark crimson of the masses stood behind a collapsible table that looked like living up to its name at any second. Scarred hands cut rough slits into bread rolls before stuffing them with a chorizo sausage straight from the homemade charcoal grill. A splash of chimichurri sauce and the *choripan* was handed to a hungry customer in exchange for a few crumpled, notes. The money pocketed and the procedure repeated. A young child, perhaps the vendor's son, stood behind the grill. A ripped square of cardboard served as a fan, which he used to coax a red glow from the coals with an artful beating of the air, one eye fixed on his father.

"*Cerveza?*" Mike asked as he came to the head of the line. A gruff shake of the head the answer, the hands not stopping their assembly-line work. Mike needed a beer. If only to chase away the headache that had been building all day, demanding attention. He couldn't even remember why he had opened the bottle last night, alone in his apartment, Dylan's *Blood on the Tracks* for self-flagellating company. He took his food. A man with a home-inked tattoo that ran the length of his forearm shouldered past him.

Mike rejoined the flow of humanity. At the barriers that led into the bowels of the Fortress a policeman stopped him with a raised hand. Mike spread his arms and legs, still holding his half-eaten *choripan*, and allowed himself to be patted down. He raised his shirt to show he wore no belt nor carried a knife or anything more lethal. The officer waved him through.

Mike pushed the stub of his *choripan* into his mouth and shoved both hands deep into his pockets, clutching wallet in one hand and keys in the other, the only protection against the attention of pickpockets.

A concrete tunnel carried the crowds into the stadium. Caged fluorescent lights threw a dull glow through the cobwebs and underground filth. The temperature felt a few degrees higher. And those few degrees were humid, heavy with human heat and sweat and swearing. The tunnel stank of beer, cigarettes, and the piss that snaked under his feet; yellow streams that flowed from beneath the shirtless, shiny backs either side of him as men relieved themselves. One shouted over his shoulder at his friends to go on ahead, another swore as he was shoved in the back.

The stream of humanity shuffled along, and Mike emerged into the bright afternoon light. The vibrant green that carpeted the stadium greeted him and set in motion the familiar internal buzz of expectation, the tingle of skin, the reflexive opening and closing of his fists as if pumping the buzz throughout his body.

Mike Costello had always been a football fan growing up in the States. Yes, he would concede there was more diving than a Jacques Cousteau Ocean Special, but football was in the Costello's Sicilian genes. As a boy he had called it soccer, an attempt to assimilate with those classmates whose surnames didn't end in O or weren't prefixed with a Del or a Di. In Argentina he had slipped into the local lexicon and called it football ever since.

He adopted Lanus as his team soon after arriving in Buenos Aires. The football club formed in January 1915. It appealed to Mike that while Europe tore itself apart on the battlefields of France, a world away the men of Lanus were gathering to form a sporting club.

If Mike had been born in Argentina he was sure he would have been born in the graffitied, gritty, contrarian streets of Lanus. He felt an affinity for the working-class people of the southern suburb with graffitied walls topped with fragments of broken glass, glorious filthy dive bars, cracked asphalt streets decorated with burnt-out car shells, and a standing warning on walking alone after dark. He identified with those who lived and died within blocks of where they were born.

In those first years in Argentina, Mike attended the Lanus home fixtures as often as he could, catching the number 37 bus from the city out to the Lanus station and making the march to the stadium. He rode the bus south from the city center, packed in shoulder to shoulder, often standing for the trip, alongside fellow supporters, his getaway at the end of the week. He didn't explain his little obsession to any of his friends or clients, who just looked at him puzzled when he turned down their offer of a weekend at the polo farm or when he made an informed remark about the southern suburb that most residents of Buenos Aires, the *porteños,* had heard of but never visited. Lanus felt like his little secret, a piece of Buenos Aires where he felt at home.

Today was the last game of the season. The team had not had a good year. Week after week, Mike watched from different city bars as Lanus put in another woeful performance, cementing their position at the bottom of the league ladder. He had tired of hurling abuse at the screen, feeling the pitiful eyes of the waiters on him even as he overheard their whispered conversations, questioning each other as to who would be mad enough to follow Lanus. But today was unmissable. Lanus versus Banfield.

The "Classic of the South", as it was known, was an intense, heated, dangerous, violent rivalry fueled by hatred, alcohol and proximity (Banfield's stadium was four short kilometers from the Fortress). For Lanus, victory today would still mean finishing last, but they would prevent Banfield, the league leader, from securing the title, for this weekend at least—a satisfaction almost as great as winning the league itself. A loss would mean watching Banfield celebrate their title at the Fortress.

Zealots dressed in team colors pushed their way to lucky spots; anonymous places on the terraces from where historic victories had been watched, opponents humiliated. Mike shouldered his way to the end of the pitch and climbed the concrete terraces behind the goal. The organized fans, the *hinchada*, packed in here at every game. Lost in the anonymity of this heaving tumult, Mike had found identity.

Mike jostled his way into the crowd, bobbing his head to the chants though not confident with either his voice or sense of rhythm to join the jumping mass. He turned and looked around the stadium, it was a sea of waving flags, flares, white smoke, arcing projectiles and thousands of bobbing heads as the fans jumped and sang in unison. Beneath his feet Mike could feel the concrete and steel of the stadium flex and tremble under the force of their fanaticism. This is what he had come for. The proximity to the zeal, to place himself at the center of this organized chaos and mayhem and absorb and savor it, to feel its current run, like low-voltage electricity, over the surface of his skin. That it could at any moment overflow into violence and destruction, as he had witnessed before, added to the addiction.

In the middle of the terrace just a few rows back, Mike made out a large figure draped in a crimson cape that hung over a matching shirt and blue jeans. Dark-caramel skin and black hair, long, hanging down to the waist. Mike smiled at the sight of *el Indio*, the Indian, and leader of the Lanus *hinchada*.

Indio appeared content, ready. By now the illegal tickets would have been sold, the counterfeit merchandise hawked at the traffic lights around the stadium, the threats to "win or else" delivered to both the players and coaching staff alike. The police had been paid off, both at the commanding level at the local station and a little extra for the guys on the ground at the stadium; the weapons and alcohol had been smuggled into the stadium; and Indio's army of soldiers were positioned around the stadium, warmed with the drink and attuned to react to any command that Indio chose to give.

The shrill of the referee's whistle and the encouraging, enveloping roar of the home crowd that signaled the start of the game ripped Mike's attention back to the field. Banfield's first attacking probe ended with the ball straining against the back of the net in front of Mike, thanks to Banfield's diminutive number 9. A ferocious strike from what, even to Mike, staring into the afternoon sun, was an outrageous offside position. Fifty thousand pairs of eyeballs lasered in on the linesman who stood still, his flag solemn and limp, hanging by his side. The goal stood.

Silence pulsed around the stadium before a cacophony of whistles and abuse erupted; flares, shoes torn from sockless feet and other objects, rained down on the field. A few meters in front of Mike, fans scaled the mesh fencing that had been erected to keep them off the pitch. Those that couldn't scale the fencing hooked their fingers through the mesh and leant back, faces raised to the skies, hands hauling against the mesh, complicating the efforts of those trying to go over the top.

The man beside Mike flung his full coterie of local insults onto the pitch with a healthy portion of spittle for company. There were the usual insults about the pussy of the referee's grandmother, mother, and sister.

Mike stood detached from the mayhem around him, an isolated observer until a missile thrown from higher up in the terraces arced over his head, and a light shower of liquid rained from the beer cup and interrupted his enjoyment. He rubbed a thumb across the droplets of amber liquid that lay on his arm and raised it to his nose. He was pissed. On and off. He wiped his arm dry on his jeans.

Play restarted, Lanus controlled the ball well and applied pressure to the Banfield defense. The attacking intent served to calm the crowd somewhat, until Banfield intercepted a sloppy pass and counterattacked in a crisp, neat transition that illustrated the difference in skill between the two teams. No amount of passion or bitter hatred would bridge that gap today.

Banfield glided downfield and the Lanus goalkeeper rushed out and shut down the play, diving on the ball at the attacker's feet before a shot could be loosed. The Banfield striker launched himself over the prone keeper in dramatic style, landed and completed three well-practiced rolls inside the 18-yard box before curling up into a writhing ball of agony and misery. The theatrics were greeted by a hysterical howl that lapped around the stadium. The referee, hair slicked back, shorts a little too high, ran towards the Lanus goal, whistle in mouth, his outstretched hand pointing to the penalty spot. The high-pitched whistles and jeers of derision transformed into a more sinister roar of battle as the referee's decision registered.

Mike looked at Indio who nodded his head. A discreet signal, that would not be picked up by the commercial-television cameras, that triggered a wave of young, drunk, angry, shirtless men storming to the perimeter fence, the first row already halfway up the mesh. Mike looked and wondered. What would happen if he joined the throng, screamed, let out the anger, frustration, and thwarted dreams that festered inside him? The thought passed, and he stood still and allowed the *hinchada* to rush by him.

On the pitch the players had confronted the referee, hands flapping in the face of the unfortunate official. The offended players were so intent on remonstrating that they were unaware of their own rioting fans.

The police that lined the sides of the pitch, dressed in full riot gear with Indio's contribution to their pensions no doubt tucked deep in their back pockets, remained seated, riot shields laying unattended on the ground beside them.

In front of Mike the first hooligan had cleared the perimeter fence and hit the ground running; a speeding, arrow aimed at the heart of the Lanus players that had encircled the referee. The hooligan arrived with a drunken, flying karate kick that found its mark in the back of the number 8 who crumpled under the unexpected attack.

The players turned on the fan and retaliated in defense of their team mate. As they did so, they at last registered the crimson tide of their own supporters bearing down on them. Prioritizing their own well-being over any thoughts of admirable defense of their colleague, the players fled in all directions like a ball of sardines that had discovered a yellowfin tuna in their midst.

The quicker players were successful in reaching the safety of the players' tunnel while the slower ones were cornered and herded into isolated groups and set upon by rabid balls of fans in a flurry of fists and feet. Mike watched clear-eyed as the hooligans stripped players of their uniforms. One player emerged dressed only in underwear and boots, blood streaming from his mouth and ears. He received a final kick to the ass, and more abuse as he was ejected from the ring of vengeance.

The message was clear. These players were not fit to wear the colors. This wasn't the consequence of today's dismal showing. This was for the season of mediocrity that had culminated in the humiliation of allowing Banfield to be crowned champions in the Fortress.

Mike's eyes scanned the stadium. At the opposite end of the pitch a small group of supporters, clad in the green and white of Banfield, jumped and chanted, flares firing off into the afternoon sky. He could feel their elation as a physical vibration through the air. On their flank a line of riot police held back a small group of Lanus supporters who were trying to get at the Banfield fans.

Another group of thugs had broken into the members' stand and were pulling at the plastics seats as if hauling a body from a burning vehicle. A chair came free, brandished skyward before being thrown down onto the field. No specific target, destruction the objective.

Mike sat down on the concrete steps. He smelt of beer and cigarettes. And piss. Smoke from the flares stung his eyes. He now remembered why he had opened that bottle last night. Yesterday was his birthday. The tenth one since he had arrived in Argentina. He looked around at the scenes playing out before him. He slumped to his haunches and held his head. Life was short and getting shorter.

CHAPTER 2

O n the sidewalk outside bar Danzon an old woman slumped against the wall, her bare feet and legs extending out in front of her. The minutely wrinkled skin of her face hung across sharp-edged cheekbones. Two eyes that looked like bullet holes in a paper target peered out. Filthy rags served as clothes, poor protection from the Arctic winds blowing from the south. Her bony hand extended in a silent plea. A small bowl waited by her cracked heels with a few coins.

Mike stopped, reached for his wallet and pulled out a five-peso note. He dropped the money into the bowl and looked at the woman. She pounced on it with alarming speed and smuggled it away inside her rags. He could smell the neglect that hung tight to her unwashed body.

"Don't waste it on food," he said. "Go and get yourself a drink or something stronger." Charity with strings was no charity at all.

He took the steps up to the bar and he considered the journey that leads to this state of abandonment. At what point does it become too late to turn around?

"Rusty nail," said Mike, straddling a stool. "Lots of ice." He watched as the bartender reached for the

Drambuie on the shelf. Johnny Cash strummed the opening bars of "Personal Jesus" over the sound system. It gave the bar a gravitas it didn't deserve.

"Any particular whiskey, sir?" the bartender asked Mike over his shoulder.

"Your cheapest," said Mike. "If I wanted expensive whiskey I wouldn't be mixing it."

He had returned from the game in a foul mood that had improved to a small degree once out of earshot of the stadium. He had ridden the taxi back to the city in silence. As he crossed the divide from southern Buenos Aires to central Buenos Aires he had let his mind wander to the Limay River, the ice-melt flow that wound its way around Bariloche far from Buenos Aires. He had fished it once, small dry flies floated down the riffling waters, the rhythm of the cast inducing a meditative state. He went back there often, in his mind, when the city became too much. Today it made no difference. His troubles were too deep to be washed away by the clear waters of the Limay.

If he hadn't already arranged to meet Alex Harper he would have been happy to sit at home with Dylan and another bottle and finish what he started last night.

He looked at his watch. Harper was late. No surprise, but still annoying. The bartender placed his drink on a napkin in front of him. Cash was asking him to take second best. What else was there to take?

Alex Harper worked at the British embassy. His cheap business card, one corner bent over from being stuffed in a wallet, standard diplomatic issue, said "Second Secretary". Mike had been around enough embassies to know that second secretaries were never second secretaries.

He had befriended Harper's predecessor, another secretary, second or third he couldn't remember, and the friendship had transferred to Harper without interruption. As second secretary, Harper had responsibility, among other things, for keeping an eye on the Argentine political scene. Any British company new to Argentina would seek out Alex Harper for his insights and opinions. Harper would give them the briefest of overviews and then suggest they speak with Mike. It was then up to Mike to turn the lead into a client.

Harper never asked for money in return. His currency was information and Mike would honor the deal by answering Harper's questions as best he could or providing his new clients with advice that may have been more in the interests of Her Majesty than their shareholders'. Mike always discharged his debt. Harper wasn't a man that Mike wanted to owe anything to. The arrangement worked well, even if it meant frequent meetings with Alex Harper.

Mike's workload was light most weeks and he was grateful for any clients that Harper pushed his way. His was not a business that could be advertised. It was word of mouth, long lunches, and discreet referrals. No matter the professional standards he reached, clients were hesitant to recommend him to family and friends. He assumed proctologists faced the same business-development struggles.

Mike heard Alex Harper before he saw him. It was still early in the evening and the bar was empty; no need to swivel on the stool to place a name to the heavy, careless footsteps that ascended the stairs behind him.

"What the fuck are you drinking?" Alex said in way of greeting.

"Rusty nail. Want one?"

"No, I do fucking not."

Alex ordered a beer. "How was the game?" An audible intake of breath followed the question, as if he was trying to suck the words back into his mouth or maybe suppress a hiccup. It was a habit he had, a sentence followed by a sharp breath, sometimes mid-sentence. It gave the impression that he was breaststroking through his sentences, emerging for a gulp of air. Whatever its genesis, Mike found it annoying.

"Next question," ordered Mike.

The two men drank in silence as the bar started to fill. Mike could feel Alex's eyes on him as he drank—those heavy eyes that stared out from under drooping eyelids, giving Alex the appearance of permanent drowsiness. He always seemed to be looking up as if using his pupils to keep the eyelids open.

A young couple came in and sat at the end of the bar.

"First date," said Mike, observing the attentive posturing of the young man.

"What's your story?" Alex asked, catching Mike off guard. He hadn't come for this.

"My story? What do you mean? What's anyone's story?"

"Wife? Family? You've never mentioned anything, but I presume there must have been something once. Man can't get as bitter as you without some help."

Mike took a deep breath. He felt about two whiskies short of being able to go into that. He never spoke about it, if one didn't count the internal conversations that formed the background chatter of his bad days. He liked that about socializing with diplomats, it was rare that talk strayed from themselves.

"No one. Just me."

"Never any one?" Alex insisted.

"Years ago," he said.

"Aha. Now we're getting somewhere. And?" coaxed Alex in that way he did that made you open up even as you tried to hold it all back.

"Emily Parisi," Mike relented. "Met at college. Talked about marrying, starting a family. Her family was from Sicily. Promised I'd take her there on our honeymoon. Sicily," he said, shaking his head. He missed Sicily. Which was odd as he had never been there. "She was one of five. Three sisters and a brother. Wanted a big family. The Italian way. But I was like any young guy. Restless, wanted to see the world first. Thought she'd always be there."

Harper sat staring ahead and allowed Mike to fill the silence between them. "I enrolled in the Peace Corps and got sent down to Peru. First night down there I thought, what have I done? I missed her so much. I decided that as soon as I'd finished my tour I'd go home and marry her. I started looking at arrangements to get to Sicily. To surprise her.

"A month later, I got a phone call from her father. Said she had been killed in a traffic accident." He raised his glass to his mouth, burying his head in the alcohol fumes. When he emerged he was in control again. "A 'Traffic accident,' he said. That always stuck with me. Not a car accident or bus accident. A 'Traffic accident' as

15

if it were nothing more than a traffic jam or a traffic light. Oh, Emily."

"I'm sorry," said Alex as he raised his glass to his mouth.

What else could he say? Mike had been hearing apologies from the innocent for the last thirty years. He'd learned to forgive them for what they were. Fillers of a void that couldn't be filled. Not by anything meaningful.

He continued, more for himself now than his listener. "I thought about going home, but didn't. Couldn't face the funeral. Never forgiven myself for that. She deserved that I be there. I had abandoned her in life and I repeated the favor in death." He swished the ice in his glass, drained it and pointed to the bottle of Glenlivet. The bartender poured a double, neat.

"Never anyone else?" asked Alex.

Mike shook his head. "No-one that didn't come with a receipt. You think you'll fall in love again, there's always that expectation, this sense that we deserve to be loved. There's someone for everyone. That's the key, the some 'one', not plural, *one*.

"You know who that one is. It's that girl you think of at 3 a.m. when you've come home steaming drunk. You're lying on your back, boots still on, focusing with everything you've got on that one bare light bulb, a wall unit doing its best to fight the night heat and you convincing yourself that if you can focus on that bulb, anchor yourself to that glow, you can stop the whole room from swirling. All you want to do is hear that girl, talk to her. She's the one, Alex.

"And every night you come home drunk, there she is. So you start drinking less until you start thinking about her in the daytime too and then you start drinking more." It was no kind of answer, but it was what he wanted to say.

"You know it's not the room that swirls? It's the bed," Alex said.

Mike ignored the observation.

"How did you end up down here?"

"I finished my tour to Peru and went home. Looked for work. Did enough odd jobs to break even. Try explaining a year in South America to a recruiter. Everyone thought I'd been running drugs. Jorge Luis Borges, José Martí, Mario Vargas Llosa, Gabriel García Márquez, Mario Benedetti, Chico Buarque, Caetano Veloso, Andrés Caicedo, Julio Cortázar, Víctor Jara. It's as if they'd never picked up a pen. A century of cultural genius relegated to oblivion by one bloke with a porn-star moustache and a fleet of Cessnas."

The list of names made no impression on Alex's face. He nodded out of the habit of the professional listener.

Mike continued his story. "I joined the army. Did that for a few years. Marching around at 6 a.m. and showering with a bunch of guys was never my thing. Then a position came up at our embassy in Peru. Liaising with local military, encouraging cooperation, curbing the excesses. Did some work with your guys there."

He noticed his drink was empty again. He called for another.

"I did that for a while. Hated every day of it. No one grows up wanting to work for government. All this talk about serving your country. They'd be serving drinks if they weren't serving their country." He paused to receive his whiskey. "After I left I did a bit of work up in Colombia, spent some time in Brazil."

Mike stared at the reflection of himself in the mirror behind the bar. "I always felt that I would do something great in life. Does everyone feel that? Probably," he answered himself.

"Life is what you make it, Mike."

Mike looked at him without turning his head. "In my experience life is a ménage a trois with fortune and destiny, Alex. And they're both wearing strap-ons."

"I never felt that," said Alex. "But I never sat around to wait for them to come knocking. There are two types of people, Mike. Those that let the world change them and those that change the world. Passion. That's all you need."

Mike let out a sigh that covered the bar. "We've all got passion and talent," he said. "Unfortunately, the two never coincide. What we are passionate about we have no talent for and no passion for what we are talented at." The words came out as a recrimination. He had intended it as an observation.

"What brought you here? Your passion or your talent?"

"Neither. I found I had a value here. Had the language skills and I understood how things worked. People valued that. The same people that had excluded me in the US, or had treated me like shit at the embassy, here they needed me.

"I could operate at the margins, I could contribute. I enjoyed that feeling of being needed. Never mind that I had to come to the end of the world to find it. No one cared where I'd studied or what family name I dragged around behind me. Amid this chaos people were looking for a face they could trust, an English-speaker, a guide who could make sense of the ridiculous. And that is what I offer, that's what's on the label. To know more, to understand more. It's neither a passion nor a talent, it's just a way of surviving."

"And it had to be here?"

"Argentina's always been a good place to hide. When you lose all notions of democracy, decency, civility, and humanity then the scraps that do survive become precious. Those scraps have a value far beyond the whole that is found elsewhere. Argentines understand that. They have an appreciation for life that we can never have. They see things in a way that I will never see. I thought I could learn to fit in here, to see life as they see it, but it's impossible. I've had enough of not fitting in, Alex."

"So, you're going home?" said Alex, as if they had arrived at the whole point of the night.

Mike shrugged. "I don't even know what home means anymore. Last time I went home they were serving salads at McDonald's." He shook his head at the memory. "May as well go to a whorehouse for a hug."

He often thought about going home, back to the States. It wasn't the leaving that scared him, it was the arriving. Arriving back with nothing to show for it. Years spent away and for what? Columbus returned home with the New World in his pocket. Mike had a bag of stories and a few dubious friends.

He filled his mouth with whiskey and swallowed. "There's a thin piece of thread that keeps you tied to home, Alex. You stay away long enough and one day it just snaps. There's no going back. Home no longer means anything when that thread snaps. No, I'm not going home. I'm going to Sicily." The words came out unplanned, a surprise to even himself. As individual words they had been floating around in his head all afternoon. Now in the fog of whiskey had they arranged themselves into a sentence that seemed logical. "Do what I should have done years ago. Start again."

"What's the difference between Sicily or the States? You're still leaving with nothing. You're quitting."

"I'm not quitting. I'm starting again. There's a difference."

"The thought of starting again fills me with horror."

"I'll do it right this time. I know everything there is to know about starting again."

"When?"

"Soon as I sell my apartment. With that I'll have enough money to set myself up."

Alex had started smiling the way he always did right before he offered something that would benefit Alex Harper. "Before you rush off and leave us, are you free Wednesday night? We're having a little *fiesta* at the embassy. I have a client for you."

"I'm not interested in clients, Alex. I told you, soon as I sell my apartment I'm out of here."

"Come along anyway, it can serve as your leaving party."

Mike stood, braced himself with one hand on his stool, drained his glass and placed it on the bar. "In that case, I'll see you Wednesday, Alex."

CHAPTER 3

The female officer handed Mike a small plastic tray. She wore an orange vest over a dark uniform; badges and insignia decorated the sleeves; a stiff peaked cap sat askew on her head. Her uniform blurred the lines between private security and police. At the officer's request, Mike produced his wallet, the keys to his apartment, and his phone and placed them in the tray. A male officer on the other side of the full-body scanner waved him through. The machine made no complaint despite the loose coins in the pocket of his trousers and his metal belt buckle. He wondered if it functioned.

The male officer blocked his way, spreading his arms wide and signaled that Mike should do the same. He obliged, and the officer made a series of quick, vertical sweeping motions with a hand-held metal detector. A disappointed grunt signaled that the inspection was over. Mike collected his wallet and keys. His phone had been sequestered by the female officer who had locked it in a small safe in the wall. In exchange she handed Mike a number scribbled on a scrap of paper.

"Which way through to the cocktail reception?"

Both officers glanced at him, ignored the question and continued the conversation that Mike's arrival had interrupted.

He climbed the stairs passing a portrait of Queen Elizabeth II. At the top of the stairs he turned right and entered a long hall with several rooms branching off on either side. Led by the trill of conversation, in Spanish or English he could not tell, he entered the second door on the right.

Once inside, the room opened into a large reception area. Well-dressed guests—smart business the invite had stipulated—milled around, broken out into small groups of four or five, conversational cells dividing and reforming around topics of mutual or no interest.

The space seemed too large for the gathering or maybe he was early and it would fill. Wait staff, flitted from group to group, white-gloved hands aloft, balancing platters of food and trays of glasses filled with red wine or whiskey. A waiter passed within range and Mike snared a red. Typical embassy do, no beer.

He looked around the room, hoping not to recognize any of the guests. He studied the high, carved wooden ceiling and the crystal chandeliers that hung low over the room, more interested in the architecture than conversation.

In the corner in and around some potted palms a three-piece jazz band played quietly. The melody seemed familiar, but Mike couldn't make out the words, or even the language coming from the singer. It might have been "Fever".

A voice from across the room reached him.

Alex Harper broke away from his group and crossed the floor to where Mike stood. "Glad you could make it, Mike."

Mike smiled in a way that showed that he wasn't as glad. "What are we celebrating, by the way? In case anybody asks me."

"Thirty-five years since we sunk the *Belgrano*." He held up a hand in mock defense. "Just joking, of course. We have the mayor of the City of London with us. This is for him."

"And my leaving party."

"Yes, that too. But first there is someone I need you to meet."

"I am not interested in meeting any clients, Alex, or hearing any stories. I am here for the booze."

"Come on just a quick chat, he's a good guy. You'll like him."

"I hope not."

"And don't be so morbid, remember it's a party. Maybe tone down your views on Argentina. I don't want to scare him off."

Alex led the way across the room acknowledging individuals in each group, moving with the confidence of a host that didn't have to pay the bill or clean up afterwards.

They approached a man standing alone in the corner. He had his back turned, hands in his pockets, staring out the bay windows. His suit was a little too big for his shoulders, a man who chose on color rather than fit. His shoes were polished to a sparkling black. His physique was unremarkable, though he possessed an air of fitness, no doubt from 5 a.m. bike rides in hotel gyms. Short hair, styled for ease of care rather than aesthetics. The man spun around to face Mike and Alex as they approached.

"I wanted to introduce you to someone, Simon. This is the infamous Michael Costello."

"Mike, actually, nice to meet you," said Mike extending his hand.

"Simon Quinn. Likewise."

"Simon's new. He's managing the project out in Cordoba," said Alex, playing his well-grooved part.

"How long have you been in town for?" asked Mike.

"Coming up three weeks."

"How have you found Cordoba?"

"I haven't even been out to site yet. There's been trouble with some local community groups. Not too happy with us being there. I'm keen to go, but the advice for now is that my presence wouldn't be helpful."

Mike stopped a passing waiter. "What are you drinking? My shout."

Simon held up his glass. "One more red won't hurt."

Mike plucked a glass from the waiter's tray and handed it to Simon along with a tumbler of whiskey to Alex. He grabbed a red wine for himself. "Here's cheers and welcome to Argentina." All three raised their glasses.

"How about yourself, how long have you been living the dream down here?" asked Simon.

"I don't know about living the dream," said Mike. "Coming up ten years now. It was only ever going to be two or three."

Alex placed a hand on Mike's shoulder. "Mike came here to find love and make his fortune."

"How have you done?" asked Simon.

"Single and broke."

"I hope you're trying to make the fortune first. That should make finding the love a bit easier."

Alex said, "He's being modest. Broke men don't live in expensive apartments in the middle of Recoleta. Still just the one maid, Mike?"

"Just the one. But if you want to talk about lifestyles, Simon, you should see Alex's place. You would think he was the goddamn ambassador. A small ranch. You could run a decent herd of cattle in his backyard if the pool didn't take up so much room."

"Nothing less than I deserve for risking life and limb for Queen and Country," said Alex, enjoying the fact that the conversation had turned to his good fortune.

"Risking your life? At these dangerous cocktail receptions?"

"You know as well as I do, Mike, that the Argies would love to get their hands on the Falklands. They may have no aircraft, boats or troops up to the task, but you know what they say, where there's a will and all that. I'm determined that the Falklands will not fall on my watch and if I'm well rewarded for that diligence of duty with a nice house, some blue sky and sunshine, weekends on a hacienda, a nice girl in the office, and, yes, the odd cocktail reception, then so be it. Not to mention how I suffered in London. You should've seen my girl there. Helen of Troy I used to call her. Had a face that could lunch a thousand chips."

Mike shook his head and grinned. He had heard the line before but still enjoyed it.

Alex looked over Quinn's shoulder. "Now, if you will excuse me gentlemen, I'll leave you two to chat. I must go and make some people like me. And be careful, Simon. I fear that Mike here has gone native. Though I don't think we have realized it yet as we keep inviting him to these things. And, Simon, if there is anything I can do for you, call me."

Mike swiveled to watch Alex move across the room. "One of the least diplomatic diplomats I've met." Turning back to Simon he asked, "What have you made of Argentina so far?"

"I'm loving it. First time in South America. I think I could get used to it. There's a real European feel about it. Compared to some places I've been, I think I am going to enjoy the experience."

He has read the guidebooks, thought Mike. "I'm sure it will be an experience. My advice is to accept it for what it is. The old bitch won't change."

"I'm sure I'll be all right. I survived three years in the Ivory Coast. I think I can handle a country whose claim to fame is red wine and steak."

"It's not a country, it's a conversation. Remember that."

Quinn took a drink from his glass. "Please explain," he invited.

"There's a lot of talk. Nothing gets done without it being talked about first. You'll have to do a lot of talking. To your secretary, she'll want to talk about her cat that died, the coffee lady will want to tell you about the niece that's just started university, the guy that fixes your car is going to want to talk about his football team that got beaten in extra time because the referee was on the take, the taxi driver's going to tell you what a basket case Argentina is and ask you how is it possible that a man with three languages and five degrees, and two of those post-graduate, who's lived all over the world can end up driving a taxi in Buenos Aires. And he'll take you the long way if it means he gets to finish the story and charge you for the pleasure. And all of them will want to talk politics." Mike drew breath. "How's your Spanish?"

"*Nada*," Quinn replied.

"For the best," said Mike, unsurprised. "If you'd learnt anything it'd be useless here. All *Castellano* here." He emphasized the "Shhh" made by the double L, a parody on the Argentine pronunciation. "They don't even call it Spanish. They say there's a historical reason why. Personally, I think it's so they don't confuse themselves with the Bolivians."

"Most people I've met have been happy to speak English. I haven't had any trouble communicating with anyone."

"You don't need the language for communicating with them. You need it for overhearing, for picking up gossip, for reading the papers. You need to keep yourself informed, don't rely on people to tell you. Then you need to make sense of it. If it sounds logical, feasible, or reasonable then it's more than likely false. The more absurd, ridiculous, and farfetched it sounds then the closer you are to the truth."

The band announced that they would be playing their last song. Nobody seemed disappointed as they started into a jazz version of "Billy Jean". Mike snatched two more glasses of red as a waiter passed and handed one to Quinn.

"The other thing you need to know about is the flush rate."

"The flush rate?"

"It's a measurement I use to gauge how fast the government is flushing the country down the toilet. The scale runs from one to ten. It's often up around nine and never dips below five. The interesting thing about the flush rate is that no matter how high it goes it never hits ten. It never all comes tumbling down. I don't know why that is. People are always saying, 'This government won't last, this will tip people over the edge, the people won't put up with this'. Believe me, they always do. They always muddle through.

"It's like dividing a number by two. Always seemed logical to me that if you keep halving a number you'll get to a point where there is nothing left to halve. But you never do get to zero. That still doesn't make sense to me. No matter how hard they try to break the country, they never get to zero.

"And don't be fooled by the architecture and the avenues and this bullshit about the Paris of South America," said Mike, aware of gathering steam but unable to locate the brake. "Buenos Aires is dirty, it's grimy, it's dangerous. It gets under your nails, you can smell it in your clothes, it makes your skin itch. She seduces you, draws you in and enthralls you, and then breaks your heart."

Quinn said, "Yet, you're still here."

"Of course. I love it." And he did, once, he thought.

"And what is it that you do here, Mike?"

A good question and Mike had spent the last ten years trying to find the right answer. Political Consultant, Risk Adviser, Security Manager at one time or another they had all appeared typed below his name in neat letters on the little business cards he had printed at the stationery shop below his office. He had given up trying to put a title to what he did. It would have been easier if he were a second secretary.

"I try to help companies stay out of trouble." As good a definition as he could come up with. He never let on that the emphasis was always on *try*.

CHAPTER 4

The morning was clear and bright and cold. Mike sat in the back of the taxi and watched the Buenos Aires streetscape slide by. The morning traffic alternated between a crawl and a standstill giving Mike ample time to admire the streets. Edwardian-style buildings dominated. A few potted plants stood on small balconies that struggled to accommodate two people side-by-side. Sculpted balustrades and antique lamps of wrought iron clung to the facades. Chipped gargoyles studied the traffic below, no doubt grateful they had no place to go. The grand structures towered into the sky and cast shadows over the footpaths.

The architecture and the scale of the buildings stood as a reminder of the immense wealth that Buenos Aires had once held. The pockmarked facades; angry, scrawled graffiti; half-clothed beggars sleeping in doorways; and the bags of uncollected rubbish piled high on the sidewalks reminded Mike that the days of abundance had gone the way of the great buffalo.

The decaying streets, rotting from the outside in, like gangrenous limbs, were the remains of a glory that refused to yield, a city that refused to accept its current state of poverty. She was a beautiful woman, who in aging is sustained by the memory of her youthful looks, the dances, the admiring glances, and the constant attention—holding on despite the knowledge that the past will never return. Regardless of her slow decay, Buenos Aires radiated a beauty and an arrogance in the face of the inevitable that bewitched Mike. He admired the city's refusal to give in, but he would listen to her lies no more.

The taxi banked by the curb. Mike glanced at the taximeter mounted on the dashboard. It read eighteen pesos. He handed over a twenty-peso note. The driver, eyeing Mike in the rearview mirror, held up a small tray and shook it. The rattle of one or two coins audible evidence that he had no change.

"Keep it," Mike said as he opened the door.

He stood on the pavement and watched the taxi pull away before turning and entering the nondescript building that was home to his preferred law firm— though "law firm" was too grand a term for the claustrophobic office that his lawyer chose to work from. The brass plaque on the outside of the office with the words "Estudio Finklestein and Knight" was the grandest aspect of the operation, though less so now that the inlaid letters had tarnished to a dark green.

Inside, the office name-partner, Tomas Finklestein, sat behind a wooden desk, piled high and loose with an assortment of files and reference books. His thermos of hot water and pewter gourd filled with *mate*, the metal straw poking up out of the green leaves like a miniature periscope, stood within easy reach of Finklestein's hand. A strip of orange peel floated in the hot water. Steam rose towards the ceiling.

Mate, the national drink, the staple of staples. Finklestein once told Mike that an Argentine could go three days without steak, two days without *mate* and a day without talking. Unlike other humans, they could go weeks without sleep.

Finklestein came out from behind his desk and greeted Mike with a kiss on the cheek and a firm hand on his shoulder. It was a traditional greeting between men who knew each other's secrets. Even so Mike still flinched at the rub of stubble on stubble.

Finklestein returned to his seat and offered Mike the *mate* gourd. Mike declined with a raised hand. He wasn't averse to the tea, he just didn't like to run the hygienic risk of sharing Finklestein's genetic matter. The kiss was risk enough.

It took five years after Mike had first hired Tomas for him to admit that the "Knight" on the name plaque was a piece of marketing fiction to give his firm an air of English respectability. Five years of Mike asking after the whereabouts of his partner only to learn that Tomas Finklestein worked in a partnership of one. However, this suited Mike's needs.

Case by case, Mike developed a thread of trust, no thicker than gossamer, in Tomas. Mike would tell friends that it wasn't that he trusted Finklestein that made him useful, it was that he knew when not to trust him. It was an important difference. Finklestein was someone Mike relied upon to do the legwork of going down to whatever public agency held the files that Mike needed and sifting through hundreds of boxes of documents and index cards where the entrails of Argentina were stored.

When Mike had come to purchase his apartment he had entrusted the paperwork to Tomas, and Tomas bit by bit had become to Mike what every good lawyer in Argentina was to their client; a consigliere, an adviser whose advice and services wandered along the outlines of the law but were not adverse to meandering into the realms of the everyday, the psychological, and even the romantic.

Having taken the decision to sell his apartment, Mike had phoned and instructed Tomas to begin preparing the papers. He did so with little understanding of what papers would need to be prepared or what the preparation would entail, only knowing that without a doubt papers, forests of them perhaps, would need to be prepared. The purchase of the property had run to five boxes of files and folders, and for a fee Tomas was happy to organize for their safekeeping in his office. Mike assumed that they were hidden somewhere in the piles that were forming like stalagmites from the office floor, his adviser's desk, and from every flat surface on offer inside the office.

"Ah, here it is," Tomas said, poking his balding head crowned with an audacious combover around the pile of folders, a single sheet held in his right hand while his left pulled his wire framed glasses down the bridge of his nose, allowing him to peer over the rim at Mike.

Finklestein's voice always carried a hushed note of excitement that never quite gelled with his demeanor. He had a face that was harder to love than other people's children. And it always wore a grim look. It was grim when he told Mike about the weekend he had spent with his family in San Pedro; it was grim when he discussed the birthday party he was planning for his children; it was grim when he spoke of his time studying in London; it was grim when he spoke about the future of Argentina. Mike had arrived at the conclusion that to be a lawyer in Argentina was grim business, day after day forced to look upon the inner workings of the country, an oncologist examining the cancer-riddled body of a patient with no hope of a cure.

"I knew it was here somewhere." His look of grimness morphed momentarily to brooding as he prepared Mike for what the document said. "Not good," he said to himself, re-reading the document, as if last time he looked it had been good news.

Mike sat in silence awaiting the information.

"I looked into the situation of your apartment. Or at least I tried to. Your assets have become of interest to the AFIP. I am sure you have seen what has been going on in the papers."

Mike felt his intestines knot. The AFIP was Argentina's tax authority. It had an insatiable appetite for the property of others. They needed no justification, but in recent weeks the AFIP was dressing up its actions with a cloak of legitimacy, justifying the repossession of property as a means of collecting unpaid taxes. That the properties were then sold at knockdown prices to friends of the government was not polite conversation.

"I haven't been advised of any issues," offered Mike, knowing that that meant nothing at all.

"Nor would you expect to be," said Tomas with an impatient wave of his hand. "I've had trouble finding out what the issue is. All I could find was that they had been flagged. Luckily for you—well, not luckily, that is why you pay me—I have a friend at the AFIP. He didn't have much more to add for now. A freeze has been placed on your assets. He couldn't say by who or for what reason, he didn't have that kind of access. I have asked him to look into it further for you." Tomas sat back in his chair and pushed his glasses back to their original position. "Of course, this favor will not be free. He is asking for fifteen thousand. Dollars."

"Fifteen thousand?" Mike repeated, his voice rising to match the elevated number. "I'm not comfortable paying a bribe, Tomas."

"Facilitation payment, Mike. It's not a bribe. Very different."

"Either way, I don't have fifteen thousand dollars to hand. I will have once I sell the house. But not now."

"Then I am afraid there is nothing to be done."

"Can't you help me out, Tomas? We've known each other a long time."

"We have. And in all that time have I ever done you a favor out of the goodness of my heart? It would not be wise on my behalf to start now."

Mike scratched his head in frustration. He clenched his jaw and shook his head. The politer option to screaming out "fuck!" and taking a wild, satisfying swipe that would send Finklestein's stacked paper towers flying across the room. Mike changed topic to avert an outburst.

"What are your thoughts on this?"

"I presume it is tax related. Though why they would freeze your assets rather than repossess strikes me as strange," Finklestein offered.

"I don't pay any taxes. You know that. You structured everything through Uruguay to evade the taxes."

"Avoid. Avoid taxes, Mike," Finklestein chastised. "And keep your voice down, please."

Tomas placed his elbows on his desk and brought his fingertips together.

"It could have something to do with the taxes that we avoided when you purchased the property," he said in a low voice, as if testing how this information would be received by his client.

A memory of walking through downtown Buenos Aires with a suitcase packed with bundles of American dollars came to Mike's mind. In an office even smaller than the one in which he now sat he had exchanged the suitcase for the deeds to his apartment. Finklestein assured him that that was how things were done.

"You said that was legal."

"It is. But you only avoid paying the taxes if you own the property. You never mentioned anything about wanting to sell one day. If I may ask, what has brought this on now?"

Mike dug into his pocket and produced a folded square of paper. Mike felt calmer just feeling the paper in his hands. He had waited until his secretary had gone out for coffee and printed it off in his office that morning. He had come across the article while searching for cheap flights to Sicily. It was a sign. The first bit of good luck he had had in five years. He spread the paper out on the desk and pushed it across to Finklestein.

Not waiting for Finklestein to read the paper he said, "The Sicilian government is giving away old houses on the island. All you need to do is to commit to investing some money in the house and have a plan to turn it into something that will attract tourists. They've been running the program for the last year. It says there that it was so successful that they have extended it for another year."

Finklestein studied the paper then placed it on the desk and looked over his glasses at Mike.

"What's your plan, then?"

"A small bed and breakfast. Something with a view of the ocean."

Finklestein chortled. "No offence, Mike, but you don't strike me as someone who has a natural aptitude for hospitality."

"Once I sell the apartment here I should have enough to do the renovations. What's left over I will leave in my account in Uruguay. I will use that money to maintain my little hotel in a permanent state of occupancy."

"Sounds like money laundering, Mike."

"But it's not. My money, legitimately earned. Using it creatively is no offence."

"Good to see you have learnt something from your time with us. Well, it seems like you have about six months left to get yourself to Sicily and claim your house. Shall I proceed with the enquiries?"

Mike sat back and looked up at the ceiling. Cobwebs connected the bare light bulb to the ceiling.

"How long do you think this will take?"

"A week. Two weeks maximum."

Mike had spent ten years advising clients to play it straight, don't get your hands dirty, and it had come to this.

"Go ahead," said Mike. He would come up with the money somehow.

CHAPTER 5

Leaving Estudio Finklestein and Knight, Mike walked south on Callao with the wind in his face. It entered his eyes and nostrils, wound down into his stomach and fanned a tiny flame deep inside. The cold energized him. He walked upright, while others made their way hunched, heads bowed down. Mike enjoyed Buenos Aires in July. When he was fishing the streams of Sicily, if he ever missed Buenos Aires, he would miss it as it was in July.

In July, the city was full. You could lose yourself in the crowds. In July, you could get things done. In January, when the city's inhabitants fled north to the beaches of Uruguay or south to the tourist beaches of Mar del Plata, Mike felt exposed, trapped in the heat and humidity, left behind to hold the fort until vacation was over.

He approached the intersection of Callao and Santa Fe. His destination, the Tienda de Café, a forgettable café like thousands of others dotted throughout the city. Its plainness made it a suitable meeting point.

Mike pushed through the glass-paned doors. In the back corner, seated alone at a table for two, back to the wall, head half-obscured by the morning paper, *La Nacion*, was the man he had come to pay. Mike raised his hand in greeting, knowing that his approach had been noted and monitored even before he had crossed Santa Fe.

"Good morning, Doctor" he said, approaching the table, his *Castellano* containing a faint trace of his native English.

"Good morning, Mr. Costello. Please, take a seat," said the Doctor, lowering his newspaper as he hoisted a grin. "I haven't ordered yet. What would you like?"

"The same as you," said Mike as he placed his leather shoulder bag on the tiled floor beside him.

The Doctor signaled to a waiter who acknowledged him and then continued his conversation with the attractive girl managing the cash register.

"What's in the papers this morning? Has it all come crashing down yet?" asked Mike.

"I haven't gotten to the comics yet," The Doctor said, referring to the political section. "I'm with the obituaries."

"Someone you know?"

"No. Just something I enjoy. I prefer to do it alone. Drives my wife mad."

"I can imagine it would."

"When I first started out in the business, as I'm sure you know, they were difficult times in Argentina. In the beginning, it was easy to keep track of who was who. You snare one and they would have diaries, address books, letters. Was easy to connect people, and satisfy our …" the Doctor hesitated, searching for the modern turn of phrase. "I think you would call them KPIs now. One would lead you to two or three more. That was in the beginning. Later you would pick someone up, a student or a teacher and nothing. No diary, no letters. Nothing to

39

connect them to anyone or anything. It made for slow work."

Mike looked for the waiter, uncomfortable with where the conversation was headed, hoping for an interruption.

"The obituaries were my idea. Every morning on my way to the office I'd buy the papers for the obituaries. Death has a special hold on us Argentines. Why else would we have a cemetery in the middle of the city, in the heart of the tourist area? Come and look at our dead! Macabre.

"Death is a time of intense emotions. Even the terrorists felt a need to pay their respects to fallen comrades. So, what I couldn't find in the diaries and notebooks and letters, I found in the messages to the lost. Hidden relationships, two people that appeared unconnected, mourning the same person. Juan David, brother to him, father to her, loving husband of … you get the picture. Painstaking work but effective."

"Very clever indeed, Doctor," Mike said, his voice dry.

The waiter appeared and took their order, two *americanos*, before skulking back to the bar, feet dragging across the tiles.

"I sense your unease. You must remember they were different times. And don't believe everything you read. We did nothing that was not approved by, or at least known by, your own Mr. Kissinger."

"I can't imagine they told him everything."

"Of course not. Nor did he ask. He was good at his job. Strong relationships are built on both parties knowing what not to ask."

"I will keep that in mind."

"My conscious is clear. My only regret is that we saved the country only for these bastards to inherit it."

The Doctor cut an urbane figure. An enviable, full head of grey hair swept back and held in place with gel, a well-curated beard and moustache, a tailored suit. He didn't look like a torturer, none of them did. He'd learnt that in Peru. He knew that the Doctor had started his career in naval intelligence. That alone made it likely he was involved in, or at least knew of, what went on. He tried not to think about it, better to change the subject.

"Are you keeping busy? You mentioned on the phone you had something on."

The Doctor leaned back in his chair, ran both hands through his hair and let out a groan. "I can rely on you to ruin my morning."

The waiter came back with the coffees. Mike's order was wrong. He let it go, happy to sit on the espresso rather than wait another ten minutes. He sipped his cup. Bitter, burnt, drinkable, just. "How so?"

"I always say never do a job for a favor. In fact, never do a favor. Money is the only justification for working."

"It's an honorable code to live by, Doctor."

"My wife introduced me to a friend of hers, some man she has known since university days. Ex-boyfriend I suspect; she is much too discreet to say. Let's just say a friend. A few weeks ago his brother died, a guy about our age, heart attack. Nice obituary by the way. The brother leaves behind two children, a house in San Isidro and a sizeable sum of money. The wife had gone a few years earlier from cancer, so the kids stand to get it all. Before the funeral another child appears, claims to be the fruit of an affair some twenty years before between our deceased and God knows who. Conveniently, her mother has also passed on."

"And this was the first the family knew of this?"

"They'd known that there had been dalliances, that's to be expected, but nothing about heirs apparent. This girl is sure of her story and insists on a DNA test. Inheritances are best split in two rather than three. The kids cancelled the funeral and put the old man on the barbecue the next day."

Mike raised his eyebrows. "Barbecue?"

"Yes, cremated, nothing left you see, no DNA. Smart under the circumstances. Like I said, death is a time of intense emotions, not always easy to think straight."

"Where do you come into all this?"

"A heart attack got him, but only after he'd battled prostate cancer. He was treated at the Palermo Clinic. By all accounts was doing well. The point is, he'd had a biopsy, the remnants of which are still at the Palermo Clinic."

The Doctor waited for Mike to put the pieces together. He didn't and the Doctor continued, a trace of impatience in his voice.

"They need me to wipe this piece of prostate from the face of the Earth."

"Impossible," declared Mike. "I hope you've got a good plan and are not working on a success-fee arrangement."

"The plan is always the same, just the amount and the person you pay differs. And that is my problem now."

"You'll never find someone to do that."

"Of course I found someone. He wants ten thousand pesos. The kids won't pay that. This guy at the clinic knows what I want and I can't move without the cash. I'm very exposed, Mike."

Mike shrugged in professional sympathy. "This is what happens when you do someone a favor, Doctor."

"Well, it ends today. When I leave here, I'm meeting the kids, see what I can work out. I might fund it myself if they cut me in. I haven't decided yet."

"If it helps, I have this month's pay for you." Mike reached down into his shoulder bag and produced a small notebook. He opened it and withdrew a check from the Banco Patagonia made out to Julian Martinelli for five thousand pesos. He handed the check to the Doctor.

"The expenses?" asked the Doctor, omitting any gratitude. He folded the check in half and slipped it into his suit pocket.

"In cash, as usual. It's in country, I just have to pick it up. I will get it to you when we catch up next." Mike sipped his espresso. "We need to discuss this arrangement. Five thousand dollars is a lot. Andrea is asking me for something to back it up."

"Andrea worries too much."

Andrea was Mike's secretary, assistant, office manager, report writer, translator, and excuse when he needed to get out of something. She also worried too much, but that worked for Mike who never worried enough.

"What does she want? An invoice saying five thousand dollars for peering into an offshore bank account? Christ, we'll all go to jail." The Doctor threw up his hands in an exaggerated show of frustration. It was the kind of gesture that would have made people stop and look if they had been sitting in a café back home. Here it was the standard accompaniment to good conversation. Mike glanced around the café. At each table well-manicured hands, both female and male, were flying in all directions. He was convinced silence could be achieved by tying their hands behind their backs.

"We need something, Doctor. I can't keep paying you in cash for expenses on top of your monthly payment. I need something from you." Mike had a long-running arrangement with the Doctor. A fixed fee of five thousand pesos per month for his services. The Doctor paid his contacts in cash and passed this expense back to Mike, no markup. Whereas the Doctor was happy to be paid in pesos, his sources worked for US dollars.

"I'll put you in touch with my accountants. They'll sell you some invoices. Just insert them into your books." He sipped his coffee.

"Sell me some invoices? Andrea would never let me."

"These are real ones, from a real company. It'll look like they did some consulting work for you for five thousand dollars."

"Let me see if there is another way first."

"Suit yourself. We've known each other too long to argue over money, Mike. What did your client think of the information?"

"Very happy. Proved what he suspected. There might be some more work. He's gotten a taste for it."

A couple had come in and sat down at the table adjacent. The Doctor lowered his voice.

"These guys are very good, Mike. Any account, anywhere in the world. Just need a passport number and a name. Tell your clients, whenever they are hiring or doing business with someone, try to get these two details. That's all we need."

"This is Mickey Mouse, right?"

The Doctor insisted on keeping his sources confidential. As a result, Mike often found himself in cafés around Buenos Aires discussing Mickey Mouse, Donald Duck, or Pluto. It may have explained their insistence on being paid in American dollars, if nothing more than to stay in character. Though the code names were dubious, Mike couldn't argue with the information. It was always good.

"Yes, Mickey. Nobody else can offer this service. If I do find someone, I'll try them. Five thousand's a lot, I understand," he conceded.

The waiter slouched back to the table and cleared away the empty cups. A gesture to say, order more or get out. Mike and the Doctor did neither.

"I met an interesting guy at the embassy the other night. He's heading up the new project in Cordoba."

"The one the government has invested in? A hundred and fifty million I read."

"Not invested. Loaned. But yes, that's the one."

"Invested, loaned whatever. Does he know what he's in for?"

"Not a clue. Doesn't even speak Spanish. He thinks he has it under control. He thinks that some experience in Africa will be useful here."

"Typical."

"What do you know about the project? From the government side. The railway appears to be the key; without it the project doesn't stack up. I'm thinking about trying to land him as a client. I want to know what I'm in for."

The Doctor straightened in his seat and smoothed his suit jacket with both hands.

"First, a question. How is it that our honorable government, that struggles to keep the lights on in Buenos Aires, that is overseeing inflation of thirty-two percent, that not that long ago defaulted on a hundred-billion-dollar debt, how is it that these comedians are able to hand out a hundred and fifty million dollars?"

"The Inter-American Development Bank. That's where the money's come from. The project ticks a lot of boxes."

The Doctor shook his head in disgust. "Boxes. That's where they all belong. I don't know much to be honest. I think it's being handled by the Ministry of Planning."

"Planning? Shouldn't Transport or Mining and Energy have it?"

The Doctor laughed out loud. Around the room hands froze mid-conversation as eyes turned to look for the source of mirth.

"The government is not going to loan these guys a hundred and fifty million and then let Mining and Energy run things," said the Doctor.

"So, what do you know about it?" Mike asked again.

"Like I said, not much. Donald Duck has a guy who works in Planning. He's close to one of the minister's advisers. They studied together, which means that they went whoring together. Nothing binds tighter than pussy. Never used him so can't vouch for his access. Shall we test the waters?"

"Not yet. I thought you might have heard something, that's all."

"I don't have to have heard anything to know something. I've lived and breathed these bad airs for sixty-two years. If the government loans money to a foreign company to set up shop in the middle of nowhere it means one thing. Somebody is going to get rich. Your new friend has a decision to make, will it be him or will it be someone else?"

CHAPTER 6

Leaving the Doctor to his obituaries, Mike pushed through the doors of the Tienda de Café, crossed Santa Fe and made his way back down Callao. He turned left at Las Heras and fell into a comfortable march. As he walked, he retrieved his cell phone from his shoulder bag.

"Alex. Mike Costello," he said, cupping his left hand around the phone to prevent the wind from distorting his words. "We still on for lunch? Same place?" A pause as Alex confirmed. "I'll be there in about forty minutes. I'm on foot. See you soon." He hung up.

He headed east along Las Heras and enjoyed the feeling of anonymity afforded by the crowded streets. He hadn't felt this way for a while. In that first winter in Buenos Aires he would go on long walks through the city and savor the possibility of disappearing, knowing that he would neither be missed nor searched for. After years of regulated life, he had felt liberated on the streets of Buenos Aires, reporting to no one, explaining nothing.

Time passed and that feeling had begun to ebb. What he once interpreted as freedom came to feel a lot like loneliness. Having made the decision to leave he felt free again, he felt unknown, alone, attached to no one and no place, and it was a blessing. This was what awaited him in Sicily.

He passed under a government billboard with the president looking down on him. The words "Argentina: A Serious Country" were emblazoned across the bottom. Mike smirked at the absurdity of the slogan. He recalled that Menem had campaigned to presidential victory on the back of "I will not disappoint you." And he had kept his word, if only to those voters who had expected to be disappointed.

The Doctor was right. The government wouldn't loan a hundred and fifty million to a foreign company out of good will, for the good of the people. Unless by the people they meant the Party, the Peronist Party—a unique political movement that could have surfaced in any country but could only have prospered in Argentina. A land that venerated the strong man, the cunning man, the one who takes what he deserves while no one is looking. And what he deserves is what he can take. Fertile ground for a politics of fear and favor. A land where an apathy fed by casual abundance allowed the darkest impulses to flourish.

It is why Mike had stayed. It was an acceptable irony that what drove him to Argentina was what drove him insane. He had felt alive like he had nowhere else before. He had lived in more dangerous countries and he had lived in prettier countries. Here he had felt that anything was possible, anything was in reach, no doors were closed to the man who wanted to reinvent himself, crawl into the skin of another. A place of no pretense, where losers are relegated and winners feted. In this environment an act of kindness meant something. In a society that turns a blind eye to human suffering, that rewards you for bending the rules, that applauds you for coveting your neighbor's wife, kindness had a value.

Mike had found this kindness. In the people who had taken him in, the ones that shared their stories with him, those that had helped him to understand this complex place. These were not the people of the Peronist Party. No, whatever the government had in mind for those hundred and fifty million dollars, it was not for these people.

• • •

Guido's was an Italian bar that had started life as a night-time refuge for taxi drivers changing shift or wanting a place to sit and talk through a slow period. The front door, painted a vibrant red, was always wide open, as were the two windows that opened on to the tree-lined sidewalk. In summer these trees provided a green canopy that embraced the street in cooling shade. Today the branches were bare of leaves, resembling arched, arthritic fingers, coming together above the traffic like those of an old man in thought.

Inside Guido's the walls and ceilings were hung with photos of Hollywood movie stars, filthy jokes in Spanish and Italian printed on tiles, football jerseys of Italian and Argentine club teams, and photos of Guido himself, arm wrapped around the shoulders of people who Mike presumed had been famous at some point in time. Anita Eckberg bathed in a fountain.

The bathrooms were wallpapered with pornographic playing cards. Guido had once confided to Mike that he had done it to stop customers bringing their kids in to the restaurant. The pornography was a crude but effective deterrent and one that ensured that even the adults didn't linger too long in the restrooms in case they be accused of going for business and staying for pleasure.

"Mr. Mike, please take your seat," said Guido, arms opened wide, head tilted to the side. He claimed to be Calabrian. Mike was unsure if he was born in Calabria or his family had come from Calabria. It was a distinction that locals didn't bother to make.

Mike took a seat by the front window at a small, wooden table covered in a red-and-white-check tablecloth. He placed his shoulder bag on the ground beside him.

"Mr. Mike, please tell me that you are waiting for a pretty girl. Every time you come, you are eating with that English man. What a waste! I don't make food to be shared between two men. It breaks my heart to see this." He held both hands to his chest to prevent further damage.

"I'm afraid it is just Alex today, Guido," Mike said, raising his hands in apology. Of course, he would prefer to be having lunch with a pretty girl. Who wouldn't? But after the lunch there would be the complaining, the fights, the power struggles, the hysterics, the you don't love me, you love me too much, and all the other bullshit.

"I don't understand you, Mr. Mike. So many girls in this city. You need a good Italian girl." He looked confused. "What can I get you to start?"

"A red wine is fine." A good Italian girl was just what he needed. A Sicilian maybe.

From his seat Mike could see across the street. A wall of green vegetation extended from behind the few parked cars that lined the curb. Beyond the wall were the grounds of the zoo. A taxi pulled up opposite and double parked. Mike watched as Alex Harper extricated himself from the taxi, yelled something at the driver, and slammed the door. The taxi lingered as if the driver were deciding whether to continue the argument.

Alex came headlong into Guido's. "Where are all the bloody coins in this city?" he asked Mike as soon as he spotted him.

His suit, as always, hung from his frame, as though it had been thrown on him from a distance, the collar crumpled and doubled under. A red rash glowed on his neck where the collar met skin. Dandruff lay heavy and visible on his shoulders, as if he had received a generous dusting of finely grated parmesan. One shoe was untied. He off took his jacket and slapped it on the back of his chair, sat down, unbuttoned his sleeves, and rolled them up. He sniffed hard, rubbed the back of his hand across his nose, looked around, and announced, "Wine!"

The difference between the man who now sat before him and the gregarious diplomat that had introduced him to Simon Quinn at the embassy cocktail party could not have been starker. These professional chameleons had an ability to blend into whatever surrounding they were thrown into. The problem was that you could never determine their original color.

"The unions," Mike said. He could hear the tiredness in his own voice.

Alex looked at him, confused.

"The Bus Drivers' Union. Reason there are no coins. The transport minister is demanding a bigger cut go straight to his office. Every Friday afternoon, some lackey from the minister's office drives around Buenos Aires and collects the minister's cut. They take it all back to the ministry, or wherever the collection point is. Because this money comes from bus fares, it's in coins. Previously, the unions would convert the coins into notes before the collect. The union isn't happy about the raise. So now they just hand over bags of coins to the ministry. The ministry can't go to the bank, that'd be laundering, so they have to sit on the coins."

"That makes sense. I read this morning that the trains are letting people travel for free because no one has any coins. No such fucking luck with the taxis. They are loving it. Have you noticed that they never round down?"

A waiter placed two glasses of wine on the table. The two men touched glasses and drank.

"How are you doing, Alex?" He had no real interest in hearing Alex's problems, he had enough of his own. Ten years' worth. But lunches went better when Alex had first rights to the whining.

"I think you've got the right idea, Mike. I'm ready to leave, too. I really am. Have you seen the cutbacks in our public service? Twenty years' service and this is what it comes to, left hoping for a decent redundancy. My fault, too—that's what hurts. I should have gone into business. All my mates did. Not me, I wanted to save the fucking world. I tell you what, they're not sitting around waiting for a redundancy now, they're fucking rolling in it. My mates, that is. And what've they done? Sold toothpaste or something. I could have done that, would have been good at it, too. Would have paid a lot better than this. Can't even survive on this wage at home. I have to leave my family and live halfway around the world just to earn something."

This was not all truth. On the surface, Alex had indeed left his family in the UK so as not to interrupt his boys' schooling. Mike suspected other reasons behind the decision.

"I need to get out, Mike. How did you get out?"

"I can remember the exact moment. Every three months our congress would send down a senator to see how US tax payers' money was being spent on the war on drugs. As liaison officer I was responsible for briefings on the coca-eradication programs. I'd take them out, fly them over the coca areas that we'd fumigated or chopped out, show them the local units that we were training up.

"This one guy comes down, from Texas I think; we give him the full tour and are back at the embassy. Everyone is there for the final debrief and he says, 'Y'all are doing a great job. I'm impressed with what you have achieved. My only question is, if we succeed in eradicating all the coca, aren't we going to piss off a bunch of chocolate drinkers around the world?'"

Alex laughed. "That is when you decided you'd had enough?"

"No, that came a few seconds later when I realized that no one in the room had the balls to call this guy an asshole. I couldn't handle that sycophantic, bullshit culture. Nothing strips the guts out of a man like seeking approval from people he despises. In the end, other events overtook me. One day I was in, the next day I was out."

"No redundancy?"

"They looked after me, but it felt like hush money. Didn't touch it for a long time, then one day I stopped caring."

"I'm going to start looking around. I'm going mad here. I've got another eighteen months left, then reassignment. I dodged Iraq last time. I can't keep dodging it forever. I'm not going there. I need to find something else."

Mike had no doubt that Alex had already planned his next move. The ability to plot your way around the globe, from one posting to another, the here and now perpetually subjugated to the potential of the future, was the essence of professional diplomacy.

The waitress returned with four small plates of antipasti. One of the pleasures of Guido's being that there was no need to order. You got what you were given.

"I may not be leaving as soon as I had hoped," Mike confessed. "It appears that there are some administrative issues to be resolved before I can sell the apartment. I am not sure exactly what the problem is at this stage. No doubt it will be expensive." Whether lawyer's fees, fines, bribes, or other miscellaneous costs, nobody ever escaped from under the AFIP microscope without money changing hands. "Which leads me to my next point. If the offer is still on the table I would like to take on MinEx as a client. What do you know about the project?"

A fleeting smile passed over Alex's bloodless lips. "You'd know more than I do. You know more than Simon. He has no idea about this place."

"None of us do. Thankfully we don't have to in our line of business. We only have to know more than the client."

"How do these guys get these jobs? Companies with money to burn. Could pick anyone in the world to send down and they pick people with absolutely no idea."

"They could pick you, you mean?"

"Well at least I speak the fucking language. That's a start."

Mike soaked up some sauce from his plate with a crust of bread. "What are your thoughts on this deal they've got with the government?"

"A hundred and fifty million dollars. Big enough to be interesting, not too big to be scandalous. A sum that could disappear in the hands of the transport minister in the blink of an eye."

"Transport aren't handling it, Planning is."

"That is a nest that we do try to avoid."

"What do you need from me, Alex?"

The waiter retrieved the empty plates and returned with two mains of pasta. The lunchtime buzz hummed through the room, accompanied by a background score of forks being dragged across plates.

"I have one goal here and that is to protect our interests in the Falklands. How do I do that? We keep a low profile. I make sure that as far as the Argentines are concerned, all things British are out of sight and out of mind."

"Sounds easier said than done."

Alex signaled the waiter for more wine. "What I don't need is a British company paying bribes to the Argentine government. Ever noticed something about the scandals down here? It's always foreign companies corrupting the honest locals, forcing honest politicians to take bribes. All I need from you is to keep an eye on Simon. Make sure he is not tempted to cut any corners or grease any wheels. I don't need him pissing anyone off and making problems for me."

"Why can't you tell him all this yourself, Alex?"

"Because corruption is like inflation down here, Mike. It doesn't exist. So it wouldn't look good if it got out that I was advising British companies against getting caught up in something that doesn't exist."

CHAPTER 7

A layer of the city's best grime coated the faded, cracked, black upholstery that attempted to cover the back seat of the taxi. Miscellaneous debris of previous passengers littered the floor. Mike kicked an empty McDonald's drink container further under the driver's seat and wondered how much time he had spent in taxis in his lifetime. Still, better than fighting the Buenos Aires traffic himself and cheaper than paying for parking.

The radio transmitted a preview of that night's game, River versus Boca, the first game of the pre-season. It was a peculiarity of the Argentine football league that they ran two competitions each year. Between seasons a three-week pre-season tournament. There was no off season, just a rolling feast of football that the cynical would say was designed to keep the masses distracted.

River versus Boca was the haves and the have nots. Mike saw from the small, souvenir pennant that hung from the rear-view mirror that the driver had an interest in the game.

"You think they have a chance tonight?"

"Not a hope! If we win, then they're out. They'll never let that happen. There's too much money in play.

Did you see who they've put in to referee it? The same prick that fucked us last year." He slapped the steering wheel with an open palm. "It's all *arreglado*."

Arreglado. Organized, set up, stitched up, fixed. Mike had heard the word used to describe election results, Supreme Court appointments, murder-trial verdicts, corruption-trial verdicts, two World Cup finals, beauty pageants, and the lottery. Anything where authority had a say. He'd heard it said that nothing in Argentina could be fixed because everything was fixed. Yet every taxi driver had a thousand fixes for the country. Mike often thought that Argentina's real troubles lay in the fact that those who should be running the country were spending their days driving cabs.

The taxi inched through the streets, approaching the destination the circumference of a wheel at a time, allowing the drivers' grievances to be aired for what he wrongly assumed were Mike's sympathetic ears. Congestion was bad with the Plaza de Mayo filled by the usual unions, paid thugs who were employed, and deployed, by the president's political apparatus.

Mike sat back, closed his eyes, and thought about floating down the Limay River, casting nymphs to willing brown trout.

The taxi came to a stop on Juana Manso. With no time to go through the ritual of discovering that the driver had no change, Mike over-tipped him and wished him well for the game. He closed the door on the hard-luck story that his words set off.

He had a good feeling about this meeting. Simon Quinn had called him. He needed help and he had been primed by Alex Harper to believe that Mike was the man to deliver it.

It begun to rain and he scurried across the street and sheltered in the foyer of the MinEx building. He could have made time yesterday but felt it gave him an advantage to appear busy. Business development wasn't that different from dating.

He flicked shut his notebook and called the elevator, riding it up to level five. The door opened onto a floor with glass doors to his left and right, both embossed with the MinEx logo and the slogan, in English, "Sustainability and Safety: It's Our Culture". Mike grimaced to himself. MinEx, a serious company.

He pushed on the door to the left where he could see the reception desk was attended. The glass door flexed and squeaked under his hand but didn't give. The receptionist saw him and buzzed him in.

"How can I help you, sir?" she asked in accented English.

"Mike Costello, here to see Simon Quinn," Mike replied in Spanish. He resented being spoken to in English, offended at the assumption that he was like all the other gringos. On more than one occasion he had exited a restaurant after being handed the English menu.

"Certainly, sir. Please take a seat and I will let Mr. Quinn know you are here."

Mike took a seat and studied the reception area. Large, glossy photos hung from the walls. They showed mining operations from around the world, large holes gouged out of the earth, the photographer struggling to capture beauty in the excavations. In between pictures were corporate affirmations of MinEx's responsibility and sustainability. Handsome, wholesome values until they got in the way of profit—that had been Mike's experience.

"Mr. Costello?" Mike looked up. "Is this your first time in the building?"

Mike nodded in the affirmative.

"You will need to take the safety induction. Just a couple of minutes, then Mr. Quinn will be with you."

It was pointless to protest the induction, as pointless as the induction itself, an exercise to reinforce those wholesome corporate values again. Statistically he had already survived the most dangerous part of the meeting, the taxi ride. He used his thumb to flick through the induction booklet provided before signing that all was understood and if an accident were to befall him it would be his responsibility. He returned his signed booklet to the receptionist who accepted it without looking at him.

"Mr. Quinn will see you now." She swiveled in her chair and pointed a well-manicured nail down the corridor that ran away behind her. "Down the hall and last door on the right."

Simon Quinn sat behind his desk, pen in hand, signing documents. He seemed smaller than Mike remembered, though that may have been because Simon was seated or because Mike was sober. Simon's head was of a form that shouldn't be shaved, and Mike imagined the dilemma that must have played out in front of the mirror as Simon weighed up baldness against skull shape. Despite this, Mike recognized in his posture an assuredness that Mike himself had once possessed.

"Signing your life away, Simon?"

Simon looked up and smiled. "I bloody hope not. Good to see you Mike, please take a seat. I'll just be a second." He applied a few more signatures, straightened the remaining papers in the pile on his left and focused his attention Mike. "Thanks for coming by, Mike, I appreciate it."

Mike noted that Simon had lost his British accent, probably from living abroad. Mike's own accent had lost the burrs and rough edges of his native speech as he planed it down to a form that the non-native English speaker could easily understand. He had found it easier to change his own way of speaking rather than repeat a word ad nauseum before giving up in frustration.

"Apologies for being late. The usual unrest on the streets, someone or other is always striking. Or protesting. Or protesting about strikes. Judging by the lack of police and the look of the thugs these ones seemed to be pro-government."

"As long it's nothing to do with us."

"Likely to do with the minister for economy."

"A show of support?"

"Yes, though not for the minister. For the president."

"What has the minister done to upset the president?"

"Since taking over a couple of months ago he made the error of believing he was the minister for economy." Mike smiled at his own wit. "Anyway, it's good to see that you are still here. How are things going?"

"Good, good. All under control. The usual stuff to sort out, nothing too untoward. I had a few questions that I thought you might be able to help me find the answers to. I spoke with Alex over at the embassy and he fingered you as the man to speak to." Simon's voice was hesitant. Asking for help was a difficult task.

"I tell my clients that I can sometimes provide the answers. What I can do is to help you to ask the right questions of the right people. Trouble arises when you don't ask questions, or you ask the wrong people the wrong questions."

"I have the questions."

"Why don't you start by telling me about the project. I've only read the papers. Assume I know nothing." The standard approach to a first meeting. Let them tell themselves why they need you. Give them time and let them spin their own web. He sat back and assumed his listening pose, right leg crossed over the left, hands clasped over his knee.

"MinEx is a mining and energy concern. We own and operate world-class assets around the globe. We like a few sectors where we're comfortable and where we think we do things better than most. We're happy to be in most countries. There are some where we won't go. Until recently, Argentina was one of those countries.

"However, our Chairman has a bit of a hard-on for the place. Cycled around the north as a teenager. No doubt had his first lay here. You can read all you like about why companies go to certain countries. In my experience it's the brainchild of an executive who met a girl there, wants to travel there, whatever. Rarely, is it strategy.

"So, Argentina's back on our radar. It's a good project, however anyone with a map can see it's a long way from any port. The Chileans won't allow anything to go out through their ports without taking a fair clip of the ticket. So, the key to it has always been the railway."

"I'd heard that the project wasn't economical if you included the cost of the railway."

"The project depends on the railway. Mining is logistics. The project has never been developed because no one wanted to risk putting money into a mine without the railway being built first. If you sink money into mine development without a way of moving the product, you're over a government-sized barrel until the rail gets built.

"We said, we'll commit to the mine development after a certain amount of the railway is built and operational. As an additional safeguard, we've insisted that the government loan us eighty percent of the railway construction cost. They've got skin in the game and need it to be built just as much as we do. If it doesn't get built, they can't pay back their loan from the IDB. We're pretty secure."

"Generous terms."

"Of course, there are conditions. We use local labor. Local investment, jobs, you know the drill. They didn't have much choice. Who else would come here? They want the world to see that people can do business here. MinEx is a big, shiny case study."

"So, you've done a good deal. And yet," Mike spread his hands wide. "Here I am."

Simon turned around in his chair and reached for some folders that were sitting on a table behind him. He placed them on the desk.

"I wanted to get your opinion on something." He added, "I am pretty sure I know the answer. Can't hurt to get a second opinion, I suppose."

Mike didn't disagree. "My priority is to begin construction of the railway. The quicker we advance, the quicker we develop the mine. There's no cashflow without the mine. We've put out a tender document and received the first round of technical offers."

Mike interrupted. "Same as oil and gas tenders? First round technical, then the technically qualified are invited to submit financial offers, best combined is the declared winner?"

"Standard procedure. We received three technical submissions."

"Surprising. The British built the railway system and the locals have spent the last 100 years destroying it, not adding to it. A testament to British engineering that any trains still run."

"That's the thing. We didn't get three submissions. Not really. We got three submissions but not from three companies." He handed the folders to Mike.

"One company lodged three different offers?"

"No, technically, three companies lodged the same offer. Different company names, registered addresses, principals, but the same company experience, employees. Haven't even tried to disguise it."

"For this to be valid you need three companies to tender?"

"Correct," said Simon.

"They're doing you a favor," said Mike as he flicked through the papers in the top folder.

"My legal counsel sees the hand of the minister for planning in this."

"Why would they want to help you? They don't do favors. They do threats, stand overs, intimidation, pay offs. Not favors." A practiced phrase that Mike had used before. No point sugar-coating things.

"You make it sound like a mafia."

"It is," Mike said without looking up. "That's exactly what it is. What's in it for them? Don't tell me it's jobs and growth, or some other fluffy bullshit."

Simon thought for a minute.

"If this project advances it will encourage other companies to invest," he offered.

"Too fluffy."

"They need us to repay the loan."

"Loan repayments have never been that important to this government. Are there local companies out there that could build this?" he asked.

"Do any companies have the experience? I doubt it. There might be one or two in the whole country that we could work with, train them up, build some capability. It's possible. We're not reinventing the wheel. Problem is it'd take time. Time, I don't have."

"And there's still a risk you come away with nothing. Have you spoken to Castelli?"

"Who?"

"Miguel Castelli. The governor of Cordoba. He must be interested in seeing you succeed."

"Never met him."

"So realistically, you don't have any option outside of these three companies. Planning knows this and knows that you can't have one bidder. They're making sure it doesn't get held up, they're providing a shortcut that gives you cover."

"How thick is that cover?

"It'll hold if they want it to hold."

"Do you see another way?"

There was always another way. The way they taught at every business school in the States. Play it straight. Corporate values, governance. Call it what you will. Mike had learnt the hard way that it had no relevance down here. He'd been preaching it himself for ten years and where had it ever got any of his clients? Quinn could play it straight but all that would do is piss off the people who wanted their cut and had the power to take it if it wasn't given.

"I don't see any other way. It's a risk but so is crossing the road. If Planning want to help you out, no point upsetting them."

Quinn tapped the desk with his pen. "I'll think it over. There's something else I wanted to discuss."

"If you insist," said Mike.

"We've been having trouble with some community groups out at site."

By community groups Mike understood activist groups. "You mentioned as much at the embassy."

"Two weeks ago we had our AGM in London. These meetings provide a chance for people in the audience to ask questions of our directors. They start to take questions and this university lecturer from Cordoba, who's already on our radar, gets up, with a translator, and starts an interrogation about destroying communities, water, and whatever else he could think of."

Simon retrieved a print out from his top drawer and handed it to Mike. It was from an online source and the picture showed the face of a bearded man holding a sign written in Spanish, his face caught in the act of screaming abuse or maybe a chant. He would have been at home at the Fortress on a Sunday afternoon. It was a determined, angry-looking face. The caption underneath identified the man as Marcelo Decoud. Mike skimmed the article and studied the face in the picture.

"Directors not happy?"

"Not happy at all. Our question is, how does a bloke from Cordoba, on a teacher's wage, manage to spring for a ticket to London and a translator?" He opened his hands as if waiting for an explanation to fall in to them. "The guys in London have asked me to look into it."

"I can help you with that," Mike said. "To clarify, the question is who is funding this guy?"

"Correct. Is he against the project or is he being paid to be against it? And if he is being paid, who's paying him?"

"Leave it with me. I'll get a proposal to you."

"What is this going to cost me, Mike?"

Mike pictured Finklestein's face in his mind. "We'll run his bank accounts, pull his phone records, criminal-record check, credit check, interview the people who know him best. We'll put this guy under the microscope. By the time I finish you'll have everything there is to know on this Decoud. But all that costs money. I can't imagine you'll get much change from twenty thousand."

Quinn just nodded, unfazed by the number. "I haven't even discussed it with my legal counsel, Mike. You are the only one I am trusting on this."

"That's the right thing to do," said Mike.

CHAPTER 8

Mike Costello licked the rim of his cup, catching a stray rivulet of coffee as it travelled fat-end first towards the tablecloth. He was ensconced in his local café Dos Escudos.

The waitresses fussed over him with a care and sympathy that young girls reserve for men who have reached an age when care and sympathy are not misinterpreted. On Monday mornings they never charged Mike for his coffees, a liberty taken with the knowledge of the café owner's inevitable late arrival, attributable to the excesses of the Sunday barbecue. In return, Mike would leave a tip that far exceeded the cost of the coffee. It was a transaction based on emotion rather than good economics.

Though the hour was past nine he was in no hurry. Monday mornings were a slow ease into the week, like those first few casts on the river to warm the elbow into the work ahead. Mike watched the snow float down through a window framed with white, lace curtains. It was the first time he had seen snow in Buenos Aires. It was the first time that anyone he knew had seen snow in Buenos Aires. According to the man on the television that was located at the back of the café, mounted high on the wall, this was the first snowfall since 1918.

The television showed clips of residents of all ages taking advantage of this freak weather event, frolicking in snow-filled streets, launching snowballs at unsuspecting friends and family members, constructing snowmen, and adorning them with the shirt of their favorite football team.

The frivolity did not extend to the government. The next news item was an interview from the Pink House, a suited-member of the cabinet reminding everyone to try to conserve energy. Yes, enjoy the snow, but please remember gas prices were rising and gas reserves were falling. And we do not want to be relying on Bolivia for our gas supply.

Mike felt like launching a snowball at the television. Instead he ordered another coffee. Two shots of espresso topped up with hot water, an *americano*. He could never remember having had one back home in the States and wondered where the name had come from. He sat back in his chair, watched the snow and waited, for his coffee and the Doctor.

His wait was short. The well-tailored figure of the Doctor materialized in the doorway, head down, collar up, a refugee from the weather outside. Without appearing to look for Mike, the Doctor made his way to where Mike sat.

"Mother of God, this is shit weather."

"I'm quite fond of it. Almost feel at home," said Mike, enjoying the Doctor's obvious discomfort and the sight of his reddened cheeks.

"Well you can take it home. You better have a good reason for dragging me out in this."

"I do. But first sit down and order yourself a coffee."

The Doctor obeyed as a man used to giving orders obeys, as if not obeying at all, master of his own movements in his own time. He called over the waiter, placed his order and paid. The waiter retreated to the counter and then returned as he had forgotten something.

"I'm sorry, sir, we don't have any change, do you have something smaller?" he said. The ten-peso note dangled from his fingertips. The Doctor fished in his pockets but came out empty.

"I do," said Mike, handing over some coins.

"Thank you," said the Doctor, pocketing his unusable note. "How have you come by so many coins? Have you robbed a bank?"

"I've started saving them. Don't tell the unions or they'll be after me."

"The unions? I don't follow," said the Doctor.

"The reason there are no coins in the city is because the transport unions are using them to pay the minister his cut. An unofficial protest of sorts."

"What rubbish." The Doctor let out a derisive laugh. "If the minister is worth his salt, he'll be taking between ten and twelve percent off the top of every bus route in the city. I'm not sure what that would be in real numbers, but I know it isn't being paid in coins. The plane south would never take off."

"Plane?" It was Mike now who didn't follow.

"Every Friday a chartered plane leaves the Campo de Mayo military airport and flies south. On board are the weeks' takings. They are unloaded and taken to a hotel.

In the basement there is a vault. That vault is the beating heart of Peronism, pumping out hard currency through the corrupted veins of this country."

"How have you come by this information, if I may ask?"

"I haven't, pure speculation on my behalf." The Doctor smiled.

"In this speculation, there are no coins in that vault?"

"None. The coins are not there. The coins I'm afraid, like the rest of us proud patriots, are victims of inflation." The Doctor explored his jacket and produced a fifty-centavo coin from the pocket that a minute ago had yielded nothing. He held it up between his thumb and forefinger. "Now, under Menem, this little beauty was worth fifty cents. Your cents, the American kind. Today it's worth about fifteen cents. The government's official inflation is running at 0.4 percent, but as you know, nothing is official in this country. The real figure for inflation is about thirty-two percent."

"On its way to being worthless," said Mike.

"Aren't we all?" replied the Doctor. Still holding the coin at Mike's eye level, he continued. "Unlike the rest of us, this little Argentine has a redeeming feature. Every coin contains 5.3 grams of copper and half a gram of aluminum. A few months back the worth of those few grams of metals were worth more than the face value of the coin. And that is what sealed their fate."

"The coins are being melted down?"

"Again, pure speculation on my behalf."

The Doctor never speculated. For confirmation, the Doctor would need to be paid. It was a game they'd played since they'd met. The Doctor would throw out information, pure speculation of course, and if Mike, or a client of Mike's, wanted confirmation, then money would need to be exchanged to check with the Doctor's cast of Disney characters, to bring facts to the table in a neat, well-written report. Mickey, Donald, and Pluto had a wide range of sources of their own; well-placed aides, a person with access to the minister, a key member of the working group responsible for the decision.

Mike was unconcerned about the disappearing coins. He was content to enjoy the pure speculation for free.

"You'll be happy to know that I did not drag you out on this summer's day to discuss the metallic content of our currency," said Mike, bringing the conversation back to work.

The Doctor straightened in his seat, crossed his legs, and assumed the pose of attentive listener. Before Mike could begin both coffees arrived. He waited until they were alone again.

"I saw MinEx on Friday. They're having an issue and they've asked me for a proposal. I wanted to discuss with you how we might best satisfy the requirements."

The Doctor nodded and stayed quiet.

"They are interested in looking at an individual who has been causing some disquiet in the local community in Cordoba and popping up in some strange places, namely London last month at the annual general meeting."

"Environmentalist?" said the Doctor, saying the word as if trying to remove a hair from his tongue.

"On the outside, yes."

"How do you want to approach it?"

"I was thinking bank accounts, pull his phone records, criminal-record check, credit check, interview the people around him."

"What's your budget?"

"Five thousand," Mike lied.

"Impossible."

"That's all there is. What can you get for that?"

"Nothing of value."

The Doctor picked up his teaspoon and stirred his coffee, the silver spoon making a slow and deliberate lap of the cup. Mike knew the Doctor didn't take sugar and allowed the theatrics to play out as he sipped his own coffee.

"I could interview him. Do you have budget for a trip to Cordoba? There and back in the same day if the flights are available." He continued to stir his coffee staring at Mike.

"Under what pretense?"

"In my role as a long-time contributor to *Environment and Modern Man*."

Mike raised his eyebrows. He had never heard of the magazine.

The Doctor continued. "A leading journal on the challenges Argentina faces dealing with an expanding population and a shrinking natural environment."

Mike played along. "What would it take to bring this journal to life? A website, business cards, a mock-up of this esteemed magazine? I'm thinking of our budget."

The Doctor feigned indignation. "*Environment and Modern Man* exists, as does the record of my contributions. I took it on after leaving the service. I did some work for Chevron who had their own environmental issues at the time. I enjoyed the intellectual stimulation. My articles have been well received. I was an influential voice in the dispute with Uruguay over the paper mill." The Doctor stopped stirring, set his teaspoon down and sipped his coffee. "The best falsehoods are true."

Mike shook his head in surprise. Surprise that he was surprised. He'd known the Doctor for over six years and it was rare that a meeting went by when he didn't learn something new.

"What are we going to learn?"

"Two concerned citizens discussing our next environmental challenge and the rape of our lands by a foreign invader. Who knows where that conversation might lead in the hands of a capable interrogator."

"Journalist," Mike corrected him.

The Doctor nodded in agreement.

"I will put it to the client and let you know."

The Doctor's product was always good, if a little expensive, compared with the other peddlers of information that he sometimes consulted. It wasn't all that he had promised the client, but if Quinn had any complaints he could track him down in Sicily.

Mike drained the last of his coffee. "I have the dollars for you. I need to stop off at the *cueva* and change some for myself. Shall we?"

On the street, the snow had stopped falling but the biting cold remained. Mike smiled as he felt a real winter's embrace. They headed right on Alvear. Before Alvear intersected with Callao they turned off into a small shopping arcade. Artefacts that could have been one hundred years old, or off the plane from China that very morning, filled the shop windows. Knives with carved, cattle-horn handles, silver-plated dinner sets, paintings of the Argentine Pampas, hand-plaited stock whips, hand-woven gaucho hats. Mementos from Borges' Argentina if it had ever existed.

Mike had frequented the arcade for the past four years and had never seen a customer in any of the six stores that lined the corridor. Now that he thought on it he couldn't remember seeing the shops open. Shop fronts in every sense of the word. At the end of the arcade, in the middle of the corridor, stood a detached shop, the *cueva*.

The *cuevas* were as Argentine as tango, though more international in outlook and less melancholic. Small, hole-in-the-wall establishments where you could change US dollars for Argentine pesos or vice versa. Whereas banks were forced to change money at a fictional rate set by government intervention, or intimidation, the *cuevas* were free to set the exchange rates that the market dictated. Free in the sense that anyone breaking the law is free.

To the right of the entrance to the *cueva*, on a shabby bar stool, slouched a man, half sitting, half standing, one leg bent back beneath the stool, clad in black jeans and a black jacket. Beneath the jacket a faded T-shirt. Off-duty policeman supplementing an income. He nodded at Mike and the Doctor and they returned the familiar greeting. The man held his hand up, palm outwards indicating that the pair should wait.

The Doctor retrieved his cell phone from his pocket and checked for messages. Mike studied an over-sized, silver-plated set of BBQ utensils that were displayed in an unattended shop window. Handy for barbecuing mammoth.

The rattling of the door of the detached store announced an imminent exit and caused Mike to forget about mammoths. The Doctor to put away his phone. The door opened and an old lady, the wrong side of eighty by Mike's judgement, high heels, a Kubanka hat and a full-length brown, fur coat, emerged. In her hand, a leash attached to a full-grown, dappled, greyhound. The door closed behind her, a rattle of shades and locks, and she progressed like royalty down the arcade without a glance or greeting for Mike or the Doctor.

Mike stepped to the door and pressed the buzzer.

"Come in," ordered a male voice from the other side.

Both men entered. The inside of the *cueva* resembled a second-hand clothes store. Dresses, jackets, jeans, T-shirts, even bras and underwear were hung from any available space around the store, which was no bigger than a shipping container. Wooden squash racquets draped in knitted scarves were propped up in shoes that had gone rigid from inactivity, or perhaps the cold. Books were piled high on any available flat space. In the corner stood a desk, an oasis of neatness and order.

A young woman, no more than thirty, her tied back in a tight pony tail, sat at the desk. In front of her a machine for counting currency. She did not look up as Mike and the Doctor entered and continued to feed stacks of notes, sometimes Argentine sometimes American, into the machine, re-feeding the notes that refused to go through the first time. She then recorded the flashing red number that appeared on the front of the machine in a leather-bound ledger. Behind her a white-haired man dressed in faded jeans and a leather jacket, retrieved the counted stacks and arranged them on another desk.

Some stacks went into envelopes, others into brown, leather shoulder bags.

Without stopping his parceling he greeted Mike and the Doctor. "Good to see you boys again." He used the word *muchachos*. Mike enjoyed being referred to as a boy, despite his obvious seniority to the speaker.

"What can I do for you today?"

Mike spoke. "We need to change some money." Erasing any doubt that they were there for the clothes.

"What are you buying? Argentine or US?"

Mike again. "Changing US for Argentine. What's the rate?"

"How much are you changing?"

"Hundred dollars," replied Mike.

"Five thirty," the man said, without looking up from the bundle of notes he was binding, his hand looping the rubber band around the bundle like a spider trussing up a fly.

"If I change two hundred?"

"I can give you five thirty-two." Still without looking up from his work.

"And four hundred?"

"Five thirty-four. And that goes for four hundred, four thousand or forty thousand. That's the best I can do. The official rate is three thirteen. There's a HSBC about a block away if you'd like to take your business there. I hear the wait in line is only three hours this morning."

Mike retrieved two rolls of dollars from his jacket pocket. The larger roll he handed over to the Doctor who disappeared it as if he had spent a lifetime conjuring. The smaller roll Mike gave to the amateur banker who took the dollars and handed them to his assistant. She fed them through her machine and confirmed the amount then punched her calculator hard, as if the velocity of its output correlated to the force of the inputs. She opened a drawer that was packed tight with Argentine currency and began feeding notes through the machine, double-checking each bundle of hundred-peso notes. Satisfied that the amount was correct she handed the bundle to her boss without looking at him. He counted them again by hand, lubricating his thumb with spit. Mike grimaced at this hygienic infringement. The man produced a rubber band from his pocket, secured it around the bundle and handed it to Mike.

"A pleasure doing business with you, sir."

Mike accepted the pesos, opened the bundle, split it in two and placed half of the notes in his shoulder bag and half in his jacket pocket.

"Like a good Argentine," the man commented, approval in his voice.

Mike laughed. "Not quite."

How's business in the banking industry?" he asked, bestowing an unearned prestige upon the *cueva*'s illegal activity.

"Unfortunately, it's good. Everyone wants to buy dollars. I can't get enough dollars. You're the only person buying pesos. It's this government. They're ruining the country. I thought this Roncelli had a chance to change things, now he's gone too."

"Roncelli was too good an economist to be the minister for economy," said the Doctor. "Has he definitely gone?"

"They announced it not long ago. Irreconcilable differences," the banker said, pointing to a small television that balanced on a stack of books.

"What will happen now?" asked Mike.

"They will print more money and the more money they print the more people will come through my door and change their money for dollars and the more money they will need to print. At least Roncelli had a plan."

"I'm sure the government has a plan," said the Doctor, with a healthy dose of sarcasm in his voice.

"They're thugs not economists. Their plan to fight inflation is to force companies to lower prices any way they can. When that approach fails, they'll start buying companies up and call it anti-inflationary measures."

Mike looked at the Doctor. "Best let him get on with it. Sounds like he's going to be busy."

They said their goodbyes and exited the *cueva*, nodding a farewell to the slouching guard, and made their way up the arcade.

"He's right you know," said the Doctor breaking the silence.

"About what?"

"About buying up companies. I've heard rumors along the same lines."

"Pure speculation?" asked Mike.

"No, you can have this for free. If inflation keeps heading north the government will look at taking over key industries to put a lid on prices. That way they can set any price they like, run them at a loss just to keep their voter base happy."

Mike thought this over as they came out onto the footpath. He never ruled anything out. He stored it all away to be cross-referenced with the other rumors, lies, vendettas, and innuendo he came across. By doing so he could put together a patchwork of possibilities of what might happen, one day, soon or a long way into the future. Never anything more and never with any real degree of certainty. It was like collecting shadows and pinning them to a corkboard.

"We should start seeding him," said the Doctor, a distant look in his eye as if mentally riffling through his old files of tactics and actions.

"Who?"

"Decoud. Get your client to start making small deposits into his campaign funds. I can try to get the details for you."

"You want MinEx to start funding Decoud?"

"Not funding. Seeding. Just small amounts that won't be noticed. We may need to use it at some point in the future. At the right time we can leak the payments to the press, make it look like he is on the MinEx payroll. It is a highly effective mechanism for discrediting someone, or for influencing them."

It sounded a lot like blackmail to Mike. "Let's just wait and see what the interview turns up first."

CHAPTER 9

"**G**ood afternoon, Sr. Costello," said the doorman with submissive formality, leaning against his broom handle. He had stopped sweeping to allow Mike to pass through the narrow corridor that ran from the door of the building back to the elevators. Mike nodded a silent greeting and turned left before the elevators, preferring to take the stairs up the two levels to his office.

He shared the level with one other office that was nothing more than a closed door on the other side of the floor. He had never seen anyone come or go, never heard any noise from behind the door. Last summer when he had enquired about renting it, desperate to escape the fierce summer sun that beat through his office windows in the afternoon, the landlord had said that it was not available. If it ever became available, he would let Mike know.

He retrieved his keychain from his pocket and shuffled through the bronzed keys looking for the lighter bronze that identified the key for the top lock. He slipped it in and with a slight wiggle felt the bolt slide back. Before he could identify the key for the second lock he heard footsteps approaching the other side of the door, a rattle and click, and the door swung open to reveal his secretary, Andrea Crespo. "Secretary" was an injustice for her role was more diverse than taking care of secretarial duties, though she did manage that with aplomb.

He had hired Andrea when he took on the office space and, like most of his corporate clients, he had hired her for her looks, though Mike's intention, unlike his clients', had been to *avoid* carnal temptation.

Andrea would arrive every morning, briefcase in hand, as if she were still the lawyer off to argue a case at the Comodoro Py law courts, where she had started her career. She had specialized in commercial law, post-graduate studies at the University of Palermo. The background checks he had run on her told the story of a career of rapid rise and promotions through the trial courts and then a sudden plateau.

"Married," was her one-word explanation when Mike had quizzed her about this. "Divorce," was her symmetric answer to why she wanted to return to work. That one word served as an effective barricade to any further progress down that laneway of conversation. Mike had hired her on the spot, one of the few decisions he had taken in Argentina which he hadn't yet come to regret.

Andrea was perfect; overqualified and underemployed, someone who was as happy to prepare coffee for client meetings as track down hidden assets, though she was much more competent at the second skill. She had a keen sense for people and Mike had lost count of the times that her warnings had rung true. Her supporting evidence for her conclusions was never more than "a woman's intuition". Mike suspected the real reason was that she was smarter than him.

The office was small with an open space occupied by two desks, his own on one side and Andrea's opposite. He had rented the office because he needed an address to put on his business card, a place for mail to be sent to, and a telephone line where calls could be taken. He would never imagine entertaining a client there and he always insisted on going to the client's office rather than reveal to them the decrepit, cramped heart of his power.

There was a tiny kitchen just big enough to prepare a cup of coffee and a functioning bathroom, though too close to the main office so that Mike would always wait until he was alone if he needed it for anything serious. The walls of the office were decorated with three framed black-and-white photos of Buenos Aires street scenes: jacarandas, a candlelit café, steps leading down to the metro tunnels. Mike had seen them in the window of a shop around the corner from his office and purchased them on the spot. Andrea had rebuked him and said he had overpaid. They seemed to capture a nostalgic mood of Buenos Aires that he had spent the intervening period trying to locate, but apart from those three pictures on his office wall he never did.

Mike moved to the picture behind his desk, pushed it upwards and lifted it from the wall then placed it on the desk behind him. He turned back to the wall and punched in the combination to the wall safe. The door swung open and he retrieved the bundle of Argentine pesos from his jacket and deposited them in the safe. He closed the safe and returned the framed photo to its place. All this he did in plain sight of Andrea who kept up a steady tapping at her keyboard, eyes averted.

Without looking up she said, "Finklestein called for you. Wants you to call him back. Has news for you." Andrea had a way of pronouncing "Finklestein" that left no doubt of her opinion of him. She reserved the same tone for when she asked him if the Doctor had provided a receipt for his latest expenditure.

"Did he say what about?" asked Mike, a note of caution in his voice. He still hadn't told Andrea about his plans to relocate. It was a conversation he wanted to leave until the very last minute. Perhaps by phone. From the airport.

"He didn't say."

Mike sat down at his desk and dialed his lawyer. He glanced up at the clock on the wall and watched it until Finklestein picked up.

"Tomas, hello, it's Mike."

Finklestein's voice came scurrying down the line with excitement. "I have some news for you, Mr. Costello."

"Go ahead," said Mike. Andrea had not stopped typing but nor had she stopped listening, though he was certain she couldn't hear Finklestein's voice.

"I have managed to get to the bottom of this little mystery we were presented with. I am pleased to say that it has nothing to do with the AFIP. Well, not nothing, what I told you before is correct. They placed the freeze on your assets. However, it was done by them, not for them. It seems that they were fulfilling a request. Your apartment has been placed under a Mareva Injunction."

The term was familiar to Mike. He had worked jobs in the past where he was commissioned to identify assets that could be targeted with a Mareva Injunction that froze the assets and allowed them to be seized. But why would anyone be going after his apartment? And who?

"I see," said Mike, keeping control of his voice, not wanting to alert Andrea. "What's to be done?"

"We must dig deeper to find out who is behind this. Once we discover that then we would look to make a deal, I imagine. Shall I move ahead?"

A pause as he waited for Mike's answer.

"I am not paying you any more money."

"I will try to keep it under the original budget."

"Go ahead then."

"Good. I am sending you the bill for the fifteen now. If there are any other costs I will add it to your monthly account."

"Just get it done, Tomas."

Mike hung up the phone and glanced at the clock again. "Six minutes, Andrea." Andrea stopped typing and produced a small notebook. She opened it and scribbled down the time. It was the only way Mike could keep a semblance of control on Finklestein's billing. He billed in fifteen-minute blocks and was notoriously slow to write three-lined emails. Mike preferred calls with a strict record kept.

"Everything OK?" asked Andrea, her senses too keen for Mike's liking.

It seemed like leaving Argentina was going to be harder than he thought; she had her hooks in.

"Everything is perfect."

Andrea pursed her mouth, raised an eyebrow but kept on typing.

CHAPTER 10

At 7 p.m. on Wednesday night the small restaurant on the corner block of Vicente Lopez and Ayacucho was empty of customers, save for one table in the back corner of the restaurant. Mike Costello sat alone, one eye on the menu, the other on the door. Outside the words "Rodi Bar" were carved into a discreet wooden sign that hung from two thin ropes attached to wrought-metal hooks.

Mike looked up as he heard the door swing open and Simon Quinn bustled into the warmth provided by the open grill fires that were burning behind the counter.

"Is this place open?" Quinn asked, shaking Mike's hand.

"It is, but you won't find any Argentines dining until at least 9 p.m. That'll be the early crowd. If you want to meet an American in Buenos Aires, hang around a restaurant at 6 p.m. They'll be the only ones there."

Quinn took off his jacket, hung it over a chair and sat down opposite Mike. "Have you been waiting long?"

"Just got here. It's a favorite place of mine. Traditional despite being on the tourist strip. I always feel like I'm eating with an Argentine family. Albeit, one that hasn't invited me to dinner. The waiters can be a bit grumpy.

That's the charm of it. No bullshit. You come in, you eat, and you go."

The interior was bare, devoid of anything that did not possess utility. The wooden tables were covered in spotless white tablecloths, relaid following the lunchtime service. Each crowned with a single salt shaker. It was a traditional place where traditional was bare bones.

"I could do with some food," said Quinn.

"Wine first?"

Quinn nodded and Mike ordered a bottle of Salentein Malbec and two glasses.

"How are you getting on?"

"Good. I'll be better when you tell me why we're here," said Quinn, cutting to the point.

"I like it," said Mike. "Straight to it." He scanned the room, lifted his napkin by the corners and resettled it on his lap. "The Cordoba job is done. Are you interested in how we got the results or just the results?" Mike had found that clients were often fascinated by his world. He felt it was part of the service to let them in for a little look if they wished.

"Just the results."

The wine arrived and Mike waited while the glasses were poured. "Well, not good. The guy is a teacher at the local university, philosophy, bit of sociology. He's from the area, long-term activist. No history of politics per se, just a long history of environmental causes. Clashed with the government over just about every project that has been put up out that way. Arrested a few times when he was younger. Prefers to stay in the background a bit these days, organizes students, writes articles—"

"Travels to London," Quinn interrupted.

"Yes, happy to do that. Point is, the guy is genuine. He believes that your project is going to fuck things up out there. That's a problem. If he were just trying to make some cash we could turn him into a supporter, MinEx shirt and cap and all."

"You sound disappointed."

"It would be easier if he were being paid to be an asshole. Then it becomes an auction. You just have to outbid whoever's paying him."

"So, he can't be bought off. What can we do then?"

"I'm not saying that. He can still be bought off, but ideologues are always going to cost you a lot more. You have to pay for their ideals."

"This could be good. If he is genuine, then I can sit down with him, explain the project to him. I've dealt with his type before. It's a good project. Best-practice environmental management. It's going to be good for these people." Quinn stopped. Mike was laughing.

"What?"

"Oh, you're serious. You don't even speak Spanish, how are you going to explain anything to anyone?"

"Someone from the team will."

"And he'll sit there, listen to your arguments, nod his head and say, 'You know what, my apologies, you're right, this looks fantastic'? Ain't going to happen, Simon. People like Decoud don't like guys like you. They don't believe guys like you. The big job, the fancy apartment in Recoleta, the meetings with the minister. They look at you and they remember that one morning they woke up and their bank accounts were empty. They don't trust your type, they never will. Guys like you have been shitting on guys like Decoud for decades."

"It sounds like we've been shitting on you too."

"I'm on your side. Doesn't mean I don't get where Decoud is coming from. How would you feel growing up in a country that *used* to be the richest country in the world? Believe it or not "as rich as an Argentine" used to be a saying. In Europe.

"Now what is it? Garbage bags stacked head-high on the streets, people having guns held to their heads in their own homes by thieves looking for the money that the family has hidden because they don't trust the banks, elections decided on who has the deepest pockets, masked thugs blocking the street so as you can't get to work, blackouts that roll on for days.

"A guy like Decoud wants to fight back, he wants to say 'no more', right or wrong he wants his country back. Can't blame him for that."

"I can't solve that, Mike. Stopping the project won't solve that."

"He feels as though he's doing something. He's not just sitting by, watching it all go to shit."

"I want to talk to him, Mike. I appreciate what you are saying and I get it. I'm sure I can talk him around."

Mike shook his head in resignation. "It's your call. I don't think it'll work though I can see I won't convince you tonight." Mike reached for the menu on the table. "I hope I can convince you to at least have the steak and some more wine," he said, refilling both their glasses.

"I must say, Mike, you don't get much for twenty thousand these days. I'd have gotten your information, the girl of my choice and a massage for that much back in the Ivory Coast." A complaint wrapped in sarcasm.

"There is something else. My guy seemed to think that Decoud was very well informed. He thinks that Decoud may be speaking to someone inside your office in Cordoba. Any ideas? You got any disgruntled employees that you know of?"

"No idea. I haven't met them yet. I haven't been out there."

Mike ordered for them both, sparing Quinn the work of deciphering the menu. An old gentleman took the order. Mike appreciated that waiting was a serious profession, too serious to be left to part-time students and failed actors.

The waiter scooped up their menus and disappeared before returning with a small basket of fresh bread rolls and two sachets of butter. Mike took a bread roll in two hands and broke the bread over the table with a sharp twist, as if beheading a lobster, shards of crumb sprinkling the white tablecloth.

"No bread plate?" Quinn asked.

"Another of the many mysteries of Argentina. They have the bread but not the plate." Mike wiped some crumbs from his mouth, spread his napkin back on his lap and reached down beside the table. His hand reappeared holding a blue folder. "Unfortunately, you have bigger issues to think about."

He placed the closed folder on the table. He wasn't sure that he was going to share the folder with Quinn until he produced it. He had considered not bringing it at all. He had done the job he was commissioned to do. The folder's pages would no doubt generate questions that he wouldn't be around to answer but Quinn deserved to know what he was in for. Though Mike couldn't help but feel that giving him the information was like handing a blind man a torch in a tunnel.

Mike had prepared the folder himself. Quinn flicked through the pages, his eyes gliding over the neat, numbered, type-written paragraphs. At the top of the front page in bold, underlined, and centered text was the title: Simon Ashton Quinn (SAQ).

"It's in English," Quinn said.

"I translated it. I can assure you that you are holding an accurate translation." Mike sat back in his seat. He waved his hand towards the folder, encouraging Simon to begin reading.

Quinn regripped the folder in both hands, gave the pages a slight shake and began reading. His eyes flitted down the page reading the text.

1. *Simon Ashton Quinn (SAQ) arrived in Buenos Aires on flight BA245 on the 5th day of May. He resides in Apartment 6A at 873 Posadas, Recoleta, a two-bedroom rental that is leased by the MinEx Corporation from a real-estate management firm that specializes in short-term corporate rentals for visiting executives. The subject lives alone and is not known to receive visitors or guests. No women have been seen leaving or entering his premises. There are no indications that he is homosexual nor are there indications that he is not. It is to be assumed that he is and is actively hiding his sexual orientation.*

2. *There are no major scandals, no criminal history, no civil complaints attached to SAQ. The subject's economic situation appears comfortable. His cred-*

*it history is clean. He holds no vehicle or proper-
ties in Argentina. He makes monthly payments to
his ex-wife and mortgage payments on a house in
London. He is the signature on a US-dollar sav-
ings account held at a HSBC branch in
Montevideo. The account, at time of reporting,
contains one thousand seven hundred fifty-three
dollars.*

3. *From Source "A": SAQ is motivated by material
   rewards. He is professionally ambitious and described as having a "win at all costs" mentality.
   Prior to SAQ's arrival in Argentina, MinEx was
   involved in an incident with a tanker that ran
   aground off West Africa. Jeff Cormac, CEO and
   close friend of SAQ, travelled to Nigeria to negotiate a deal. Cormac was jailed upon arrival. There
   is no indication that SAQ was involved, nor is
   there evidence he was not involved. SAQ has professional experience in the Ivory Coast as well as
   Malaysia.*

4. *From Source "A": SAQ speaks no Spanish,
   watches no local television. On weekends he purchases the* Buenos Aires Herald, *which he reads
   over a cup of tea on Saturday afternoon. He is
   confident in his own abilities, bordering on arro-
   gant. He doesn't smoke or gamble, and though he
   is always willing to go for a drink he is never the
   last to leave.*

5. *From Source "B": He is polite to his staff though
   they believe him to be standoffish and unaccus-*

*tomed to leadership. They feel he is a "soft touch"
and can be taken advantage of due to his lack of
understanding of the local context. His relationship   with   other
senior executives is strained. He struggles to maintain
relationships outside of work. His staff doubt he
can be successful. Inside the office it is openly
speculated that he will not last until the end of the
year.*

6. *From Source "C": SAQ has shown a willingness to
   circumvent company procedures and protocols to
   progress works.*

7. _SAQ is a driven, ambitious man determined to
   forge a successful corporate career. His actions can
   be influenced with appropriate incentives and rewards, most likely monetary. That he has already
   violated company protocols is a promising development and one that can be used as leverage in
   future operations._

Point seven was underlined in the original, an attempt
to emphasize or enlarge, the truthfulness of the conclusion.
Mike had done the same in the translation.

Quinn looked up from the folder, opened his eyes
wide, and took a sip from his refilled glass, not yet ready
to put thoughts into words. He placed the glass back
down on the table with care. He looked ruffled as if he
had just stepped off a roller coaster.

Mike leant forward. "So, bullshit?"

Quinn shook his head. "The information is accurate, the conclusion less so. Where has this come from?"

"From Planning. They've had their eye on you."

"This is a lot to take in." Mike could almost see Quinn's mind taking an inventory of every conversation he'd had since arriving. It was the usual reaction to finding out that you have been watched, violated. "I can't think who I'd have told all this to."

"Don't bother. Pointless to do so. They've had you under surveillance, human and electronic."

"Electronic?"

"Phone taps, emails, they've run your bank accounts. They've spent a lot of money getting to know you, Simon, you should feel flattered." Mike's attempt at humor went unacknowledged.

"They've hacked my phone and email?"

"They've hacked your email. They've tapped your phone. Look at the last few pages."

Quinn thumbed through to the last pages of the dossier. Mike had left them in the original Spanish with the speaker's name in italics down the left-hand side of the page, matched with paragraphs of transcribed speech.

"Transcripts," Mike said. "Nothing you don't know."

Quinn slumped back in his chair and ran his hands through his hair. His stare went past Mike who turned to follow it but saw only the toilet door. A small brass figure in top hat and tails indicated the way for men.

"How much is true?" asked Mike, bringing Quinn's attention back to him.

"I'm not homosexual."

"And here I am wasting good money on dinner."

"I don't know." Quinn appeared to search his past trying to match it to the words in the folder. "Some of it's true. Yes, my wife left me, yes, I have a bank account in Uruguay. I set it up when I arrived. I thought I might squirrel some away from the lawyers. A little something for myself.

"I was in Malaysia and the Ivory Coast. I wasn't involved in the Nigeria stuff. That was all Cormac, my old boss. He thought he could pay our way out of a situation. Paperwork, grease the wheels, he'd said. At the time, we suspected that the Nigerians had been tipped off about what Cormac planned to do but it wasn't me."

Mike leant across the table and tapped the page where it read Point 6. "What else?" he urged.

"I read the *Buenos Aires Herald*." He shrugged.

"A willingness to circumvent company procedures," said Mike, his eyes widening in accusation as he quoted from the page.

"A few little things I suppose, just to get the project going. It's not a big deal."

"Isn't it? If you've cut corners these guys will be watching you. Every corner you cut, they are storing away for later use."

Quinn accepted the logic though still disputed the spirit. "Sometimes in these places you have to take calculated risks. I'm managing that. What would you have me do?"

"That's of no concern to me now, Simon. I got you the information on Decoud, my job's done. You will have my bill tomorrow morning. And I didn't charge you for the extra you're holding."

A waiter appeared carrying a tray with two steaks and the sides. Mike cleared a space on the table and motioned for the waiter to set the plates down. The revelations had made no impact on his appetite.

CHAPTER 11

The ceilings of the function room inside the Jockey Club were high and dominated by a low-hanging, crystal chandelier that flung shadows and light around the room. Mike had to arch backwards in his chair, almost to tipping point, to see the highest spot of the ceiling. A room for balls, flowing dresses, and affairs of state.

Mike sat in the front row of the chairs that had been set out for the audience. A lectern stood unoccupied at the front of the room. Against the lectern someone had positioned a cardboard sign with the Argentine–British Chamber of Commerce logo printed on it. The printing had faded.

In front of Mike, on a raised stage, stood a table, set with four chairs and covered in a plain, white tablecloth, the kind found at the cheaper, local restaurants that Mike often walked past. Beneath the hem of the tablecloth he could make out the folding, rusted, metal legs of the table. Though he could not bring the metal legs and the chandelier above him into the same field of vision, he could feel them clashing; past decadence meeting present reality.

The room filled with businessmen, politicians, and hangers on, most of who Mike recognized though none acknowledged him. He scanned the room looking for the familiar combover of Finklestein. It wasn't so much a needle in a haystack situation, rather a needle in a stack of needles. Even with the relentless advance of years, Argentine men were reluctant to let go of their shoulder-length hair, no matter what grade of deforestation was going on up top.

Finklestein never missed these gatherings. Membership of the Argentine–British Chamber of Commerce, and attendance at every event they held, was a crucial cog in keeping up the very British appearances of Estudio Finklestein and Knight.

A quick word with Finklestein and Mike could go. He had no appetite for sitting through another chamber event. The morning's agenda had been emailed out the week before. A prominent politician, name not supplied, was scheduled to provide his views on the current political climate. The talk was entitled, "Muddling Through: Argentina Post-Debt Default".

The email spoke of unique insights and a frank discussion of the current political outlook. Excellent networking opportunities were promised. Mike had heard it all before. The talks, the roundtables, the prominent politician, the subject-matter expert, the privileged insights from the sector analyst. Same shit, different lips—that was his privileged insight.

As if on cue, Finklestein came bustling through the door and headed straight to the tables that were set out with coffee, tea, and assorted pastries. Before Mike could stand to approach him, he heard his own name called and turned in his seat. Alex Harper came striding down the aisle that separated the two blocks of seating, hand raised in familiar greeting.

"Saved me a spot did you, old chap?"

Mike hadn't but he removed the gift pen with the chamber logo and the papers advertising member rates from the chair to his left. He placed it on the floor with the materials that he had banished from his own chair.

"I'll have that pen, thanks," said Alex, bending to retrieve it from the floor and depositing it inside his crumpled suit jacket. "I hate these bloody things," he continued, taking his seat. "The events, not the pens."

Mike looked at Alex, silently questioning the excellent networking opportunities that had been promised.

An officious-looking woman, an organizer, in a drab, brown business suit, wearing a small lapel pin of entwined British and Argentine flags, approached the lectern. Mike sat still and shot a look back at Finklestein who took a chair near the back of the room. Mike tried to catch his eye but failed.

"Good morning, ladies and gentlemen, and welcome to today's chamber event. We are very lucky to have use of the Jockey Club's facilities and we must thank our member, Horacio Bianchi, for organizing that." A polite round of applause and all eyes on an elderly, besuited and bespectacled, balding gentleman in the front row who held up his hand and dipped his head in acknowledgement.

"We are also very fortunate to have speaking to us this morning a former President of Argentina." She glanced at the empty chair beside her. "Unfortunately, the President is running a little behind schedule. We have been advised that he will be with us shortly. Meanwhile, there is coffee, and tea, of course, at the back of the room."

Mike seized the reprieve and stood up. Finklestein's seat was empty. He scanned the room. No Finklestein.

"You in a rush, Mike?" asked Alex.

"Just trying to find someone I need to speak to. Preferably before the speaker arrives."

"I'm only here because I can't face the office today. I had Lloyd's of London on the phone all yesterday about this bloody ship of theirs. In the diplomatic service, one hour of phone calls equals about four hours of paperwork. You private-sector guys have got no idea how lucky you are."

"What happened to their ship?" asked Mike, abandoning his attempt to locate Finklestein and turning back to Alex.

"You've not heard about the infamous *Polar Mist*?"

Mike had seen some headlines but not followed the story. It was all the invitation that Alex needed.

"Last month a fishing boat left a port down south. For some reason, it isn't carrying fish. It's been loaded with gold bullion from one of the mines out of Santa Cruz. This boat hits a storm and the crew radio for help, the ship is sinking. They don life jackets and throw themselves into the sea, motors still running, all the hatches open. The Argentine Coast Guard sends a chopper. Everyone is rescued. But the ship doesn't sink. Two days later a Chilean vessel finds it still turning circles in the middle of the ocean. The Chileans hook it up and begin towing it back to their coast.

"The Argentines see what's happening and order the Chileans to turn around and tow the ship back to the Argentine coast, which they begin to do. But before they make the Argentine coast the *Polar Mist* begins to sink, so they cut the old girl loose and down she goes."

"And is the gold recoverable?"

"Was it even loaded? Is it at the bottom of the ocean? Lloyd's suspect it was never on board. The mining company are asking for the insurance payout, Lloyd's want to raise the ship."

"What's your view on it?"

"I'm not concerned with what happened. I am more concerned with the why and what happens next. A few things worry me; that it happened in the president's home province and that the insurer is English. It looks too much like the government is laying groundwork for a media attack on all things British. Speaking of all things British, how goes it with MinEx?"

Before Mike could answer the organizer returned to the lectern. She tapped on the microphone with a bent index finger, as if testing the shell of a meringue. Satisfied, she looked towards the back of the room. Mike slumped in his chair. There was no escaping now.

"Ladies and gentlemen, I am pleased and honored to welcome here with us today the ex-President of Argentina, Mr. Eduardo Camano."

The applause in the room was almost loud enough to cover Alex Harper's exclamation of, "Shit."

Eduardo Camano had been President in 2001. A position he held for two full days. Mike applauded and glanced sideways. Alex lent in closer, reducing his voice to a more appropriate whisper, as Eduardo Camano made his way, every inch the president, in Mike's opinion, to the lectern.

"I'm not sure he can even use the title. He definitely won't be getting a bloody statue out on the avenue," said Alex as the applause died down.

Mike returned his focus to the former President who assumed his position behind the lectern. President Camano charmed the audience with dry, English wit that he had picked up in his days at Oxford in the 1970s. Mike liked him against his better judgement.

"They are born to it these buggers," Alex whispered. "None of this self-deprecating bullshit that hamstrings us."

"He is a natural," Mike conceded.

"Politics. They're made for it. Look at this smarmy bugger waltzing in here like he really was President, joking, smiling. And look around. Everyone enthralled. I'd vote for the bastard if I could. He's taking me for a ride and I love it."

The speech lasted forty-five long minutes. To Mike, politics was the art of the intangible, producing nothing that could be pegged down, a shadow of the real and only objective; power.

Camano wrapped up his speech and started doing the rounds of the room, shaking hands and smiling, ruthlessly gregarious in his manner. Mike retrieved his shoulder bag from under the seat, and without farewelling Alex, who had lined up to press the flesh, made his way to the back of the room where Finklestein had appeared as if by miracle at the coffee tables.

"Tomas."

Finklestein turned and greeted Mike with a wct smile. "Mike, I didn't expect to see you here. I thought you had given up on these events long ago."

"I wanted to catch you, Tomas. Do you have any news for me?"

Finklestein dipped his head into his coffee, took a long sip and re-emerged with an apologetic look on his face. If it was meant to draw sympathy from Mike it had the opposite effect.

"I am afraid not. It is proving a lot harder than I expected. My man is trying his best, but he is not getting any answers."

"Listen, Finklestein, I don't want excuses. Two weeks maximum, you said. You've got your money, now I need this cleared up."

"It's not just a question of money, Mike. If only it were. But that is not how these things work. I expected you of all people to know that by now. We have to find the right person inside the AFIP, build a relationship, bring him, or her, onside. This takes time."

"I don't have time, Finklestein," said Mike as loud as he dared without raising attention. He could feel the vein above his ear begin to throb. He was sure it was visible from across the room.

"I am doing my best," Finklestein offered in defense.

"Well your best had better get a whole lot better or I might just start asking questions around here about where the esteemed Mr. Knight from the famous Finklestein and Knight is."

"Mike! I told you that in confidence," Finklestein whispered. "I said I'll do my best and I will. Now, if you'll excuse me." With that he sidled off without a goodbye, leaving Mike steaming by the coffee urn.

"Trouble with the AFIP still?"

Mike turned at the sound of Alex Harper's voice. How long had he been there? Long enough.

"We have a guy at the AFIP that we deal with. It would be irregular, but I could ask him to look at your situation. As a favor."

Mike considered the proposal. "I wouldn't want to trouble you, Alex."

"Would be no trouble at all." He smiled as if happy to help.

"Let me see how it goes with him," he said, nodding to where Finklestein hovered on the edge of a group that refused to open to let him in.

"As you wish. If you need me, just say the word. How are things going with MinEx?"

"All done. It was just a small piece of work they needed. Don't worry, I impressed on Simon the need to act with probity as you asked. It all went well."

CHAPTER 12

Mike Costello squinted his eyes against the morning sun that reflected off the bleached concrete sidewalk. He kept his head down, a half-opened eye on the holes and crumbling edges that served the sole purpose of tripping up distracted pedestrians.

The walk to Chinatown was a Saturday-morning ritual—a few purchases then walk back to the barrio of Las Canitas for lunch. He was enjoying these habits that he had acquired over the last decade, knowing that he would soon leave them behind. Mike had spent the previous evening on a website inspecting the houses that were available in Sicily. A two-storey villa with an ocean view had caught his eye. The pictures from inside suggested it needed some work but there would be spectacular views while he renovated.

Among the Korean immigrants, for Chinatown consisted mainly of Koreans, Mike hunted the ingredients that mainstream Argentina had shunned. An excess of premium-quality meat meant that there was little need, or desire, to embellish meals with flavor-masking additions. For a man of spice, Buenos Aires could be a frustrating place to eat. Though salt was standard, black pepper was as spicy as it ever got. Until Mike discovered Chinatown, he had had to forego any attempts at culinary adventure. The tastes and flavors of the far east, which he had come to love since his time in Peru, were relegated to memory.

At this hour of the day the streets were all but empty. The small groups that were out were more likely returning home from Friday night than going out on Saturday morning. Mike stepped off the sidewalk and into one of the larger supermarkets that occupied the main strip of Chinatown. He was hit by the familiar smell of all Asian supermarkets. It was a smell he had once associated with pet shops—dry, musty, invasive. Now, he associated it with those hard-to-get ingredients that he would combine in his wok at home on the original four-burner gas stove.

Years ago, when still dating, he had invited a lady over for dinner. He had spent the afternoon measuring, grinding, and combining his own spice mix. By the time his date arrived his creation, a fish curry, had been simmering away, filling the house with the aromatics of Goa. He had gotten it just right.

His guest took one smell as she stepped through the doorway, ran to the sliding doors on his balcony, threw them open and jumped outside, gasping for air and swearing not to return until "that stink" had been expunged from the house. Mike had turned off the stove, grabbed his coat and gone out for steak. She wasn't the one, and these days he preferred to eat alone.

He strolled past the dried-fish section, a little too exotic, stopped and checked out the prices of the egg noodles and grabbed two packets, which he placed in his red, plastic hand basket. He moved to the sauce section that carried a variety of Indian and Thai flavors. He had run out of chili sauce during the week and needed to restock. He searched the shelves and couldn't locate it in its usual place. He backtracked down the aisle and started his search afresh. Curry pastes, mango chutneys, oyster sauce, soy sauce, hoisin sauce. No chili sauce.

He called to the young attendant who was slouched over the counter at the front of the shop. She came towards him with a shuffling of feet.

"Good morning, I can't find the chili sauce. It's usually right here," said Mike, pointing at a space now occupied by an ordered row of mirin bottles.

The girl turned without a word and walked towards the back of the shop. She yelled something in Korean. Mike wondered if she had understood his Spanish. A small man appeared, a father or uncle Mike guessed by his age.

"Good morning, sir," the man said in accented Spanish. "Can I help you?"

"I was asking about the chili sauce. I can't find it."

"No more chili sauce. No more."

For fuck's sake, thought Mike, but instead asked, "When will you have it in again?"

"No more, no order any more. Government don't allow. They make now in Mendoza." The shopkeeper threw his hands up in disgust as if to ask, *What would Mendoza know about making chili sauce?*

"You can't import it anymore?"

"No, no more. Regulation."

"Fuck," said Mike. "They're killing me. Bit by fucking bit they are killing me."

"Lots of other good products," said the man, trying to guide Mike's eyes to the rest of his wares.

Mike thanked him, picked up a few more things, and made his way to the counter. He paid the languid girl who had returned to her post and exited.

He walked back down the length of Chinatown, under the lucky red arches, a non-believer that knew better than to tempt fate, turned onto Virrey Vertiz and headed towards Luis Maria Ocampo.

The walk would take forty minutes, maybe a little longer carrying his bag of shopping. The morning was still warm and some overhead cloud had taken the glare off the street. He made a mental note to buy some sunglasses. He remembered a shop near his apartment that sold knockoff Ray Bans.

At a small kiosk adorned with a cross section of magazines and newspapers, the majority carrying headlines about local football, he picked up that day's edition of *La Nacion*. While he often read the *Buenos Aires Herald*, reading *La Nacion* made him feel less an outsider and more in touch with the local pulse. And the reporting was good. *La Nacion* was evidence that a country needed much more than a strong press to be a functioning democracy. If *La Nacion* was labelled anti-government, it was because the current government was anti-governance.

La Nacion was embroiled in overt conflict with the government and Mike followed the tactical battles as a loyal partisan. The first shot was the government withdrawing its advertising spend. This had minimal effect on the wealthy media group behind the paper and, if anything, increased circulation among the more educated classes. The Ministry of News and Public Affairs then tried manipulating the content. This approach also met with limited results. Having attacked the news element of the newspaper they then went after the paper stock, buying up the largest newsprint supplier and then refusing to sell to *La Nacion* until they changed their editorial tune.

Mike had thought this a cunning tactic until he heard that it was a rehash of what Menem had done in the 1990s when he engaged in his own conflict with the paper. Wrongfooted for a week or two, the paper located a supplier of newsprint out of Finland. The additional production costs were offset by the increased circulation, which had continued to rise.

Mike arrived at the Las Cholas restaurant located on the corner of Arce and Arevalo. The shaded streets in the heart of the Las Canitas area were a favorite haunt, cozy in winter and refreshing in summer. Less touristy than Palermo or Recoleta there was an eclectic selection of traditional establishments dotted throughout Las Canitas.

The restaurant staff were opening the doors, unhurried and making rudimentary preparations for the lunch rush that would soon hit. A full two hours out and Mike could see that they would not be ready.

He settled into a corner chair and organized his paper into its proper reading order. Front page, politics, business, and sport. He didn't bother to call the waiter. When they were ready they would approach him.

He gripped the paper in both hands, extended his arms, and shook out the crinkles in the Finnish newsprint. The front page proclaimed that the incoming minister for economy had vowed to tackle inflation. Mike checked the date at the top of the paper. He had the feeling of having read the same announcement a few months earlier, from the then-incoming Eduardo Roncelli.

A separate headline read "AFIP Takes Action". The accompanying photo montage showed various houses from Buenos Aires' wealthier suburbs. All had been repossessed the day before, all belonged to prominent businessmen who had been vocal critics of the government's economic management. Fuck Finklestein, he was taking too long. He considered calling Alex. There would be a cost, there always was, but it was better than placing all his faith in Finklestein. If it got him out of here, then it would be worth it. He could regret it later, on a beach in Sicily.

Mike took out his phone and dialed. "Alex? About the AFIP. I'd like to take you up on your offer."

Alex's voice came down the line and into his ear like warm water. "Happy to help. Just send me through the details and I'll get on it."

"Thanks. It really is appreciated."

"Happy to help you out. There is something that you might be able to do in return."

That was quick, thought Mike.

"I need you to keep Simon Quinn on the straight and narrow. But I need you to *do it*, Mike." The warmth was gone from his voice.

"I already told you, Alex, there is nothing to worry about. I made it to clear to Simon that he needed to keep a low profile."

"You obviously haven't read today's papers."

"There's one right here in front of me, Alex."

Mike opened up the business section. A half-page headline jolted him: "MinEx Suspend Tender Process Over Inflation Fears".

"I'll save you the trouble of reading it. Quinn has suspended the tender process indefinitely. Because of inflation! He says he is hopeful that the government will put in place the right measures to tackle inflation that would benefit the MinEx project along with all Argentines."

Mike skimmed the article, matching the words he saw with those that Alex spoke down the line. If Quinn had set out to ruffle government feathers, Mike could think of no better way.

"Mike, this is going to draw international media attention. I need you to get Quinn to pull his fucking head in. And stay close to him this time."

It wasn't just the international attention. To blame inflation, which the government continued to report as running at 0.4 percent, would not go down well within the corridors of power. They had already jailed one pollster who had dared publish alternate inflation figures of eight percent. For Quinn to say that the government should fix inflation was akin to blaming them for it in the first place. All true facts and not ones that should be stated if Quinn wanted to continue working in Argentina. The government would be plotting a rebuttal that would hit hard at MinEx.

"Leave it with me," Mike said and hung up.

CHAPTER 13

On Monday morning Mike waited for Simon at the front of the MinEx offices. As Simon hurried towards him, head buried in his phone, Mike stepped out in front of him.

"Just a few questions if you don't mind, Mr. Quinn." Simon's head snapped up and Mike saw the anger in his eyes. "Sorry, I misjudged that," he apologized.

Simon relaxed. "I'm a bit on edge."

"Coffee? There's a place around the corner."

"Tea and I'm in. I can't drink the shit they're passing off as coffee down here."

Mike led the way to a small café tucked away on a side street. They took a seat at the back of the room at a white metal table.

"What are you having?"

Quinn swiveled in his chair to look at the front counter that held an array of small pastries.

"Just a tea and a croissant."

"You mean *media luna*, that's what they call croissants. They have a passion for renaming things. Go anywhere in the world, dip a chicken breast in egg yolk, roll it in breadcrumbs, fry it, and you have a schnitzel. Not here.

Here it's a *milanesa*. And it's not a language thing either. Go anywhere in the Spanish-speaking world and a strawberry is a *fresa*. Here, it's a *frutilla*. And nor does this unique ability limit itself to food. Take your Prince William for example. He gets off a plane here and now he's Prince *Guillermo*."

"He's not mine. But I take your point. I've noticed they also refuse to call a spade a spade."

"I hadn't thought of that one," said Mike, getting the attention of the waitress with a raised arm.

They ordered tea and a few of the *media lunas*. Smaller, denser, and sweeter than a croissant, they were Mike's favorite breakfast in a country that had failed to embrace the egg as a breakfast staple.

"I see you've been building a media profile."

"You saw the article then."

The waitress arrived with two cups of tea. Hot milk with a tea bag lurking below the surface. Mike sent them back after explaining the tea-making process. The waitress stared without blinking before moving off and returning with two cups of hot water, two unopened teabags and a glass of cold milk. She dumped them on the table as if to say, "Make it yourself." Mike prepared the teas.

"As you would have read, I've suspended the project." Quinn paused as if deciding whether to continue. He ruffled his hair with his hand and looked out the window. "Planning told me that there were no companies from Cordoba that were capable of building the project. I thought that if the company that Planning had put forward could do the work and there were no repercussions from other companies we'd be fine just qualifying one company. Planning assured us that there would be no issues if we were to move ahead with just the one bidder."

"So, why haven't you then?"

"We received the financial offers—offer, I should say. Technically, we have to accept the financial bid, but it would have bankrupted the whole project. The costs are around four hundred percent higher than we have budgeted for." Quinn dipped his *media luna* in his tea. Mike looked on in disapproval.

"That's high, even considering inflation."

"The inflation line was my own thinking. Put a bit of pressure back on them. When you deal with these governments you can't let them steamroll you. If I'm going to get this job done, I needed to set down a marker. Let them know that I can't be pushed around."

"I'm not sure it was a smart move. If you piss these people off, they will shut the whole thing down. For good. You are dealing with the same people who defaulted on a hundred billion dollars of debt. And what did congress do? They stood and applauded. World opinion doesn't cross the River Plate, Simon."

"They won't shut us down. They need us more than I realized. We've been talking to Planning. We explained that there was no way we could go ahead with the quote that we had received. It would blow the economics of the whole project."

"And their response?" asked Mike through a mouthful of yellow pastry.

"They said that costs were higher now because everything would have to be manufactured locally, that there were new import regulations that meant nothing could be brought in from abroad."

"It's an anti-inflation measure. They are trying to stop dollars going overseas so they've banned the importation of anything that can be made locally. Unfortunately, they believe they can make anything. Including Thai chili sauce as I found out on Saturday. There's a bloke making it out in Mendoza." Mike's tone made it sound as if this was a greater problem than Simon's.

Unoffended, Simon continued. "That's what they said, they are combatting inflation, they need us to do our part, for the good of the country. Even if you manufactured the whole thing here, that doesn't explain these prices. We ran the numbers. The profit alone for the construction company would have been near enough to 150 million dollars. The entire IDB loan," Quinn added though it wasn't necessary. He put his cup down, a full stop on his point and stared at Mike.

"Planning's view is that I am making a big deal out of nothing, that I needed to understand how things work in Argentina. They let it be known that if I reopened the tender, no questions asked, I would be looked after."

"They said that? Looked after?"

"They said I was in a country of abundance. Said there was plenty to go around. It was clear enough."

"Are you open to that?"

"If they were willing to reduce the tender prices. Why not? Once the project is built we'll be printing money. We'd recover any additional costs in no time. Problem is, with what they are asking now I will never get it built."

It was always the economics, never the morals. If the numbers made sense the ethics could always be massaged. In Quinn's situation it was the easiest option. Take a piece of the pie, the government gets what they want, and Quinn would get his railroad built.

"I don't recommend going down that path," Mike said.

"I am going to see what Planning comes back with. They'll cave and resubmit new prices."

Mike arched his eyebrows. On the list of the top-hundred things that were unlikely to happen, the Argentine government caving into Simon Quinn was number two or three. Mike fucking Gabriela Sabatini was number one.

Mike felt an anger begin to simmer. Not at Quinn, at Alex. Why would Alex expect that Quinn could get this project done playing it straight? That's how things were done here. Inflate the prices and skim the cream. Alex knew that. That is what Mike wanted to tell Quinn. Jump in! Grease their fucking palms, graft away, take your piece, it's your only fucking hope! But he stayed silent.

"I will see this out for as long as it runs, Mike. Quitting is not an option. I didn't tell my boss that we only qualified one bidder. If I go, Head Office will review what I have been doing here. They will go after me for sure. Corruption is not part of the corporate culture," he added.

Before Mike could speak Quinn cut him off.

"I have to make this work. And to make it work I need to know what is going on inside the Planning Ministry."

"I'll be happy to help. But I need you to keep your head down, Simon. No more press releases. If you want me to do this for you then the less attention on us the better."

"Whatever you say, Mike, but I want my money's worth this time. I want everything you can get on the minister. And if he so much as farts in my direction I want to know what it smells like. Got that?"

"You'll even know how loud it was," Mike promised.

Spying on the minister of planning had not been on Mike's to do list that morning, but if it was the only way to stay close to Simon Quinn then he would find a way.

CHAPTER 14

T he armchair retained the impression of the Doctor's
ample ass. The black leather was worn from use and
the arms were tattooed with the overlapping, ringed stains
of the thousand saucer-less cups that had been rested on
them. With the two matching armchairs, floral throw rug,
outdated television with a thick layer of dust on the screen
and extensive library with shelves that ran the length of
the wall, the room stood as testimony to a life without
children and of a couple who had settled into a familiarity
that Mike would never know.

It was a strange setting for the discussion he needed
to have. But what setting would have been appropriate to
discuss the surveillance of a government minister? In any
other country even the idea of doing so would be in the
realms of the fantastic. Here it was not only believable but
possible. If the money was right there would always be
somebody willing to assume the risk.

Mike's visit had been unannounced. After a quick,
surprised greeting, a kiss on the cheek, the Doctor had
retreated into the back of his house to search for more
appropriate dress than the tartan dressing gown in which
he had opened the door.

By the armchair, with its cushioned seat in no hurry to retake its form, next to the ubiquitous *mate* gourd and thermos, a book lay face down on the carved surface of a stained wooden table. Mike leant forward in his chair in an unsuccessful effort to make out the upside-down title written in inlaid gold print on the light-blue cover. Inching further forward he picked up the book and hauled it in for closer inspection. Careful not to lose the Doctor's page he examined the cover. *A History of British Naval Battles 1785–1805.* He flicked through the well-read pages, words and phrases had been underlined in lead pencil. Riveting, he thought.

He turned to the inside jacket. In careful writing in the top-right corner of the first page, "Julian Martinelli" was written. Below, an inscription:

To My Dear Friend, Julian. I hope this volume serves as a reminder that in life, as in the navy, we should always remember to pick our battles wisely.

Sincerely, Jeffrey Wainwright.

The name was familiar to Mike. Wainwright had been the British Defense Attaché in Buenos Aires several years back. Mike had met him at a few embassy events before Wainwright was sent home following an indiscretion with an embassy secretary. Mike leant forward and replaced the book on the table as the Doctor entered the room.

"I didn't know you were friends with Jeffrey Wainwright," said Mike.

"Wainwright? One of the world's great bastards, Mike. No friend of mine. That was not a gift. More a facetious threat. I had just published an article on lessons from the Malvinas war. The Brits considered it an attempt to incite nationalistic feeling. A few days later I received that at my office. My immediate thought was to send it back, but it's a first edition, hard to come by."

"You thanked him I presume?"

"Of course. Well I tried to. Before I could, the embassy received an anonymous tip-off that Wainwright had been dallying with his secretary. A gorgeous young thing, much too young for Jeffrey, and photogenic. Even through a bedroom window at night. It got some press at the time and was all of a bit of a mystery to be honest." The Doctor's smug grin told Mike that it was anything but a mystery.

"Reliving old memories?" asked Mike, pointing to the book.

"No, I'm translating it. I intend to make a gift of my translated version to the Argentine Maritime Museum. Sadly, we are very short on our own successful naval battles and there are lessons to be learned from the British." The Doctor scooped up the book and returned it to the bookshelf.

"Translating?" Mike had never heard the Doctor speak English.

"As you know, I don't really speak English. But I can understand it written."

Mike tried not to appear skeptical. It was a claim he often heard from those embarrassed by their lack of English.

"I hope I will receive a copy when it's done."

"First on the list, I promise. But you didn't come here to discuss British naval history, or did you?" asked the Doctor, raising an eyebrow.

"Indeed, I did not. I did want to ask how you were getting along with the prostate case. I forgot to ask when we caught up last."

"Where was I, last time we spoke?"

"You were trying to convince the kids to pay up."

"Ah yes, well that went nowhere. Idiots. They didn't want to spend ten thousand pesos, so I had to find someone who would."

"You bankrolled it yourself?"

"No. I went to the bastard child. She was a smart one. For her it was a no brainer, invest ten thousand pesos to make God knows how much. You should have seen her face, she thought I was Willy Winka come to save her from a life of poverty and abandonment."

"Wonka," Mike corrected.

"Yes, Willy Wonka, of course. In the end a satisfactory result. And no more favors, I can assure you."

"How have you explained this to the kids? They must be livid."

"Not at all. I kept my word. I destroyed the sample. The old man has departed from this earth. All of him."

"You said—"

"I said that the bastard child paid the money to pay the nurse. Unfortunately, for her, and this is unfortunate, the prostate didn't come back a match. It appears that her mother had lied to her all these years. She was quite upset."

"Or someone switched the prostates," said Mike in disbelief.

"Highly unlikely, Mike," said the Doctor, without blinking. "Now, my turn to ask you something," he said, moving on. "I read that MinEx has suspended the project. Don't tell me that my friend Decoud has won the battle? We have kept up quite the correspondence since our meeting. Passionate fellow."

"Nothing to do with the environmentalists. They're still being a nuisance, but not enough to stop the project." Mike paused. "You're not collaborating with them, are you? I know that you might consider making more trouble for MinEx as marketing. From my perspective, it would place me in a difficult position."

The Doctor uncrossed his legs and adjusted himself in his arm chair. "I can assure you that I would do no such thing. My correspondence with Mr. Decoud is of one concerned citizen to another. Any action he takes is of his own doing. Well, not completely. I am convinced he has someone on the inside of MinEx who is feeding him information." Mike ignored the bait. He had no intention of chasing more shadows than the ones he already had.

"There was an issue with the tender process."

"Inflation was the official reason. Though I have been around long enough to doubt any sentence containing the words 'official' and 'inflation'."

"In this case, it's accurate. It was inflation. The prices they received on the bid were inflated."

"All the bids?"

"They only received one bid."

"Well played," said the Doctor with what Mike sensed was a degree of nationalistic admiration.

"They ran the numbers on the bid, using their own cost estimates. The net profit matches or is somewhat similar, to the total of the government loan."

"All is revealed," said the Doctor. "MinEx has been lured to the Argentine to launder the IDB loan for our government. That is quite the conundrum. I must admit I haven't seen this play before. It does show a nice evolution of procedure."

"You seem impressed," said Mike.

"One can only hope to see the country moving forward. Let's face it, Mike, at their heart these are not new issues. You could trace it back to Spanish colonization if you wanted to go back that far. Better to start with Peron himself. Do you know when Argentina entered the Second World War? About a month before it ended. I know we have a reputation for tardiness, but six years? Why do you think that was?" He didn't wait for an answer. "Because neutrality was a lucrative business.

"Peron was available to the highest bidder and rather than pick a winner early on he wanted to make sure he was on the winning side. So, he made promises and took money from both sides. The promises he never kept, the money he did. All squirreled away in a bank account in Switzerland.

"After his death, some of his followers dug him up. In the dead of night, they crept into the Recoleta cemetery and exhumed his corpse. You know what they took? His hands! They lopped them both off. Why would they do this? I'll tell you why, because all the money he had sent off to Switzerland was held in an account that could only be opened with Peron's fingerprints."

"Why didn't they just take the fingers?"

"And risk losing one? Much more sensible to take two hands rather than ten fingers."

"What happened to the money?"

The Doctor crossed his legs again and sat back, deep in his chair. "I've no idea. It's probably still up there with the Santa Cruz funds. The point is, Peron never got to spend it. After the war, there was speculation that any money taken from the Germans was Jewish money, the Americans were looking for it, they felt guilty. They hadn't been able to save Jewish lives; they wouldn't make the same mistake with their gold. Too much attention. Peron could never claim the money."

"How do you know all this?"

"Everyone knows this, Mike," said the Doctor, dismissing the question with a wave of his hand. "Exhibit B, Carlos Menem," the Doctor said, moving his thesis along. "His play was a little different. He started out selling off state assets to his cronies. Lucrative work that didn't interfere too much with the running of the country. Like all small men, Carlitos always felt he was bigger than the country that bore him. He wanted the world to know his greatness. He sought bigger and bigger gains. That's how he got involved in selling arms to Ecuador. He wasn't interested in the cash for the arms. He was interested in what he could gain in return for backing a winning side. He didn't realize that the US were backing the other side. If they had backed the same side, no problem, as soon he opposed the US he was doomed."

"That was the only fact in his downfall. And it wasn't just arms. There were the drugs. I think the whole region had an interest in stamping out that kind of activity," said Mike, embarrassed by the sanctimony he heard in his own voice. It was the North American in him, the one that still made a token appearance every now and then.

"And Mr. Oliver North?"

"Ended up in jail."

"And has been forgotten by history. The aura of Carlitos lives on, and not because he was caught. He's admired because ultimately, he has escaped punishment. We respect that. But that's not my point.

"My point is that our current administration has learnt these lessons well. They have stolen no more or no less from the country than those that have gone before. The methods are evolving. You will hear no stories of stashing war loot or selling arms to insurgents. This administration has made corruption boring. That is their legacy."

"Boring?" asked Mike.

"Boring so as not to attract the attention of the US and your, I must say, hypocritical agents of good. An agency for every vice; drugs, weapons, terrorism, religion, ethics. This administration has focused their looting on the most boring, uninteresting, unwatched sectors out there. Public works.

"It's big money and it's on sovereign territory, another plus. You build a road from Gualeguaychu to Trelew and you budget one billion pesos, the budget blows out to 1.2 billion and then 1.3 billion. Who's watching? Who even knows where these places are? And who can tell how much it should cost? A bridge over the Paraná River, budgeted to cost four hundred million, extras and add-ons and adjustments and it comes in at four seventy-five million. Who cares? It's a bloody bridge.

"You land a small plane on the border of Venezuela and Colombia, unload a crate of weapons destined for the FARC and you've got more red flags than Mao's funeral. A public-works budget for a road from nowhere to nowhere blows out by ten, fifteen, twenty percent? Who gives a shit? Maybe the road never even gets finished. Again, who's going to care? That is what is brilliant about these assholes in power."

"So, how do you stop them?"

"Unless somebody takes an interest in what they intend to spend their laundered funds on, you can't. You must wait until the money runs out. The US are not coming to help. Luckily, it appears that the money *is* running out. And without cash, Peronism as a political force is nothing. So, what you are telling me makes sense. The government needs that money back from MinEx. MinEx is just an intermediary, a launderer of the bank loan. They weren't counting on MinEx caring about the budget. Or they may have thought MinEx may be interested in getting some of that money back themselves. A la Skanska."

Mike nodded his head. "The client did suggest that an offer was made."

He saw now what the Doctor was saying. The play had evolved, now the prices would still be inflated, but the work was real, a railway would be built. It would just be expensive. Best of all, they weren't skimming company money or government money. It was Inter-American Development Bank money; a victimless crime.

Mike could hear the Doctor's wife through the open door, busying about the kitchen.

"And what makes you think they are running out of money now?"

"The fights they are picking and the people who are picking fights with them. That tells me people are not getting paid."

"For example?" asked Mike.

"For example, the British government and the Argentine navy. Articles are starting to appear about the Malvinas. Always a sure sign that the government is worried about things on the domestic front. This time it seems to have been triggered by the sinking of that boat in Santa Cruz carrying, or not carrying as the insurers claim, a cargo of gold."

Mike remembered the trouble that the *Polar Mist* was causing for Alex. His attempts to placate Lloyd's of London were failing. The papers were calling it another case of the English impugning Argentina's international reputation.

"The English claiming something that is not theirs. It's a narrative that plays well down here. The government embellish a bit, throw out some smoke. Maybe Lloyd's sunk the boat. Now we have an international conspiracy to defraud Argentina. And there is precedent. In the Malvinas war, the president reminds us, the English sunk the *Belgrano*, a non-combat ship, sailing away from the zone of combat, torpedoed by the British in an act of treachery and cowardice."

"Non-combat?" interrupted Mike. "It was a battleship. In battle."

"Exactly, and this is where we see who is picking fights with the government. The navy. Now if the navy is on side they go along with this, for the national interest.

However, that is not the case. The Admiral, a good man I will add and a personal friend, has come out and refuted the president's version of the sinking of the *Belgrano*. You now have the unusual situation where the head of the Argentine navy, to save the navy's honor, insists that the *Belgrano* was indeed sunk by the British in combat. But the president, to paint the British as immoral bastards, is saying, no, the *Belgrano* was sailing away from the battle, heading back to the mainland. Imagine, accusing your own navy of an act of cowardice to score a political point." Mike saw the Doctor's fist open and clench on the arm rest.

"You were on the *Bouchard*, Doctor. Where was the *Belgrano* headed?" Mike had spent countless hours sitting through the Doctor's tales of life on the *Bouchard*, the Malvinas war, and the respect the Argentine navy and military had felt towards their English enemies. The Doctor often said that British had treated them better than their own political masters.

The Doctor wore his impenetrable smile. "We were at war, Mike. The *Belgrano* was in battle. They were doing what they were trained to do. The *Bouchard* is only remembered today as first on the scene to rescue the *Belgrano* survivors, but we were lucky to survive ourselves. A torpedo grazed our hull. I saw the damage done. For some reason it didn't explode." The Doctor placed both hands on the arms of his chair and pushed himself to his feet. "If you believe the president, a passing whale did the damage. An English whale no doubt!"

Mike watched the Doctor circle the room. He stopped at the window and with thumb and forefinger pulled aside the floral curtain that matched the throw rug and looked out on the garden.

"No, they're desperate for money," he said to the roses. "Don't think that makes them weak, Mike. That makes them dangerous." He turned to face Mike. "Will you be staying for dinner? I can ask Martha to prepare us something."

"No, I have to get going back to the city. I have a request."

"Of course. What can I do for you?"

"I need information on the Planning Minister."

The Doctor nodded registering neither encouragement nor approbation.

"His plans, movements, his weak spots. Everything we can get. Dirt. All the skeletons. All the bodies."

"And how does your client intend to use this information?"

Mike's intention was to buy one package of information and then drip feed it to Quinn for as long as Alex needed him to stay close to him. What Quinn did with it didn't concern Mike.

"I don't know. Has that ever mattered?" Mike knew that it didn't. If the Doctor got paid he never asked questions.

"I can't guarantee anything. And I will tell you now. If you have other sources out there, I suggest you contact them. Donald Duck has closed up on me. Thanks to your client."

"Why would he close up?" asked Mike, with equal parts surprise and concern.

"Can you blame him? He hands over Planning's KYC file on your client and the next day the tender is suspended."

"I explained why he suspended the tender. Nothing more sinister than awful timing. I advised the client as we agreed. Change nothing. Show nothing. Business as usual." The explanation didn't appear to mollify the Doctor.

"That may well be what happened, Mike, but that is not what Donald Duck believes happened. He says his guy in Planning is spooked. Of course, I will transmit this new information. As I said, no promises. I'm not sure we can count on him to continue his work for us."

Mike sensed that Donald Duck could be convinced to continue. He would just require more financial incentive to do so.

"Like I said, if you have other sources best throw a few lines out."

"I'll do that, Doctor." Mike stood up and made for the door from where he had entered. The afternoon had dragged on and the last light of day spattered through the garden.

The Doctor remained by the window. "Mike, if collecting a dirt file on the Planning Minister is their solution, then they have no solution. Your client should go to Cordoba and speak to Governor Castelli. Go over Planning's head. Make a deal. Castelli is no friend of the president. He could also look into his leak while he is out there." The Doctor turned back to Mike. "Boots on the ground. That's the way to get things done."

CHAPTER 15

"So, Andrea, what have we got today?" Mike asked, placing his feet on his desk.

"It's not good, Mike." Andrea tilted her head and tugged at her earring with thumb and forefinger, stretching her earlobe, repeating the movement as if tolling a warning bell in her own mind.

"Not good, as in same old not good, or not good as in getting worse?" asked Mike.

"Not good as in getting worse," said Andrea, moving from behind her desk. She opened a newspaper and laid it before Mike. She sat down opposite, crossed her legs, and placed the remaining papers in a neat pile on the floor beside her. Her fingers went back to the unconscious tolling of her earlobe. "Every day it is getting worse. And every day you have me going through these papers, translating the same stories about Simon Quinn, and sending them over to him. Does he even read them or am I wasting my time? Because if he is reading them then he would be thinking the same thing I am. Their project is fucked and, by association, so are we. What is it about this client, Mike? Why are you so fixated on them?"

Mike ran his hand over his head, feeling more scalp than hair. Where would he start? That the work for MinEx was just an excuse to stay close to Quinn? And he was staying close to Quinn so that Alex would pull some strings so Mike could sell his apartment and abandon the country and Andrea? She'd have his balls for any one of those reasons. All of them combined and she might just take off his head. He opted for the most benign option.

"I'm doing it as a favor for Alex Harper," he said, hoping his comment would go through unexamined.

"Alex fucking Harper? From the British embassy?" Andrea shook her head in disgust. "What has he got on you? The only reason you would be doing him a favor is if he has something on you."

"He doesn't have anything on me, Andrea. I'm just trying to help him out."

Andrea cocked a well-manicured eyebrow. Mike understood why. The last place he wanted to be was in a quid pro quo with Alex Harper. He hoped Finklestein would come through before he had to do any spying on the minister of planning. How did it get to this? His escape from Argentina, his golden, Sicilian future directed by Harper and Finklestein. It sounded like a fucking opera.

"Why don't you just tell me what's in the paper that has got you so upset, Andrea," said Mike, trying to lead her and himself down a different path.

Andrea closed her eyes and breathed in through her nose and out her mouth. Mike could hear the passage of her breath. Diaphragm breathing, she called it. When she opened her eyes the red mist had passed and the eyebrow had settled back into its natural position.

"There's the usual, that suspending the tender is illegal under Argentine law. They are still failing to specify which law. I presume they are drawing one up. However, and this is where things have changed, anonymous sources within the government have expressed sympathy with MinEx's local management." Andrea paused to allow her boss to register his surprise. Then the kicker. "The decision to suspend the tender process has nothing to do with the economic conditions of Argentina and everything to do with MinEx's own financial situation.

"It is understood, it doesn't say by whom, that MinEx is having cashflow and liquidity problems that are affecting its Argentine project and the viability of several projects across Latin America. There is speculation that MinEx may sell off several tier-one assets across Latin America. The unnamed source has been in contact with government counterparts in Brazil, Ecuador, and Venezuela and can confirm that MinEx projects are suffering similar delays there."

"Do they have anything in Venezuela?" Mike asked.

"Not that I can find," said Andrea.

"How do they make this shit up?"

Andrea remained unmoved, expressed no opinion either way. "Shall I continue?"

"There's more?" asked Mike.

"According to another, unnamed, source, the decision to award MinEx the Cordoba project and the subsequent loan arrangement was engineered by the former minister for economy, Eduardo Roncelli." She looked over the paper at Mike. "You will recall that Roncelli was ousted from the government not long ago."

"I recall."

"They are saying, alleging, that there may be links between MinEx and Roncelli, that a deal may have been done."

"That's absurd."

"It justifies an investigation and that creates the opportunity to put more pressure on MinEx. That is what they're after. Search their offices, sequester documents, make arrests. Anything they like."

"Arrests? Let's try to stay calm here, Andrea. No one is getting arrested." Not yet anyway.

"Anything is possible. MinEx have upset people who are not used to being upset. Suspending the project was one thing. Blaming it on inflation. Putting a number on that inflation. The government is trying to negotiate its way back into the World Bank's good books and MinEx accuses them of being unable to run the economy and lying about it too."

"Accuse them, Andrea? You live, here don't you? Inflation's not the reason Simon took the decision he did but that doesn't make it any less out of control."

"I do live here, Mike. And when you live here, you learn to keep your head down and you get by. You make do with what life deals you. The way things get done here might be different to what our client is used to. Might offend their sensitivities. That's how it is. And in some bizarre, mixed up way, it works. There are winners and losers but tell me, where is that not the case?

"Going public, calling out the government, scream-ing from the rooftops, is not the way to go about it. You are supposed to be advising them, Mike. Sometimes I wonder who is advising you?"

Mike was never offended by Andrea's outbursts, scared yes, but never offended. He admired the passion, the authenticity. He was always happy to admit when she was right, which often meant admitting that he was wrong.

"I have advised Simon to keep his head own. It just doesn't seem to be Simon's way, unfortunately. What do you suggest I tell him?"

"Sit tight. And stop pissing people off."

"You sound like Alex Harper."

"Sorry?"

Mike ignored the question, not wanting to stoke the flame.

"There is something else. Finklestein called again."

"Yes?" Mike asked, as if probing for a land mine.

"He said to tell you there was still no news on your apartment."

"What did he say exactly?"

"There's no news on Mike's apartment." She raised both eyebrows in expectation of an explanation. Mike's shoulders slumped and he looked out the window. He could tell her, but he couldn't look at her and tell her.

"Fuck Finklestein," he mumbled. Then louder, "I've asked Finkelstein to prepare the apartment for sale."

Andrea's laugh filled the office. "Selling the apartment? Moving again are we? Where to this time?"

"Sicily. I'm sorry, Andrea, I should have told you, but I can't take it anymore. I've had enough," said Mike hands raised in defense.

"Sicily? You are not going anywhere," she said, still laughing. 'Remember last time you had had enough? Where was it you were going to? Mexico? And how did that end? You had me do all that research. House prices, office space, the annual fucking rainfall. Then what? You decided you didn't like the smog or the food or the Mexicans. Didn't you learn anything from that, Mike?" Her voice had morphed from mirth to pity.

"I've tried to change, Andrea, you know that. I have tried accepting it, I have tried loving it, and at times I really do. I've tried living in a little bubble down here, blocking it all out. But it always gets in, gets at me, and eats me up. I swear someday I am going to explode and kill someone. Or myself. I don't get it, I just don't get you fucking people. And I never will!"

"What's to get, Mike? You can do anything you want here, be anyone you want. You don't need to go anywhere. Changing country isn't going to help you. You need to change here," she said, tapping her breast with her finger tips. "What you need is a woman, Mike."

Mike searched her face. Where was the rage?

"Don't look at me like that. I am not that woman. You made that clear already. What were your words? Don't shit where you eat?"

"Come on, Andrea, that was four years ago. How do you even remember that stuff? And you shouldn't be listening to my phone calls."

"Is that what this MinEx case is about? Somehow part of your plan to get out of here?"

The woman was a witch. "No," Mike lied. He had had enough of this conversation. "What do I do about MinEx?"

Andrea relaxed her grip. "If the government see that their pressure is having an effect, they will go to MinEx, see if they are ready to make a deal. Be patient, *ragazzo*."

Andrea rose from her chair, still smiling, smoothed her skirt against her thighs, collected the unread newspapers from the floor and left Mike to his thoughts.

He had to admit it was good advice. He had no intention of following it. Quinn couldn't be trusted to make the right decisions. Mike would have to do it himself.

"Andrea, I need you to book me a flight to Cordoba. For tomorrow."

CHAPTER 16

M ike Costello stopped in front of office number 36 and knocked on the wood-paneled door. The sliding of chair legs and sounds of shuffling feet could be heard in response.

The door swung back and he was greeted by a lady dressed in a serious, dark-blue jacket and office pants of a matching color. Her hair was grey with a faint blush of purple and held up in a bun.

"Mr. Quinn," she said, smiling. "Please, come in. The governor is expecting you. How was your flight?"

Mike greeted the governor's secretary and entered. The secretary commanded a desk that was covered with files in neat stacks of two and threes. Another table held a small television set that was tuned to the 24-hour news station. The residue of a political life in Argentina hung from every wall. Plaques of thanks, photos with dignitaries, both foreign and domestic, recognizable and unrecognizable, honorary degrees, and reams of ribbon being cut in front of bridges, libraries, buildings, boats, and statues. Front and center of each photo stood the beaming figure of Miguel Castelli, Governor of the

Province of Cordoba and leader of the unofficial opposition, or what was left of it.

From the photos, Mike could track the progression of the youthful man that stood in some of the black-and-white photos to the man of more advanced years that looked out from the color photos. A hard, political life.

"Can I offer you something to drink while you wait? The governor will only be a minute."

"I would accept a glass of water." Mike was always left dry after a flight.

"Certainly, Mr. Quinn." The secretary left the room and returned with a glass and handed it to Mike. At once, the door behind the secretary's desk opened and Governor Castelli's large frame emerged. If the governor had ever seen a picture of Simon Quinn the game would be up in this instant. It wasn't.

The governor was a tall man. A good height for television, Mike thought. He must have been well over six foot with wide shoulders. His head was a little too big for his admittedly large body. From his ears, also in matching large size and set a little low as if they had slipped down, sprouted hairs that needed a trim. He had a robustness about him that bode well for the meeting. Only the governor's hands were delicate, policy hands.

"Mr. Quinn, please come through. I see Angelica has already given you some water. Can I offer you something else?"

"The water is fine." Mike picked up his shoulder bag and followed the governor back into his office. It was a cramped affair, the kind of office you chose if you didn't want to spend large amounts of money on sweeping for listening devices, a service that Mike charged out by the square meter. A large, wooden writing desk that featured carved borders on all sides dominated the room. Mike ran a finger over the border in appreciation. The governor took his place behind the desk in a green leather chair, leant back, clasped his hands in front of him and studied Mike.

"So, Mr. Quinn, as I have heard them say in the movies, to what do I owe this honor?" the governor asked in impeccable English. Mike thought he detected a slight British accent.

Mike had his pitch well prepared. He lubricated his throat with some more water.

"Thank you for seeing me at such short notice, Governor Castelli," said Mike, keeping his mode of address formal. It was his experience that the further you got from the capital, the more respect these officials demanded. A president would be happy with "John". The mayor of San Martin de los Andes would take offense at anything less than his "Esteemed Excellency the Mayor".

"I have been expecting you for some time, Mr. Quinn. I thought you may have paid me a visit by now."

"I apologize that I did not come sooner. I wasn't sure of the welcome I would receive. There are some misinformed elements of your community that would prefer that I never came here at all."

The governor smiled and relaxed further into his chair. He raised a delicate hand to his head and took the tufts of hair protruding from his ears and gently, almost tenderly, rolled them between thumb and forefinger, clockwise then anti-clockwise, as if enjoying the sound of the fibers entwining and untwining, a tiny stringed orchestra that only he could hear.

"You refer of course to Mr. Decoud. He is a passionate man though I am sure he means you no harm." The fingers played on.

"Even so, the advice from my security was to stay away until things had calmed down somewhat," said Mike, believing he was making a more than passable impression of what Simon Quinn would say in the same circumstances.

"Yet here you are, in my office and, as you say, at such short notice. A more cynical man than myself might be forgiven for thinking that you've come to ask a favor."

Mike met the eyes of the governor.

"Of course, I have been following MinEx's predicament, Mr. Quinn. The government has cornered you into using contractors of their choice. You are refusing to do so but you need to find a way to advance the project. So, let us not dance around the issue. How can I help you? Or more accurately, how do you believe I can help you?"

"I think that there is an opportunity to work together here, Governor. MinEx were led to believe that your province did not have any companies with the capability to build the railway. Having reviewed the technical offers from the bid process I saw that the companies intended to hire their employees locally." After the first lie it was easy to find more. "I will be open with you. You are correct in saying that the company that has tendered for the work on this project is connected to the federal government and is controlled by front men for the government.

"What I'm suggesting to you, Governor, is that MinEx works with your office to cut out these middlemen and that MinEx hire these employees, on fixed-term contracts, for the duration of the project. We've already received the government loan; we have run the numbers and they make sense. A lot more sense than the financial bid we have already received. Importantly, we will be in compliance with our agreement to hire locally."

"Technically," interjected the governor.

"Correct, technically we'd be employing local contractors just not through a local company. The benefit to your province will be more direct, the money will be going straight into the pockets of your constituents." Mike concluded his pitch. He was not sure of the business logic, but from a political point of view it had to be compelling for the governor. He studied the governor's face for any reaction.

"Mr. Quinn, I appreciate your offer. It's an attractive offer. I can assure you it makes a lot of sense. In London or New York or Paris. Unfortunately, we are not in any of those places. We are in Cordoba. As you may be gathering, things work differently down here. Did you notice the roadworks on the way in from the airport?"

Mike nodded.

"Did you notice that while there were roadworks there were no road workers? If you had of flown in last month you would have seen the same sight. I can think of no better window onto politics than those roadworks. They are both the carrot and the stick that the Federal government uses to drive its agenda. My senators vote the right way, the government frees up the funds for public works; we vote a different way and the funds freeze, the works stall, the traffic backs up, people are late for work, a child can't make an emergency medical flight, and my constituents come after me. They do the work of the government for them.

"Look around the country, Mr. Quinn, look at the public works, the roads, the bridges, the tunnels, the infrastructure. Where is it progressing, where is it stalled? That is your political map of Argentina. What do you suppose will happen to me if I go along with this idea of yours and cut the government out of, what? A hundred-and-fifty-million-dollar business? Like I said, it's a brilliant idea, but what would happen to me? I can tell you. I would never see another federal peso. Without money I cannot govern. I would not last until the end of the year."

"MinEx is the largest single investor in your province. That must count for something."

Castelli shook his head as if embarrassed by the suggestion. "That means very little here, Mr. Quinn. Your company will come and go, that will not change these things. We will not become the US or the United Kingdom because you build a railway. Not if ten MinExes build ten railways. This is how we are. I must deal with the realities of my situation.

"The great mistake that people like yourself make is to think that your western countries are more advanced, more developed than us, and that one day we will catch up if only we can get the investment. It is an error. We are developed. We have developed on a different path, at a different time." Castelli paused. "Look at the trees out that window Mr. Quinn."

Mike followed the governor's order. Having played himself into the office as the naïve envoy of MinEx he realized he would now have to sit through the lecture.

"That tree started as a seed. It grows, matures, and decays. That is the way of the natural world. The birds who make their home in that tree will follow the same path, as will the worms that those birds feed on. Nations, economies, democratic systems, all products of us humans, also of the natural world, why should they be any different? From where do we get this certainty that progress is lineal, forever trending upwards? A country's development can only follow that of the natural world, the same development path of the units that compose it. We are born, we grow, we have our glory years, and then we begin to decline, naturally, as it must be."

"And you just accept this decline?"

"Of course. All nations of a certain age are in decline. We cannot be saved, Mr. Quinn. Your hope is that we will become like you, my certainty is that you will become like us. What you see here, you will see in all nations. Just like humans, in some the decline will be rapid, in others slow. But it will only be delaying the inevitable.

"In that sense, education is like daily exercise that strengthens democracy, keeps decline at bay, even if only temporarily. Argentina was once a beacon of education, until we killed it. Strikes, politics, militancy, unions, stolen funds. And now we pay the price. A country that abandons the education of its citizens sickens. It has happened here, Mr. Quinn, and I see it happening abroad. It opens the door for populism, or in our case worse, Peronism. It won't kill a country outright, just make it sick enough for something else to finish the job."

"You make it sound like HIV."

"A good analogy."

"If it's so hopeless, why are you here? What's the point?" challenged Mike, warming to his role of innocent questioner.

"The decline can be rough, or it can be smooth. I like to think that I am performing a service. I try to manage the decline, comfort my constituents. Consider it palliative, political care."

Mike shifted tack, emboldened by his false identity.

"If MinEx could make a change, Governor, at the very top? Could you not do more than just manage the decline as you put it? Show some leadership?" It sounded insolent to Mike's own ears. He didn't care, it wasn't his reputation he was playing with.

"How do you propose to achieve that change, Mr. Quinn? At the very top?" asked the governor, cocking his large head to one side.

"I'm compiling a report on the minister for planning." Mike paused to allow his words to bury into those large, low-set ears. "Our intention is to provide it to the media, here and abroad. We want to use MinEx's profile to expose what is happening, Governor. People will listen. I don't expect you to do anything beforehand. Afterwards I will need political support. If I can create enough of a bang there will be a political space that you can fill."

The governor pushed his chair back from his desk and stood up. A green, porcelain vase sat on the desk. He upended it. A small, bronzed key dropped into his palm. He turned to the cabinet behind him. In a practiced movement, he used the key to unlock the sliding, wooden door, jiggled it a little on its runners until it rolled back to reveal a row of folders of various thicknesses. He ran his finger over several binders that were neatly labelled. He paused over a large one before retrieving it from the cabinet. He returned to his seat and placed it on the table in front of Mike.

"Here you go. Feel free to take it. It's everything I have gathered on the esteemed minister for planning since he first raised his reptilian head in Rio Gallegos. It's all in there." He pointed over his shoulder to the still-opened cabinet. "The presidential inner circle is all in there too. The scandals, the cover ups, the fraud, the casinos, the hotels, the real estate. I don't even have it all. These bastards are like Aloe Vera, the more you investigate the more properties you find.

"Take it. It will do no good, it means nothing." He waggled a smooth index finger at the folder. "These scandals, they are tiny bargaining chips at best, insignificant pawns in a game of Kings and Queens. Politics are won and lost on the streets, not in folders in an old man's cabinet."

Mike leant forward and opened the folder. He flicked through a few pages. Newspaper clippings that had yellowed with age and neat typed paragraphs that had been produced on typewriters gave an indication of how far back the reporting went. Mike closed the folder and sat back in his chair. He imagined the price he would put on this for Simon. In Sicily it could pay for new floors or maybe even a whole new deck.

"Are you familiar with Borges, Mr. Quinn?"

A shake of the head. Another non-verbal lie.

"One of our greatest writers. He wrote: 'The best place to hide a leaf is in a forest'. Our political class has learnt this lesson well. Each scandal is covered up by another scandal, and another, and another. The people lose track, the courts can't process them, the police can't investigate them. I believe in English you have a saying: When you find yourself in a hole, stop digging. Our local version would be: When you find yourself in a hole, dig another!"

Mike laughed as expected and extended his hand across the desk. "Thank you for your time, Governor."

"Will you join me for lunch, Mr. Quinn?"

"I would be honored, Governor."

"Mr. Quinn?" Angelica's head had appeared around the door. "I have your office on the phone. They said to tell you that the reporters have arrived. They want to know if you will be much longer."

"My office?"

"Yes, here in Cordoba."

No one could have known Mike was in Cordoba. It was his golden rule not to alert the press when impersonating clients.

"Can you tell them that I will be having lunch with the governor. We may have to reschedule."

"I see you share my fondness of the fourth estate. Well their bad luck is my good luck. I am very keen to pick your brains on some of the engineering aspects of the project. I graduated in civil engineering, did my Masters in heavy infrastructure, and I have been fascinated by some of the things that you are intending to do with the railway around the Champaqui mountains."

Mike felt his face drop. "Yes, it is, it is, quite innovative," he stammered. "What we are intending to do," he said. "Though I must admit—" he broke off and dug into his pocket for his phone. "I am sorry, Governor, I have a hundred missed calls here from my office. Maybe it is best if I get over there. I forgot that we have a media call."

"That is a pity. Next time perhaps," Castelli said, showing no obvious offence.

"Yes, next time. I'll look forward to it. I will take you through the whole project," said Mike, grateful to have avoided a conversation he was nowhere near qualified to have.

The governor picked up his dirt file from the table. "Take this with you. Consider it a gift. And look after it. I don't want this coming back on me," he said with a practiced wink.

"Would you mind calling me a taxi?" asked Mike.

"Nonsense. I will have my driver take you straight there. Safer and cheaper."

And no chance of diverting to the airport, thought Mike.

When Mike emerged on the street the governor's car was already waiting for him. Mike got in and without a word it took off. At the MinEx offices, once the governor's driver was gone, he could catch a taxi to the airport. A short but necessary detour.

CHAPTER 17

On the car radio, tuned for the driver and not the passenger, Andres Calamaro was wondering who would write the history of all the things that could have happened but didn't. To Mike it was a pointless, if beautiful question, and in Argentina's case would have resulted in a formidable tome. Sad and unreadable.

The streets passed by the window of the governor's car. Mike disengaged his mind from the world outside his window, more concerned with replaying the governor's conversation, examining it for any wormholes that he could follow down towards some kind of solution. None presented themselves. Impersonating Simon Quinn had been a risk but looking at the folder in his hands it had paid off in an unexpected way. That was Argentina, ready to give you something when you least expected it.

The car pulled up in front of the MinEx offices. Mike recognized the building from the brochures that papered the coffee table in the Buenos Aires office. An example of MinEx's commitment to being part of the community. A global company with a local presence, that was how it was sold.

Mike stood on the pavement and waited for the governor's car to pull away. It didn't. The driver loitered, waiting for Mike to go inside. With a quick glance around he crossed the gravel parking spaces and approached the glass door. MinEx was splashed across the pane in black lettering like a discount sale. The windows facing the street were stenciled with the same corporate messages that decorated the reception in Buenos Aires. Mike wondered who had decided to have them printed in English.

He tried the door handle and entered the building. The reception was unoccupied. No reporters. No staff. He leant across the desk. The computer screen was lit. An Excel document was open, a few cells filled in with numbers. A window with a half-finished game of solitaire overlaid the excel document. A mustard-colored knitted cardigan hung across the back of the chair.

"Hola," Mike called out. No response. He could feel the silence in the building like a physical presence. He placed the governor's dirt file on the reception desk and walked through to the offices to confirm what he already knew. They were empty.

Noises outside the office snapped his attention. He checked his watch. The staff returning from lunch, he guessed. He was always too quick to judge, to think the worst. Andrea's influence no doubt. He returned to the reception area. Through the window he could see a crowd of people forming on the other side of the gravel parking lot. Too many to be staff. Too hungry-looking to be arriving from lunch. He felt the saliva in his mouth dry up.

He shuffled a few paces to his left to better see the group. Around twenty people stood on the footpath, the back rows were swelling with new arrivals. Most were men, bare chested with dirty T-shirts wound around their faces to form make-shift masks. As he saw the group they saw him, and a uniform chant erupted. He could have been in Lanus on a sunny Sunday afternoon awaiting kick-off. He could feel their voices even through the office walls.

He looked at the telephone behind reception. Who would he call? The governor? He reached for the phone and held it to his ear. Dead. He looked again through the window to the mob outside. If they were looking for Simon Quinn he might be able talk to these people. Why would they suspect he had anything to do with MinEx? Just an unfortunate visitor. He took a step towards the door. The chanting grew louder. A visceral hatred carrying through the air. He turned and grabbed the dirt file from the reception desk and placed it under his arm. It gave him some comfort, some aspect of authority.

He opened the door, stepped outside, then turned his back on the crowd as he shut the door with deliberate care, trying to appear calm, in control. He faced the baying group that stood on the opposite side of the gravel parking lot. The first missile was launched from the back of the crowd. Mike saw its arching trajectory, a dark shadow against the blue of the cloudless sky. He threw his arms up in defense, the folder under his arm falling to the gravel. The missile sailed by and smashed through the office window behind him. A pause then a whoosh as flame burst out of the broken window. A cheer went up and, as Mike stumbled away from the fire, a second projectile caught him a thudding blow on the arm that he still had raised in protection of his face. He turned his back on the crowd, shaking his arms, trying to get free of his jacket in anticipation of the burst of engulfing flame that was to come but none came.

As he struggled with his jacket a third projectile caught him low on the back of his head with a crack that shook him and wobbled his knees. He fell to the gravel and as the smoke that poured from the window covered him he could see the advancing shoes attached to legs that stretched in vertical lines to the sky, then felt their jackhammer kicks into the small of his back, his legs, his groin, and his stomach. Other feet stomped from above, driving his body into the gravel of the parking lot. He felt his shoulder bag pulled on until the strap broke.

He balled up, using his arms to cover his head and face. The blows did not abate and felt to be increasing in intensity. He knew to resist was to invite further punishment. He felt rough hands clasp on his shirt and begin to drag him across the gravel. He heard his shirt tear and the hands regripped and the dragging began again. He kept his hands and arms held tight over his head as he felt himself being hauled and lifted and then he was on the backseat of a car, glimpses of cracked upholstery visible through his arms that he dared not remove from his face. He ventured a glimpse at the window and as the car accelerated he saw the flats of palms being banged against the glass.

He remained laying down on the backseat, panting animal-like through his nose, his mouth clenched shut. If he opened his mouth he would vomit. The driver said nothing. Mike ran his fingers over his face. It had come out unscathed, either by miracle or design of his attackers he was unsure. His body pulsed with the echo of the kicks and blows he had taken but nothing appeared broken. It still hurt to breathe.

The man in the passenger seat turned. Mike blinked hard as if to confirm that the stone-hard face that watched him belonged to Marcelo Decoud. Mike attempted to decipher the meaning of Decoud's presence in the vehicle, but his mental Enigma machine was scrambled. No triumph or even pleasure told in Decoud's demeanor. He appeared detached from the attack that had taken place.

In Spanish tinged with the distinctive Cordoba lilt he said, "This attack was not organized or condoned by me or the group I lead. I condemn violence in all its forms. The destruction of the earth or the destruction of an office or a human life are all equally unforgiveable." His face was drawn with what looked like resignation.

After what seemed like a few minutes the car stopped.

"Out," barked the driver.

Still prone, Mike fumbled with the door handle near his head, pushed the door open and crawled out head first onto the asphalt. The car accelerated away, the back door flapping back and forth a few times before catching shut.

Mike pulled himself into a sitting position. He was in a parking lot. Beyond the parking lot he could see a long, squat, white building with large, black, stenciled letters across the facade: Aeronautical Engineer Ambrosio L.V. Taravella International Airport. Some airport drop-off, he thought.

Mike hobbled into the airport. It had been a mistake to go to the offices. That was clear. The MinEx staff had to be in on it or maybe they had been warned to get out.

He sat in the departure lounge and watched scenes from the afternoon play on the television screens. The cameras had turned up after Mike's departure. Angry youths, their faces covered against the smoke, smashing in the windows and dragging office furniture into the street, not to steal, but to destroy, utter destruction, to remove all trace of MinEx from their town. It wasn't just the young men that Mike had seen; they had been joined by old men, young girls, their mothers. The whole town had turned up, a demographic radiograph of hatred, assembled to send a clear message that MinEx was not wanted.

As his flight back to Buenos Aires took off and climbed over Cordoba he could see a plume of smoke rising into the afternoon sky. He followed it back down to earth, imagining he could see it begin its ascent snaking from a broken window of the MinEx office.

Mike rubbed the lump on the back of his head. If Decoud was not behind the attack, and Mike was not convinced that this was the case, then it had to be the government. It would have been easy for them to discover he was in Cordoba. From the airline. From the governor. He realized it may have been a mistake to use Quinn's name to get the meeting with the governor. Impersonating a man with so many enemies in Cordoba was not smart.

CHAPTER 18

A t the Café Richmond, located on Florida Street in the heart of Buenos Aires, a small army of uniformed waiters moved between the tables, delivering coffee, retrieving plates, stopping every now and then to share a joke with a familiar customer. None stopped to chat with Mike.

The room bubbled and percolated to the sound of the Portuguese language, the Brazilian version. In the late 90s when Menem had pegged the Argentine peso to the US dollar, Argentines, having no access to world class beaches themselves, flooded to the beaches of Brazil, using their overvalued currency to buy hot cheese, cold beers and generally lord it over their bitter rivals. Nowadays, the tables had turned and the overvalued Brazilian real, pegged to nothing more than Brazilian hubris, allowed Brazilians to flood the shopping and café districts of Buenos Aires. From the sounds of the café, they were enjoying their revenge, decades in the making.

He surveyed the room. He saw the exchange of rumors, plots, secrets, and conspiracies. There was no evidence that any of these men and women with whom he shared the café had any idea that his client had become front-page news around the world, that the stock had fallen further, that he himself was under surveillance, that the MinEx office in Cordoba was now reduced to ashes. Nothing to indicate that any of his fellow diners were aware of the forces of power, retribution, and money that were at play and that somehow he had managed to entangle himself in the center of it all. It seemed like years had passed since he had first dreamt of Sicily.

The paneled walls, the high ceilings, the obscure, darkened corners, and the dripping chandeliers; elegant accoutrements to disguise the true nature of things. Always chandeliers, he thought, always elegance. Beside him an elderly lady sat by herself, feeding an éclair into her lipstick-rimmed mouth with manicured fingers, a constant, smooth movement that reminded Mike of a butcher feeding mince into a sausage machine. The empty plates stacked around her hinted that she had been there since mid-morning, her enormous size suggested that she had been there since the mid-seventies.

Two men approached the table in front of, and a little to the left of Mike. Without shifting his head, he observed the men exchange an emotionless greeting and take their seats. A waiter approached their table. Mike caught the word *americano*. They entered into discussion as the waiter retreated.

Mike's coffee arrived in a chipped, white cup matched to an off-green saucer. He picked it up and stared straight ahead over the rim, blowing a small stream of air across the top of his coffee. The chandelier above him was reflected and rippling on the dark surface of his drink. He was certain that the two men were there for him, to observe. He imagined that they were now

157

exchanging their own rumors, plots, secrets, and conspiracies as cover for their real job. Watching Mike.

No doubt at the appropriate time they would leave and retreat to a rundown office that could use new furniture and a coat of paint. By the glow of a bare bulb they would write up their notes, copied from yellowed notebooks, detailing Mike's nervous demeanor, his painful movements, his clothing, what he ordered, who he met, and who he looked at. Yes, his face was fine, the boys did a good job.

He held these racing thoughts steady in his head and watched as the elder of the two gentlemen, who was still yet to smile, a lawyer no doubt, rose from the table and exited Café Richmond. He left behind the tanned leather briefcase that moments earlier he had arrived with.

Mike observed that the younger gentleman, still in his overcoat despite the room temperature being a few degrees too high, noticed the abandoned briefcase but did not call back his somber-faced friend. Rather, he waited for five minutes, timed by the clock above the espresso machine behind the bar, asked for the bill, overpaid, and then left with the briefcase that he did not arrive with.

A tall waiter glided to the table, pocketed the fifty-peso note that had been left under the untouched coffees, and returned to the kitchen. Mike smiled to himself, pleased at this authentic sighting of local culture that no quantity of chandeliers and shadow could hide. Gentlemen with business to conduct at Café Richmond ordered the coffee and paid for the discretion.

The heavy-set woman finished her éclair and pushed the empty plate, smudged with chocolate, to the side with a delicate movement that drew more attention to her size.

She caught Mike watching and smiled a coquette's smile. Mike's mind was on other matters.

"Good afternoon, Mr. Costello."

Mike started, his body jerking with a bolt of pain at the unexpected voice. He grabbed for his ribs.

"My name is Luis Lopez. I am with the Ministry of Planning. Adviser to the minister on special projects."

"What the fuck do you want?" growled Mike, in no mood or physical capacity to be pushed around again.

Lopez ignored the question and settled himself into the seat opposite. He flagged over a waiter and placed his order before returning his attention to Mike.

Lopez wore a grey suit over a blue shirt, offset with a red tie. His hair was cut short and matched the color of his suit. A grub-like moustache perched provocatively on his top lip like a toupee for his terse little mouth. The mouth pissed Mike off. A mouth that was only big enough for eating olives one at a time or getting punched.

"Mr. Costello, it is customary to start a meeting with a bit of, how would you say? Chit chat? Something light, no matter how unpleasant the conversation to come is expected to be. You can get a lot from this chit chat, maybe even discover you are not so different, common ground."

"I would be very surprised if you and I had anything in common." Lopez knew Mike had been at the MinEx offices or he wouldn't be here. The Ministry of Planning must be watching him too. "Nice job your boys did."

A look of feigned shock covered Lopez's face. The moustache twitched. "I am aggrieved that you would accuse me of such a despicable act. The government is a partner in this project. Like yourself, we have a vested interest in seeing MinEx succeed. Destroying their offices does not align with that objective. You should be directing your anger at those environmental activists that, as you know, have long opposed MinEx's presence in Cordoba."

"They didn't do it," said Mike, not realizing until the words were out that he had exonerated Decoud.

"You seem sure of this."

"I've been in contact with Marcelo Decoud." It was one way to describe Decoud's exfiltration of him. Lopez looked surprised.

"Decoud is speaking with you? I find that surprising after everything. You are a more forgiving man than me. It proves nothing, even if we are to accept his word. You know how these groups are. Everybody wants to be the leader; everybody wants to be on television. To do so, you must be bold, you must do something to stand out, to show that the current leadership is outdated, that it's not militant enough, that it is in the pay of the corporates or in the pay of the government. Anything is fair game; the objective is control of the group.

"Decoud may claim to have nothing to do with yesterday's incident. I can assure you that as soon as he created that group, as soon as he set public opinion against MinEx, he set in motion a chain of events that resulted in what took place yesterday. What this may show is that he has lost control of his own creation. And that is not good for you, your client, and most importantly for us." Lopez sat back and smiled, pleased at this turn of events.

Mike looked around the room. He wondered who had come in with Lopez. Who was watching? Who was listening?

"You need to assure me that there will be no more incidents like yesterday. A repeat and MinEx will exit the country. How would it look to the world if you lose your biggest investor?" Mike looked into the eyes of the man from Planning, attempting to fill the words with an intent and gravitas that would send the message that he was not fucking around even as he knew he had no right to be making such threats.

"There are no guarantees in life, Mr. Costello. I can assure you that I will do my best, that this government will do our best to support the project. We will need something in return. No more games. Tell Mr. Quinn to award the tender and let's get started. As partners."

Mike ran his eyes over Luis Lopez, his sharp suit, his slicked back hair, his confidence.

'MinEx doesn't need a partner. They just need a level playing field to get started. They're not interested in politics; they're not interested in games. That's your area. You handle your side of things and let them get on and do their thing. That way everybody wins."

"Exactly, win-win. We all get what we want. The question is, what do you want, Mr. Costello? I understand that favors of this kind are not free. I cannot make any guarantees, but a man of your talents could be quite useful to the party. A few years working with us could set you up with the lifestyle you deserve, enough to retire on down here. We would be better friends than the ones you have now. How does that sound, Mr. Costello? Citizenship even if you like. You can while away the rest of your life in the most magnificent city on earth, drinking the finest wine, eating the best steak, chasing the tastiest pussy. Not a care in the world."

It sounded like purgatory to Mike. Maybe these slick suited fucks didn't know as much about him as he thought. The rest of his life in Argentina.

"Have your company resubmit the tender, Luis. With new financials. Financials that make sense. That is what I want and then you will get what you want."

"That is not what I want, Mr. Costello. What I want is for MinEx to accept the tender they have. No questions asked, no more delays. That is what I want."

No more delays sounded good to Mike. If he knew how to proceed without delays he would already be in Sicily. But delays were what made the world go around. And round and round.

"That's not my understanding of win-win, Luis."

"Win-win." Lopez seemed to test the words in his mouth as if fondling the syllables of a new language for the first time. "Do you believe that's possible? Such a quaint notion," he said. "This kind of thinking will get you nowhere. Do you think that is how we got here today? By letting our opponents win? Letting them have what they want? Do you think that is how we came to be in government? There is no win-win, Mr. Costello. It is fuck or be fucked. It always has been." He raised himself in his seat, warming to his topic.

"Let me tell you a story about Juan Peron. Three times he led this country. Three times he ploughed these seas. Can you imagine what that must have taken? To three times battle for control, vanquish enemies, to dedicate your life to fighting for those that never win? If you can understand that, then you can understand why Peron is the most important figure in our country's history.

"His legacy is to continue to fight for those that cannot win. That fight never stops. After his death, a group of thugs in the pay of the opposition raided Peron's tomb and desecrated his resting remains. They took an electric saw and cut his hands off." Luis held his own hands in front of Mike.

"Even in death Peron was still in battle, at his most defenseless, his enemies still pursued him. They wanted to take those hands that had fought so long for the Argentine people, to severe them, to destroy them forever. We cannot let that happen. We are those hands. We are the embodiment of those hands that are still fighting for the Argentine people, the poor, the disenfranchised, those that do not know what it is to win.

"We cannot be disappeared, like so many of our brothers and sisters were disappeared. Make no mistake, the battle continues. We are winning, but that does not mean that the enemy has given up." Lopez paused and looked at the table beside them. An elderly couple sharing a piece of cake over afternoon coffee had stopped their conversation and were staring at Luis, his hands now bunched into fists.

He lowered his voice and continued. "In 2001, I was an adviser to Senator Jenefes from Jujuy, a northern province, very beautiful. But insignificant by any measure that means something. It was a difficult year, we were coming out of a period of sustained abuse under the presidency of Menem. The lost decade. The government had lost its grip on power. Menem had gone and the people who had grown fat on his regime did not want to accept that their time was over. They sowed chaos, they drove the country to the edge. Their aim was to throw the country into such a state of anarchy that the army would be forced to intervene. In that chaos, they came for us.

"For two days I was locked inside my office, inside the congress. I could hear the crowds outside, howling for our blood, like barbarians. Nothing to eat, nothing to drink. On the second day, I had to leave the office. I didn't know if the congress had been overrun or what I would find.

"I unlocked the door and made my way down the corridor that connected my office to the senator's chamber. The place was empty. As if the congress had been frozen in time. Everybody had left, nothing had been packed up, books were open on desks, files on chairs, cups of coffee had been abandoned, briefcases lay open. And from outside this terrible roar. Adjacent to my boss' office there was a janitor's closet. I tried the door, it opened, and by some miracle, hanging on the peg behind the door, a pair of blue janitors' overalls.

"I stripped off my suit and my shoes. It was absurd. In the Argentine congress, the center of power, in my underwear. I grabbed my shoes and rubbed them against the concrete wall of the janitor's room, roughing them up to take off their shine. I dressed in the overalls and put my shoes back on.

"From the sounds outside, the bulk of the crowd had concentrated at the front of the congress. I crept to the back. I tried a few doors to offices and found one unlocked. I went in and there was a window that opened onto the congress gardens. I lifted the window just enough to squeeze out and flopped down into a flowerbed."

Lopez smiled at the memory. "The day before, I had come to work, suit and tie, through the front door of the congress. Six years at the country's most prestigious law school, two years at the London School of Economics, Senior Adviser to a Senator of the Nation, dressed as a janitor, escaping from a window like a common criminal. I've never forgotten that lesson."

Luis looked into Mike's eyes. Mike returned the stare and waited for Lopez to blink. He didn't.

"We can never stop fighting, Mr. Costello. The day we stop they will come for us again. There is no win-win." He shook his head as if to confirm the fact. "That is not possible. There is victory and there is destruction."

"Destruction you do well. It is time you started playing by the rules."

"We do play by the rules. You may not recognize those rules, but we do. I smile when I read articles in your press, about our institutions and democracy and rule of law. Do the people writing these articles think that the political class here has just magically appeared one day? Just dropped from the sky? We are from here. We are born here. We were raised on our own history, on stories from our fathers, we have lived and breathed the history of this country. Do you think that if you put any other Argentine into government he would act in a different way? We are of the people, by the people, for the people; this is who we are. The people understand this. They know what is needed to get things done, they understand what it is we need to do. And they have lived through the consequences of doing nothing."

The chatter in the room had grown louder as the afternoon crowd thickened. Lopez leant backwards, arching his back, spread his arms wide, his fingers pointing inwards to his chest. "This is us, Mr. Costello. Your client can work with us or not. We will not change."

Mike stood up. Pain accompanied him.

"Mr. Costello, before you run," said Lopez, enjoying the joke. "You are playing a very dangerous game. We know you are working for the British. We have enough to shut you down today and have you on the first plane out of here."

"Why don't you then?" asked Mike neither denying or accepting the accusation. As far as threats went it sounded a lot like a pretty good solution to Mike.

"Because you still have a use. You are what your British friends would call a 'cut out'. Tell your client to award the tender. Get things moving. There are ways that we can make sure that he is rewarded down the line when he shows that he is a trusted partner. You won't be forgotten either, Mr. Costello. The alternative is that we just place MinEx in the hands of someone who is willing to act like a good partner."

"Nationalize MinEx? You don't have the power to do that."

"Believe me we do, Mr. Costello. We just need the excuse to do so."

CHAPTER 19

The building at 2811 Lavalle was identical to 2809 and 2813 either side of it except for the graffiti. Someone had scrawled the name of the band "Patricio Rey y sus Redonditos de Ricota" across the facade in a defiant, angry spray-can scrawl.

The neighborhood was not affluent, and the owners had spared expenses on the building's upkeep. Mike stepped forward and pressed the button labelled apt 808 in scratchy black ink. The bruising on his body was still visible when he had dressed before his mirror in the morning, but the pain no longer bothered him. The lump on his head had not disappeared and he often found his hand going over his head to locate it. An unconscious reminder of the need to keep his eyes open.

The Doctor had still not appeared with any information on the minister, Donald Duck unable or unwilling to convince his source to continue as an informant. If Mike didn't come up with information for MinEx, Simon would no doubt cut him loose.

His arrival that morning at 2811 Lavalle had been prompted by an article in *La Nacion* that had outlined hostilities between the mayor of Buenos Aires and his chief of police. Mike cared little for the fortunes of either man but there buried in the text, in black-and-white print, he came across the name Consultora Tigre. The chief of police had accused the mayor of hiring Consultora Tigre to monitor his phone calls. A classic smear. The mayor denied this credible accusation and Consultora Tigre had not responded to requests for comment.

Consultora Tigre was a new name in the game that Mike had been playing since he left the employ of the United States government. Identifying a new player felt like finding a wallet on the street; who knows what it would contain or who it could lead you to.

The accusations of wiretapping didn't concern him. It may well be that the chief of police had hired Consultora Tigre to spy on the mayor and to muddy the waters, accused the mayor of the same. In which case, it was high praise indeed that of all the suppliers that the chief of police could trust with the job he chose Consultora Tigre. You couldn't buy publicity like that. Even better, it could be that Consultora Tigre had planted the article themselves, a new outfit that wanted to get the word out that they were open for business. Either way, Mike was intrigued enough to make a few phone calls and it did not take much to locate the company, giving weight to Mike's theory that the article may have been nothing more than clever marketing.

A thin voice came through the intercom, frazzled by a failing connection. "Yes?"

"Costello." A buzz indicated that the locking mechanism had opened. Mike pushed on the door a little too late. The door didn't budge. He pushed the buzzer again.

The same voice, irritated this time. "Yes?"

"Still me, I didn't push in time." Mike thought he heard his name used in vain as the door buzzed again, he shoved hard, and went through the doorway. The door was still buzzing for good measure as it swung shut behind him, the lock clicking back into place.

He rode the stylish old elevator to the eighth floor, the antique, steel cables groaning. He arrived at the eighth floor, pulled back the metal, concertina-like door, and stepped out. He watched the elevator return down the shaft. It arrived at the first floor with an audible clunk that made Mike consider the return journey.

A threadbare, reptilian-green carpet covered the floor. A musty, stale smell rose from it. It was hard to imagine that it had ever been brand new. A small plaque affixed to the wall informed that offices 801 to 810 could be found to his left. Offices 811 to 820 to his right. He went left and approached office 808. Seeing no doorbell, he knocked with a single knuckle on the door.

A chair scraped and then there was a rhythmic clunking of boots on wood. Mike waited. The door opened to reveal a heavy-set man, early sixties by Mike's guess, grey hair slicked back with a local variant of bryl cream, dark business pants matched with a white, short-sleeve business shirt that gave the man the appearance of a waiter.

"Mr. Costello, a pleasure to meet you, please come in. I am Villagra, Hector Villagra, retired major." He took Mike's hand and pumped it. "Let me introduce you to my partner. Jorge!" he bellowed as if Jorge was hard of hearing. "Mr. Costello is here."

Retired Major Villagra led Mike down a short corridor to the doorway of a second interior office. Mike stopped on the threshold of the office and Jorge, a thin, frail man raised himself from behind his desk. Perched on a small stack of tatty magazines, was an ashtray, overflowing with stubbed-out butts. Jorge pushed and twisted and added one more stub to the pile before making his way around the desk.

Mike saw that he was afflicted by palsy, both his hands were bent inwards at the wrists leaving his twisted fingers in permanent contact with the inside of his lower arm. He walked towards Mike, his gait a swaying, stilted, locomotion that betrayed the fact that his feet had suffered the same distortion as his hands. Mike avoided looking down as Jorge extended an arm in greeting and Mike, looking him in the eyes, gripped him by the forearm and returned the greeting.

"Jorge Batelli," he said, failing to give a rank, retired or otherwise, though Mike suspected Intelligence of some kind, maybe naval, maybe federal. There was a shiftiness in the eyes that came from a life of watching and lying and lying in watch.

Introduction completed Mike watched him tick-tock his way back to his desk where he plonked down, exhausted by the physical exertion that good manners demanded, and lit up another cigarette. Without another glance at Mike he began banging away on his keyboard, his face obscured by an expanding cloud of smoke.

"Please, let's come through to my office. We can speak in there without the risk of lung cancer," said Hector, risking a humor that was foreign to a retired major.

Mike sensed he was uncomfortable. Common enough among military men that had lived their life in regimented structure and were then forced to survive in a corporate world, governed by self-interest and greed rather than chains of command and indisputable orders.

Mike followed his host back down the corridor. The office was tidy, the walls lined with shelves that held detailed, plastic miniatures of the instruments of war. Tanks, jeeps, battleships, artillery, fighter jets. Hector caught Mike looking at his collection.

"My wife refuses to let me keep them at home. She says that part of our life is over. Time to move on. I suppose she's right." He sighed. "It's hard. Did you serve, Mr. Costello?"

"No, I didn't," Mike lied for no reason.

"Twenty-five years, I did. I loved it. Now, I'm here," he said, eyebrows raised. "Would you like me to give you a rundown of our services? I suppose you know most of it or you wouldn't be here. We don't get many customers who are just browsing in our line of work."

"I don't suppose you do," said Mike as he took a seat on the opposite side of the desk where Hector had made himself comfortable. "How do you work?"

"50 percent up front and 50 percent on delivery of the material. We don't work on success fees. We do the work, we get paid. Only dollars. Always cash."

"How do you charge?"

"Depends on the service. You want somebody watched we will charge you a daily fee per man on the ground plus an administration fee to cover our report-writing time. All incidentals that the surveillance team incur will be charged back to you at cost. Receipts provided.

"Due diligence we charge a flat fee per job. Price can vary on the target's profile. If you're looking at a businessman, no profile, no friends, then it's one price. A politician or somebody with a public profile, then our fee will vary according to the risk we're taking. We're happy to take risks, Mr. Costello, just as long as we get paid for doing so."

"Fair enough," said Mike as he considered the extra zeros that the minister for planning would add to the quote.

"We also have other services that you may not find amongst our competitors, Mr. Costello."

"I had hoped you would have," replied Mike, encouraging his host to continue with a conspiratorial smile.

"Phone services. We charge a daily rate, 100 percent up front. You tell us the days and hours you need it monitored and we monitor those times. The target goes away, loses his phone, changes his phone, not our problem. This isn't cheap so if you contract this service I recommend you do so sparingly and only when you know that the target will be making a call or is likely to be making a call that you need to hear. Monitoring a line in the hope of hearing something is a waste of time. We can provide the recorded material in audio or in transcripts. For transcripts, we charge per word for a written report."

"And high-profile targets?"

"If it's not an encrypted device. Again, the fee will correspond to the level of risk we run." Hector paused, allowing time for any question or comment from Mike. When none came, he continued. "We also provide a bank service."

Mike assumed he was referring to laundering, an activity that Mike considered on the black side of the grey area where he was comfortable operating.

For clarity he asked, "What kind of bank service?"

"I can see I have piqued your interest," replied Hector, confusing Mike's alarm for curiosity. "We can find any bank account anywhere in the world held by a target." Hector grinned with pride at the revelation of his criminal reach. "I'm confident that nobody else can offer this service, at least not here in Argentina, maybe Brazil. Definitely not here."

Mike knew this to be untrue. This was the same service he had been paying the Doctor's Mickey Mouse a lot of money for.

"Accounts attached to a name?" probed Mike.

"Much more than that, Mr. Costello. We can look inside the account, see the movements, see the balances, everything. We cannot make changes, just a peek, no touching," Hector said.

The turn of phrase sounded familiar.

"And cost?" asked Mike, trying not to appear too interested. He knew that Simon would be interested in finding out just where the minister for planning hid his money and who was supplying it.

"I think about two thousand US. Jorge handles this work."

"Two thousand? Regardless of the target?"

"Yes, the risk is the same. Zero. No one can detect this."

Mike tried to hide the smile that was forming inside. Mickey Mouse had been charging the Doctor five thousand US for this service. If Hector charged two thousand and Mickey Mouse charged five thousand then Mike had stumbled on Mickey Mouse's source of banking information. He needed confirmation.

"You think two thousand or it is two thousand?" asked Mike.

Hector swiveled in his chair to face his open door. "Jorge!" he yelled. "How much did you charge Martinelli for that last bank report?" He sounded all the world like a credit analyst with none of the discretion.

"Who?" came Jorge's muffled reply through the walls.

"Martinelli, Julian Martinelli. How much did you charge him?"

Receiving no audible reply Retired Major Villagra stood up, apologized with his eyes and left the room.

Mike sat solid in his chair. His blood frozen, his heart accelerating under his shirt. He could hear the two men conversing through the office walls. Hector returned looking pleased with himself.

"Sorry, I misspoke."

Mike was relieved. He hoped that the corrected number out of Hector's mouth would be five thousand US dollars. That was what Julian Martinelli, the Doctor, his friend, had charged him, no markup. That was the cost for just a peek, no touching.

"It's actually two thousand five hundred," said Hector.

"For Julian Martinelli?" insisted Mike, assuming the same level of discretion as the retired major.

"Yes, you know him? We do a lot of work for him."

Mike felt sick. He hadn't stumbled on Mickey Mouse's source; he had stumbled on Mickey Mouse.

CHAPTER 20

G reen shoots covered the branches of the trees that arched over Republica de India, throwing a dappled shade over the footpaths. Spring was beginning to win the battle with winter and the cold southern winds that blew up from Antarctica were making fewer appearances. As if raised from an urban hibernation, the residents of Buenos Aires were emerging, populating sidewalk cafés and restaurants that were empty only a few, short weeks earlier.

From his seat inside Guido's Mike watched the *porteños* stroll past the red-paneled windows, chattering about the mini-scandals that filled their lives. Mike was an avid eavesdropper, listening in on the conversations of students on buses, taxi drivers taking calls from their wives, the table next door at a restaurant, slowing down in the street to follow the dialogue of couples behind him, one ear cocked.

Everyday language intrigued him; how it was used, what phrases were employed and by whom. Today the only conversations he heard were those in his own head as he went through the mental files of all interactions he had ever had with the Doctor, Julian Martinelli.

Yesterday he had left the offices of Consultora Tigre, thanking them for their time and assuring them that yes, he was interested, and would be in touch. His first impulse had been to call the Doctor and confront him. What would he say? He would deny, as all spies are taught to do, regardless of their service, if ever caught in a lie. Deny, deny, deny.

He thought about revenge, running through elaborate plots in his mind that ended with him the victor and the Doctor humiliated. He considered continuing as normal, waiting for the day when the Doctor slipped up and he would be there to pounce, to tell him that he had known all along.

None of the plots and plans that ended with Mike winning seemed plausible. He had lost as he had lost numerous times before. Wasn't this why he had decided to leave Argentina? The acceptance that he could never make sense of the complex moral and social webs that drew him in and so intrigued him. Wasn't he tired of always being the one caught? Tired of being unable to disentangle himself from his own desire to immerse himself further into a system that refused to reveal itself to him. It always felt just within reach, but he knew that it would always stay that way. He had to digest that fact, as stomach churning as that process was.

He blamed himself. A lifetime had taught him that there are no friendships, only alliances and partnerships and even these are brief at best, vulnerable to be carried away, destroyed by any fresh wind of opportunity or self-interest.

In the end, as the coffee rings in his espresso dried to the walls of the tiny cup, a visual marker of each sip, he picked up his phone and dialed the Doctor. He attempted to strip his voice of the anger, the humiliation, and sense of betrayal that roiled inside him.

The Doctor's phone was off so he left a voice message; something has come up, I will explain later, don't do any more work on any projects until you hear from me. Mike hung up, firm in his commitment to never see the Doctor again.

As Mike sat there and waited for the eternally late Alex Harper, he moved past the emotional inventory and begun to count the lost dollars that the Doctor had taken him for. He retrieved all the jobs they had done together, all the dollars that had exchanged hands in *cuevas* and cafés all over Buenos Aires, always at cost; *this what I'm being charged, I can't get it any cheaper*. And all the while the Doctor was putting on fifty percent. Or more, in all likelihood.

He remembered the times when he confessed to the Doctor how he was struggling to keep his business afloat. How funds were tight. Promising to pay the Doctor up front and in full, even when he had to take it out of his own pocket.

Mike sat studying the rings of his espresso, lulled by the rippling shadows playing on the tabletop, pockets of light scampering left and right across the checkered cloth as if controlled by invisible strings attached to the branches that swayed outside the window.

Fifteen thousand dollars. Surveillance job on a mercurial oil trader who had appropriated two tanks of crude from an international client that had made the mistake of trusting his local partner. The Doctor had set up an observation post under the cover of a kiosk selling grilled steak sandwiches. So convincing was the stand that an irate local vendor saw them as unfair competition on his corner and chased them off.

Twenty thousand dollars. Information on how a small company with only two directors, grandmothers from the southern Buenos Aires suburb of Lomas de Zamora, with no funds, no infrastructure, and no experience could import 70,000 packs of cigarettes over the Paraguayan border and then manage the logistics to resell them on the local black market.

Thirty-five thousand dollars. Track down a desperate man from Corrientes who had borrowed two hundred thousand dollars to purchase life insurance and then disappeared, presumed dead the following week. A situation that had set off corporate alarm bells from Buenos Aires to Hong Kong until somehow the Doctor had found him living, under his own name, in Curitiba, Brazil.

Mike terminated his mental accounting. Too painful. He'd considered the Doctor a friend, a consideration that Mike now saw for the weakness it was. Could he blame the Doctor for exploiting that? Not really. Mike knew the rules; he was no Simon Quinn. If he knew the rules, he knew that others would be playing by them.

"Jesus Christ, what the bloody hell is wrong with you? You look sadder than an empty restaurant."

Mike had not seen Alex approach.

"Problems," said Mike as way of explanation.

"Plenty of my own, Mike. First things first," he said, pointing to Mike's empty espresso cup. "I see you've made a poor man's start."

Alex called over the waiter and in his broken Spanish ordered two glasses of red and asked that the food should begin arriving.

"And can we get a fucking bread plate, please?" Mike asked the back of the departing waiter.

Alex ignored the outburst. "I'm in trouble, Mike."

"I'm all ears."

"This may come as a bit of a shock. For the last few months I've been seeing someone here. Not my wife," he added for redundant clarity. He paused to allow Mike to take in what he thought was news.

The expat community had spoken of nothing else for the past weeks. Alex's affair with his twenty-two-year-old secretary had replaced the ambassador's problems with a light-fingered maid as the number-one topic among the bored expatriates of San Isidro. That Alex was having an affair had surprised very few; to Mike it had even seemed a little contrived. That the young consort was female had surprised many.

"I had heard rumors, Alex, I must admit," he said as he looked up to receive the wine and first plates of food that had arrived.

"Really? Who else knows?" Alex asked, with neither surprise nor concern, just a hint of pride. He didn't wait for an answer. "Things have taken a bit of a turn in the last week or so. The poor little thing has fallen quite in love with me."

Mike had met Alex's secretary and poor was the only accurate descriptor. She had a poverty of looks that could have justified another Band Aid album.

"She knows about your wife and family?"

"I told her everything. I told her about the wife, the children, the marriage, the whole truth. Only some of the circumstances and tenses were false," said Alex, the last part of the sentence lost to a sharp intake of breath.

"How very Borgesian of you, Alex."

"Perhaps, but your vocabulary prevents me from agreeing with any certainty," said Alex. "She has been seeing a psychologist. They all are down here, aren't they? It's like going out for milk for these people. She's been making some real progress with her therapist. She feels awful about having an affair. She's coming to terms with being a homewrecker. I, of course, assure her she is not a homewrecker, that I'm in love with her and that one day, when my boys are old enough to understand, we'll marry. We'll have our whole lives ahead of us."

Mike swirled his glass of red as he did the math in his head. Based on his vague knowledge of the ages of those involved, by the time the kids left school the secretary would only be 31.

"Plenty of time," he agreed.

"A few days ago she comes to me and says that she wants to have a baby."

"With you?"

"My reaction exactly! She said her bloody psychologist suggested it! Bring us closer together, a life project I think she called it." Alex gulped at his glass of wine. He looked fearful. "There's a small problem, though."

"You already have a wife and family?" asked Mike, failing to remove the facetiousness from his voice.

"OK, there are a few problems. Of varying sizes." Alex leaned in, drawing Mike into the conspiracy though there was nobody to overhear them. The nearest tables were unoccupied at this early hour of the day.

"I've had the snip." He sucked air through his teeth with more vigor than usual and emphasized his point by imitating a pair of snipping scissors with his fingers, a bit too close to Mike's face. "Can't have kids. I haven't told her that, you see. I said, 'I'm not sure that it's a good idea, I'm too old to go through raising a child again'—which is true, wouldn't be fair on the kid, wouldn't be fair on her. 'Couldn't we just get a dog or a cat?' Though I bloody hate cats. However, under the circumstances in which I find myself I'm happy to be flexible on the cat."

"How was this magnanimity received?" asked Mike, suspecting he knew the answer.

"As well as could be expected. She said if we don't have a baby she'll throw herself into the River Plate."

Mike couldn't prevent a smile forming on his lips, his own troubles forgotten for a while. "What's your plan?"

Alex raised his glass above the table. "We're trying for a baby!"

Mike shook his head and laughed. "You awful man. How do you think she's going to feel when she can't fall pregnant?"

"What option do I have? I can't solve this. I must push it forward. I think the best I can hope for is to get that posting in Iraq."

"The one you don't want."

"Then I can claim a trauma-induced condition. I'll be damaged goods, no good for anyone, unable to commit, wracked by fevers and nightmares. It's a long play I know. I can't think of anything else. Last night she told me that if I ever left her she would stab me. In her mind that was a declaration of love."

Mike let out a low, slow whistle. He couldn't imagine that this pasty Englishman could evoke such desire in another human being. Conclusive evidence that in matters of love, the grass was always greener.

"And to top it all off, this morning I had protestors outside the embassy, throwing stones, demanding we give back the Falklands. Luckily it started raining and they dispersed. Doesn't take much to wash away their political will. Still, not a good look. All this agitation comes from high up."

Alex looked around the dining room signaling a change of topic. A few other diners had begun to drift in. The waiter brought more plates of antipasti.

"So that's me. Now, what's got you looking so down at heel? I can only presume its work."

"I came into some information yesterday. I went to visit a firm, Consultora Tigre, a new consulting company that has come on the scene. Two guys, one ex-cavalry and the other federal intelligence, I think. He's disabled, palsy or something. All bent up, walks like a grandfather clock and smokes like a chimney. An odd couple. You know them?"

Alex shook his head in the negative.

"I'm there chatting about what they can and can't do and it becomes apparent that they are the source for another source I have been using for the last few years."

"Not your infamous Doctor?" asked Alex.

"Yes. The Doctor." Mike had no recollection of ever having told Alex about the Doctor. He made a mental note to drink less at embassy cocktails. He would have to consider acquiring a mental cabinet for the mental notes he was forever producing.

"That's good, right? Now you can cut the Doctor out, go down the chain a link."

"That's an option. I also discovered what they had been charging the Doctor. They had no idea who I was or that he has been working for me. My arrangement with the Doctor was that I pay him a flat monthly fee, every month regardless if we do ten jobs or no jobs. The idea was to give him some stability. Any expenses that his sources charged him get passed back to me at cost—at cost, no markup."

"Oh dear, really, Mike?" said Alex, not needing to hear the rest.

"I trusted the guy."

"You're a sailor getting upset at the ocean. What did you expect?"

"I know," said Mike, regretting having opened his mouth. But that was what Alex did. Invited you to open up and then used it against you, made you feel humiliated. You then felt the need to defend yourself and ended up telling him more than you wanted to.

"The damage?"

"Who knows? Whatever he could take and I was stupid enough to pay. It seems that everyone made money on these jobs except me. I could be in fucking Sicily by now!"

Alex ignored the emotion, stacked up the antipasti plates and caught the attention of the waiter.

"I can't use him anymore," said Mike.

"Why not? You can't blame a man for acting exactly how you knew he would act."

"I don't trust him anymore."

"That isn't the problem. The problem is that you trusted him in the first place."

Mike placed his fork on the tablecloth and rubbed his face with both hands. "I know. But that's it. It's over. I can't do the fucking job. Without any information there's no way Simon will keep me around."

Alex lowered his glass from his lips and leant forward. "Mike, I need you on this. You're the only guy I can trust. You know that. Can't you just make something up? Get something from the papers. Who cares where it comes from?"

"Make it up? That would be going native."

"It won't be for long, just until I clear this tax office thing for you. Meanwhile, I need you close to Simon. I don't want to open my paper tomorrow morning and read 'British Company Caught Greasing the Wheels of Argentine Democracy.'"

A waiter cleared away the plates and another brought the bowls of pasta, red and white sauce, to share. Alex ordered more wine.

"Are you making any progress with my AFIP issue?"

"Yes, yes. All very positive. I have raised a request internally for information on your case. It is sitting on the ambassador's desk awaiting his signature. He is down south for a few days casting flies. As soon as he is back we will get his autograph on it and send it off. Shouldn't take any more than two or three weeks."

"I've been thinking. How about I pay you something for your trouble on this. I know I haven't come through for you on MinEx."

"Pay me something? A British diplomat? Who has gone native now, Mike?"

"I am in a bit of a rush on this, Alex. You can't speed it up somehow could you?"

"Nothing can happen without the ambo's scribble, I'm afraid. Just have to be patient a little while longer. Don't worry, you'll be in Sicily in no time," he said. "And I do appreciate the job you have done with Quinn. I know it hasn't been easy. If you can stick to him a little longer, just until I can sort this AFIP stuff for you that would be grand."

Mike nodded, more in frustration than acceptance. Nothing was fucking grand on his side of the table.

"I sometimes wonder what Quinn is trying to achieve here. Why doesn't he just say, 'stick it up your ass' and leave?" asked Alex.

Mike considered the question before answering. "I'm not sure, to be honest. The problem appears to be that he fudged the tender process. He advanced with only one bidder qualified."

"So, he played ball with the Argentines, got the project moving and left himself exposed to accusations of corruption. Not very smart. I do recall asking you to keep an eye on that."

"What option did he have? Play it straight, nothing gets done and his boss cans him anyway and he pisses off the Argentines, which I believe you also didn't want to happen."

"Quite the dilemma," said Alex.

"If he leaves now, his replacement would realize what has happened. The only way Simon can keep a lid on what he has done is by staying on and playing by their rules. Quietly."

"So, he's fucked," Alex said. "Good. Does he know this?"

"No. He has this unshakeable faith that he can bend the world to his way of working. That everything is manageable."

"All he needs to manage is to keep his head down. I saw the little incident at the MinEx office out in Cordoba. What did you make of that?"

Mike shrugged his shoulders. Something told him it was better not to reveal his own involvement. "The usual, environmentalists trying to make a name for themselves. I assume it was just a bit of negotiating pressure being applied."

"A little bird told me that Quinn was in Cordoba that day," said Alex.

Alex was a box of surprises today. Mike had had enough surprises. He stayed quiet and raised his eyebrows a little to register the news.

Alex continued. "He went to meet Governor Castelli. He must have then decided to visit the offices. This bird also told me that at 5 a.m. on that same day two busloads of the Truckers Union members left Buenos Aires, headed for Cordoba. They knew that Simon was going to be at the MinEx office that day and wanted to apply, what was the phrase you used? Negotiating pressure? I don't believe for a second it was the environmental groups."

Mike stopped, his fork hovered above his plate, a few skewered fusilli still bouncing, carbonara sauce dripping. Harper was an information iceberg and he enjoyed revealing the depth of his knowledge an icicle at a time.

Alex continued chewing on a mouthful of pasta, some red sauce making a dash down his chin. He didn't bother to wipe it away. Mike averted his eyes.

"Quinn will rightly be upset at what happened in Cordoba. I need you to make sure that he doesn't go off piste on us. We do not need him playing ball with Planning. The last thing I need is a bribery scandal involving a British company."

Alex found time to take up his napkin and wipe his chin. He placed his plate to the side. Personal hygiene completed, he continued. "The president has instructed Planning to draw up a list of companies that are of public interest and suitable for expropriation. Nothing concrete yet, it will still have to go to congress and they will have to go through a few legal formalities, most likely involving changing a few laws. I have been given the tricky task of ensuring that no British companies appear on that list."

"How do you propose to do that?" asked Mike, tracing circles around his plate with a crust of broken bread, mopping up the last of his carbonara.

"By making sure that MinEx, and all the other companies like them, stay below the radar."

"That may be too late. I had a visit from an adviser from the Planning Ministry. He said that if MinEx don't play ball they could be nationalized."

Alex's face lit up. "There you have it!"

"Have what?"

"Your ongoing relevance to Simon. You have heard from a well-placed contact, a person with access to privileged information, a human source asset, whatever the fuck you want to call it, that plans for the nationalization of MinEx are underway. Simon will want to know all about the ministry's plans."

"I suppose so," said Mike. In truth he had gone back to thinking about the Doctor's treachery.

"You suppose so? Cheer the fuck up, Mike. You help Simon steer through these waters and you won't just be his hero, you'll be mine too. If any British company gets nationalized, I am fucked. That will be the end of me. Because once these bastards get the taste for one then you can rest assured they will go for the rest."

"I'm not sure what MinEx can do, Alex. They can't go backwards or forwards now. The easiest way to avoid being nationalized is to start greasing every palm they see."

"Not an option, Mike. I've already told you that."

"If they don't play ball with the government, you're not happy, if they do play ball you're not happy. What the fuck do you want them to do?"

"You remember Greg Stelton? He's with that oil company Chief Energy, down in Ushuaia."

"I remember him."

"I had lunch with him a while back when he was up here. I asked him how the bloody hell is Chief Energy making money when the price of oil all over the world is one hundred and forty dollars a barrel and Chief is forced to sell it in Argentina at forty dollars. You know what his answer was? Chief's got nothing to sell. They've stopped producing. They are exploring and discovering and then capping the wells. Stelton is booking the barrels and getting the value on the stock as the Chief's oil reserves increase. Then they leave the oil in the ground. Stelton's view is that, sooner or later, things will change and when they do he will just turn the tap on. Brilliant!"

"It's a long play," nodded Mike in approval.

"Argentina is a long play, Mike, anyone who tells you any different is full of shit. Tell Simon to hang in there. In the meantime, I don't want to give the government any reason to be looking at British companies. For the time being, Britain and Argentina are best friends. In fact, next week we have a special working group coming down from London. Bunch of graduates on a mission to save the world. The Special Working Group on Good Governance and Oversight." Alex's chest swelled with a stifled laugh as if he'd named the group himself.

"And Mike, next time you are thinking of going to Cordoba, I'd appreciate you letting me know beforehand," said Alex with a very non-diplomatic wink.

CHAPTER 21

The Oak Bar was situated in the Park Hyatt Palacio Duhau. On this afternoon, which was cool enough to remind a man that spring was a promise, never a guarantee, Mike Costello alighted from a taxi on Posadas, argued over the change, lost, slammed the door, crossed the street, and entered the grounds of the Palacio Duhau, as he preferred to call it. He leant forward into the incline and marched upwards through the ornamental gardens, stopping once, to see if he was accompanied.

Satisfied he was alone he continued, climbed the stairs of the main hotel area, passed the elevators and exited on Alvear Avenue. He waited five minutes, and confident he was still alone, retraced his steps to the elevators, took a sharp left, a quick right and then proceeded to the end of the hall and entered the Oak Bar.

Mike's intention was to meet Simon and give him an update on the progress, or lack of, on the work that he had commissioned. He was unsure how Simon would react.

The bar was empty, as he knew it would be at this time. He chose a leather, wingback chair in the corner of the room from where he could survey the bar, the sliding doors that opened onto the terrace, and the main door. A waitress in black jeans and matching button-up black top that stretched at the buttons appeared. Park Hyatt was embroidered in white cotton over the pocket of her shirt. Mike declined her invitation to order a spirit, explaining that he was waiting for a friend.

Years ago, Mike sheltered here on a squalid Buenos Aires day. He waited out the storm in the company of the crackling fireplace and an off-duty manager who shared the story of the engraved oak paneling that gave the bar its name.

The paneling had been carved for a French castle sometime in the 1600s. Upon the death of the castle's last owner, the man who had built and named the Palacio after himself, Luis Duhau, approached the widow and acquired the paneling for a song, as the off-duty manager related with a touch of pride. A natural transfer of wealth, prestige, and opportunism in the 1930s, as Argentina rose and France floundered.

Mike had spent many an afternoon examining the panels, picking out St. George, languid lilies, or the lute-playing tiger over the fireplace. More than the paneling, Mike enjoyed the Oak Bar for Luis Duhau. On numerous occasions, he had sat with clients and told them Duhau's story.

An agricultural engineer by trade, a politician by design, a land owner by birth, and a wealthy man at death. By the 1930s Duhau had risen to the post of minister for agriculture from where he oversaw a policy—scheme was a better word—that allowed British companies to buy Argentine beef at low prices whilst simultaneously avoiding taxes. Duhau did not discharge this service for free, accruing immense personal wealth in the process. As was bound to happen, opposition senators, led by Lisandro de la Torre, levelled accusations of corruption.

In defense of his good name Duhau appeared before the senate to face down his accusers, speaking for thirteen days straight. On the thirteenth day, an unimpressed de la Torre confronted Duhau in the senate and attempted to achieve with fists what the rule of law could not.

Duhau, forewarned, had arranged for a hired assassin to be lurking. As de la Torre attacked Duhau, Enzo Bordabehere, a senator and friend of de la Torre, intervened to maintain order in the house. For his troubles, Enzo was shot twice in the back and, as he turned to identify his assailant, again in the chest. He died a short time later.

Duhau, chastened if not punished, resigned, and retired to the Palacio Duhau where he lived out the remainder of his life in luxury and no doubt happiness. De la Torre, disillusioned and impacted by the death of his long-time colleague, withdrew from politics. A few years later, alone in his apartment on Esmeralda, just a few blocks from where Mike now sat, de la Torre drew the curtains against the afternoon sun, took a revolver from the drawer of his writing desk, placed it to his sad heart, and pulled the trigger.

For Mike, the complete history and future of the Argentine Republic could be written and recorded in two syllables. Everything that ever was and would ever be, enunciated and implied by one word: Duhau.

"Mind if I join you?" Simon asked and sat down.

Mike caught the eye of the waitress.

"Two whiskies, please." Then to Simon, "Ice? Water?"

"Just ice, no water thanks."

"Neat for me," said Mike.

The waitress, with a youthful roll of hips, hurried away to fill the order. She returned with the two glasses and a small bowl of olives, and set the order on the small table.

Mike, never a confident bearer of bad news, started. "Thanks for coming, Simon. I've been making some good progress. I will need a little more time, but it is looking good. I met with a source yesterday. Let's just say someone with access to privileged information inside the ministry. They mentioned that it might be better if MinEx adopted a low profile for the time being. The government is beginning to discuss nationalizations. They advised against any actions that could be interpreted as antagonistic towards the government. I think that spying on the minister for planning may fall into that category." A brilliant synthesis of insinuation, half-truths, and outright lies. Taken together it had that tinny ring of truth.

Mike took a sip of whiskey, swirled the spirit around his mouth and inhaled as he swallowed, enjoying the burn.

A look of concern passed over Simon's face.

"I'd prefer it if you stopped the work anyway. At least on the minister himself. I would still like to know what kind of trouble is coming my way though. For example, when my offices might be about to be burnt down. Did your source have any information on that?"

Mike shook his head. He had decided against admitting to Simon that he had been in Cordoba. That was something best kept to himself, no matter how good his synthesizing skills were.

"I've been thinking a lot about what happened in Cordoba," said Simon. "Why now?"

"Impossible to tell," said Mike, uncomfortable with where the conversation was heading.

"You were right, no point talking to these barbarians. I want Decoud's head on a stick."

Mike was unsure if it was a commission or just a desire expressed. He weighed up sharing Alex Harper's thoughts on the subject that it wasn't Decoud or even Decoud's group that had destroyed the MinEx offices, but union thugs connected to the government.

"I can tell you what I've been told. Decoud wasn't behind it."

"Then who was?"

Some of the truth needed to be told. "I had a chat with one of the advisers from Planning. Slimy, little bastard, Luis Lopez. You ever come across him?"

If Simon was surprised that Mike was speaking to Planning he hid it. "I know of him."

"He blamed Decoud's group. He gave me a story about how these groups often get out of control, young guys coming up the ranks, trying to make a name for themselves, and can't be held by the leadership."

"You think that's what happened here?"

"No," said Mike.

"What's your view then? You've no doubt got one." He studied Mike over the rim of his glass.

"The government. What happened in Cordoba was government sanctioned. I don't know by who. The guys who did this were Truckers Union, and not from

Cordoba, they bussed up from BA on the same morning. I think they thought you were going to be there."

"Why would they think that?"

Mike had reached the limit of his truth telling. "No idea."

"And why do you think this?"

"Can't say," said Mike, avoiding the question in his glass. "Doesn't matter where it came from. I believe the Planning Ministry organized for your offices to be burnt to the ground. Doesn't mean it's true though. Let's just add it to the puzzle. Another piece to be considered."

Simon seemed to swallow the explanation like a brussels sprout. He turned his head to the door of the bar where two men in dark-blue suits, no ties, had entered, and were chatting in loud voices. They proceeded to the terrace. Simon's eyes followed them until they were out of sight.

"Nobody followed you in."

"Since you gave me that dossier I haven't stopped looking over my shoulder. And I haven't seen a thing. They all look suspicious to me. The guy with the suit, the guy with the bag, the guy with the tie, the guy without the tie, the guy that comes into the room, the guy that leaves the room."

"Forget it," counselled Mike. "The government is watching your every move. That's all you need to know."

He called over the waitress and asked for another round of whiskies. Two were brought. Mike handed back the empty glasses.

"Where are we at, Simon?"

"You tell me, Mike. I never know what is around the next corner."

"Not such a bad thing. The only people who know what is around the next corner are the ones going in circles."

"Well I seem to be doing that too."

"What if you were to do nothing?" It was a thought that he had been kneading in his mind since his lunch with Alex, working it into a form that could be presented to Simon.

"I have to show some progress back home. I'm already responsible for the largest share-price drop in company history. There's an expectation, to say the least, that I will generate some good news out of here. To stop the bleeding if nothing else." He cupped his whiskey in two hands, considering the amber liquid, rocking the ice cubes back and forth.

"What does progress have to look like?" coaxed Mike, his idea beginning to firm in his mind. A plan to suit the environs. He was careful not to show too much enthusiasm. His last idea of approaching the governor had almost got him killed.

"Tender awarded and signed off."

"Then what should happen? Under normal circumstances," pressed Mike, like a doctor probing for where it hurts.

"After that comes the usual administrative process you'd do before any large-scale project begins. Check all the contractors are compliant, final review of your environmentals, construction planning, review all your licensing and permitting, make sure that everything is in place."

"How long should that take? Under normal circumstance."

"No more than a couple of weeks. It's a review of what's already been done, a final check. What are you thinking?"

"What if you award the tender then do nothing? Well, not nothing, just nothing substantial." Mike placed his glass on the table and sat forward in his chair, hands clasped together, elbows on his knees, warming to his own idea. He could almost feel the tug on the line as the trout mouthed the fly. "What if these checks and reviews took longer than expected? Maybe some plans need to be resubmitted, maybe you need extensive documentation on the employee health plans of your contractor company, maybe you need to rejig some plans, which means resubmitting your environmental approvals."

"To what end?"

"To push forward the moment when you have to commit to spending money. You just keep pushing it forward," said Mike, quoting Alex Harper. "You may have noticed that things take time here, Simon. Whatever documentation you have, whatever approvals you need, you throw it back into the system. Take advantage of their own bureaucracy. You are seen to be doing your bit. It gets your boss and the government off your back. You repeat the process for as long as you need to."

Simon nodded as he thought it through. "To HQ I'm doing my best to move forward. Things move slowly here, not my fault. To the Argentines, the same. I want to move this forward, but I have certain requirements I need to meet, compliance wise. So, I push it forward. I agree, it's doable. For what purpose?"

Mike exhaled. He hadn't got that far. He didn't care. The plan suited his needs. The government would see the tender signed off and be happy. No nationalization would be required. That would save the government an international backlash. Quinn would not be paying any bribes to the government so Harper would be happy. At some point the stalling tactics would wear thin and someone would have to do something.

But by then, Mike would be long gone. They could all work it out themselves. He'd read about it in Sicily, if his Italian was up to it by then.

"We'll burn that bridge when we come to it. For now, stay patient and outwait planning. That's easier than trying to outwit them."

Mike reached for his drink, took a swig, placed his glass back on the table and spread his hands wide. "Anything can happen".

Simon sat looking at his hands. He looked up. "The night I met you at the British embassy. You said something odd at the time. I thought you were pissed."

"I was," Mike confirmed.

"You said that Argentina's not a country, it's a conversation. I can see that now. Let's have that conversation. We talk about it, talk about it, and talk about it, and we don't do anything. We buy time, see what happens." Simon smiled for the first time all night. "So, we have a plan, for now. It's not much of a plan, Mike, but as you say, anything can happen." He raised his glass in the air. "To doing nothing!"

"To doing nothing," echoed Mike. He drained the remains of his whiskey in a single draw. The empty glass smelt of Sicily. Or at least what Mike imagined Sicily would smell like when he was sitting in a bar in Taormina drinking whiskey.

CHAPTER 22

Spring advanced. The purple bloom of jacarandas cloaked and carpeted the neighborhoods of Buenos Aires. Simon Quinn was busy doing nothing. On the Monday morning Mike read with satisfaction that MinEx had awarded their tender to Austral Construcciones. Mike knew that awarding the tender in a process where only one company had been qualified further compromised his client, but he saw it as one more leaf to the native forest.

The news was picked up in the press with several articles in newspapers spanning the full political spectrum, trumpeting MinEx's progress as a sign that the government was winning the battle with inflation. Headline writers seized on the news to hit back at the self-righteous preaching of the armies of naysayers; the World Bank, the International Monetary Fund, and the Paris Club chief among them.

The fewer people that knew of Mike's emergent strategy, the strategy you had when you had no strategy, the better.

Finklestein had reappeared and advised that real progress was being made on Mike's apartment. He hoped that he would have some information soon. In his mind,

Mike took bets on who would come up with a solution first, Finklestein or Harper. On one level it was an interesting socio-cultural experiment; one working for money and the other out of self-interest, both culturally appropriate motivators. At this stage, as far as Mike could tell, they were neck and neck, on the start line. It was just one more frustration that he had to push to the back of his mind for now.

The path forward for MinEx was clearer, even if only temporarily, but temporarily is all Mike needed. He watched on as Quinn threw himself into his work with a vigor and dedication that if applied to more productive circumstances would have achieved remarkable results.

The genius of Mike's plan lay in its simplicity. The building blocks were already in place. All MinEx needed to do was to proceed as if they were trying to get things done and let the machinery of Argentina's multilayered, labyrinthine bureaucracy work in their favor. It would be business as normal where normal meant endless delays, obstructions and dead ends.

In the evenings Mike and Simon met to discuss their encouraging lack of progress. Simon told of how he had called his engineering and planning teams into the boardroom and dragged together three desks around which his team huddled. As Quinn explained how they had studied the blueprints for the construction of the first tranche of rail line, Mike could almost see Quinn frowning, eyebrows close to touching above the bridge of his nose and mumbling to himself in a way that projected real concern until his face unfolded itself and he tapped a knowing pencil on an unsuspecting area of the blueprint.

"I told them that it would be necessary to widen the existing safety zones by fifty centimeters, possibly sixty, on either side of the rail corridor. This would give us an extra meter, an absolute necessity if we wanted to avoid what had occurred in the Ivory Coast." Quinn laughed to himself. "Thankfully nobody dared ask what had actually happened in the Ivory Coast. I presume you don't get very far in Argentina by asking tough questions of your boss."

"More likely they thought it best not to reveal their ignorance of the Ivory Coast incident."

"Either way, they all nodded in agreement and got to work."

Over the following weeks Quinn kept Mike informed of whatever the opposite of progress was as draftsmen and women redrew plans and boundaries, engineers reviewed gradients and calculated weights, loads and load-bearing limits. "It's done," Quinn announced proudly over beers one night. "We've got the blueprint."

Mike nodded in approval and laid out what Quinn should do next. The following day, armed with the new blueprint—Quinn, without an appointment or previous announcement, as Mike had instructed—marched down to the Ministry of Transport, then proceeded to the Ministry of Environment and then the Ministry of Urban Planning and submitted their revised plans.

At each ministerial reception, a blank-faced clerk accepted the nondescript, white envelopes, marked with the MinEx logo; along with the powers of attorney—duly signed and notarized in original plus one photocopy; a color photocopy of Quinn's National Identification Card—enlarged by one hundred and fifty percent and duly signed and notarized; MinEx's business registration and statutes—in original and photocopy, duly signed and notarized.

After Quinn had provided a full set of fingerprints and wiped his fingers clean with a small square of recycled paper, and the clerk had declined Quinn's offer to provide a blood sample, the clerk handed Quinn a small paper chit with a reference number that could be used to follow up on the envelopes' progress through the system.

"The Ministry of Environment got back to us today," Quinn said a few weeks later. The official note from the ministry that Quinn showed Mike officially informed whoever may be concerned that the Federal Ministry of Environment was not competent in this matter and that the plans would need to be first lodged with the municipal council in whose jurisdiction the project was to be executed, in this case Cordoba City, which would, if approved, then need to be forwarded to, and approved, at the provincial government level. Once the provincial government had added their approval to the plans, then, and only then, could the plans be submitted to the Federal Ministry of Environment who will be delighted to assist with your project.

A further three weeks passed, a period of six weeks since the day the plans were lodged, and both the Ministry of Urban Planning and Ministry of Transport followed up with similar advice.

Quinn, respecting the rule of the land and the advice of his trusted adviser, dispatched a team to lodge the plans with the Cordoba Municipal Council. A lengthy period of study elapsed before the municipal council returned with the news that it had come to their attention that the revised plans had not been submitted to a community-consultation process before arriving at the council. It would be impossible to approve the plans without first completing a consultation process. However, due to the importance of the project to the regional economy, the municipal council was prepared to discuss ways in which this process could be expedited. Would MinEx be interested?

"There are three reasons for slow bureaucracy," Mike said. "Reason number one is that your file lands on the desk of a corrupt employee who will place it at the bottom of a pile, never to see the light of day. They're banking on you losing patience. They want you to ask, 'Isn't there another way to get this done?'. Then they'll smile and say, 'Well, actually there is.' Next thing they will be suggesting to meet somewhere discreet, to discuss solutions that could be arrived at, and off down the slippery slope you go.

"Now, the second reason can often be more trouble-some than the first. God forbid your file should land on the desk of an honest employee. There are a few lone rangers out there who are surrounded by corruption, suspicions of corruption, accusations of corruption, and the watchful eye of colleagues and bosses anxious not to miss an opportunity for themselves. You want to try and avoid these employees. They are fearful of being tarred with the same brush as their corrupt colleagues, so this employee is meticulous in crossing every *t*, dotting every *i*, and leaving no room for error or for even the tiniest doubt to shadow their probity and sense of moral rectitude, their only defense against the barbarians seated to their left and right." Mike compared these employees to a beacon of light emitting a dull glow in a murky system from which they cannot escape. And in an environment of limited information, untrustworthy sources, and incomplete records, the work that a lone ranger must do to reach a point of absolute certainty, of absolute conviction, to a point where there exists no crack into which a sliver of doubt could be inserted, can indeed be long and arduous.

"The third, and most common, reason for the inbuilt tardiness was the lazy, disillusioned, bored, and incompetent party-faithful who are hired throughout the system, precisely because they are the least curious, least likely to raise an eyebrow to sleights of hand, the least likely to twitch an ear at the rasping sound of corners being cut." Mike downed the last of his beer for emphasis.

It was into this stymied, inefficient system that Quinn threw his revised plans and Mike was confident that it could be weeks, more likely months, before MinEx would be given the green light to proceed to the next step.

So, as advised by Mike, Quinn declined, he would not like to explore ways in which the municipal council could facilitate or expedite or circumnavigate the community-consultation process. Indeed, as he noted in his return correspondence drafted by Mike himself at the Oak Bar, Quinn thought it essential that the community-consultation process be completed and that he himself would like to attend and supplied a list of dates, providing ample time for the required planning to occur, in which he would be available to travel and make the MinEx case in person.

Around that time, Quinn started receiving the phone calls. Anonymous calls at odd hours, whispered offers of assistance from faceless men, bureaucratic sharks attracted from the depths by an ailing fish that had become separated from the school, they sniffed around MinEx's plans and sensing no free meal retired to the murky depths. The origin of the calls, from this ministry or that council, tracked the journey of the MinEx plans through the underworld of government bureaucracy.

Spring was now a reality and the giant, metal architectural flower on Libertador began to open further each day. Every time Mike walked past this flower he wondered to himself how a country could invest the time, knowledge, and resource to come up with such a spectacular engineering feat, even if ultimately useless, but a decent loaf of bread remained unattainable.

Despite these pockets of grumpiness, Mike's winter of frustration receded into the distance. He realized it had been weeks since he had thought of Sicily, which in turn reminded him that he needed to check in with Finkelstein on his apartment situation. If he didn't continue to push forward towards the exit he knew that Buenos Aires, that crafty old bitch, would begin to suck him back in. He had still heard nothing useful from the lawyer, which could only mean that when he did hear something it would be costly.

As MinEx's plans ground to a pleasing halt, the flush rate increased to levels that Mike estimated had not been reached since December 2001.

"They're planning to nationalize Aerolineas Argentinas, the national airline, from a Spanish investment group." Mike said over media lunas one morning. Between mouthfuls of pastry he explained how the government had pushed through congress a law that deemed the airline of national interest and eligible for expropriation. The airline had been owned by the state before being sold off by the administration of Carlos Menem in the early nineties. The buyers then took the next decade to run the company into the ground. Rumors at the time said that Menem and his inner circle had profited from the sale. This was just one of a wave of privatizations under the Menem government and nobody had the time, or newsprint, to investigate every rumor. As with the privatization, the nationalization was now plagued with accusations of corruption, the Spanish owners complaining of being lowballed on the takeover price.

With the help of the unions, always willing to down tools in the national interest, the president was able to leave the Spaniards with no choice. They cut their losses and left with nothing more than a lesson learned in free lunches. And like in the nineties there was just too much happening for anybody to investigate with any thoroughness. Because if a keen-eyed journalist, eager to make their name in the cut-throat world of journalism, had lingered on the smoke and mirrors and heavy hands behind the airline deal, they may well have missed the unusual case of Antonio Zanetti.

Mike explained that Zanetti was a close friend of the president and was a man who had made two very astute business decisions in his lifetime. The first was in 1990 when, while working as a bank teller, he leaked confidential bank documents to the mayor of Rio Gallegos, a small town in southern Argentina.

Thirteen years later that same mayor, following a stint as governor of Santa Cruz, would become President of the Republic. During that time, Zanetti cultivated his relationship with the future president, always on hand for a favor, always willing to make something appear or disappear as was needed. His friendship, cultivated with such attention, would not be forgotten.

Zanetti's second astute decision was, upon the assumption of the presidency by the ex-mayor of Rio Gallegos, to have the foresight to found a construction company, Electroingenieria Ltd. That company went on to be an outstanding success, winning more than four billion dollars' worth of government building contracts. And Zanetti, the humble bank teller, became a very wealthy man. This arrangement may have gone on into the future if not for Zanetti's, and perhaps the president's, mistrust of their own banking system.

The Swiss authorities had opened an investigation into suspicious transactions originating out of the southern province of Santa Cruz. Around the same time a leaked tape had appeared and was gracing the televisions of every bar and cafeteria in Buenos Aires. Subtitled and with the light adjusted for cinematic effect, it showed alleged associates of Zanetti and the president discussing the dilemma of moving the profits of Electroingenieria Ltd.

From what Mike gathered over the following weeks, from the television, newspapers, taxi drivers, and his own less-reliable sources, was that all up, the operation was a little too successful. Moving the money out of Argentina had become a logistical nightmare. Even for an ex-bank teller, keeping track of the profits proved difficult, with talk of money being weighed rather than counted in an effort to save time.

Making the money was an easier affair. A picture emerged of a well-oiled operation whereby Electroingenieria Ltd would win tenders for public construction work, inflate the price to the government and skim off the top of the contract.

A slight twist was the construction company's incredible streak of buying land prior to the government announcing that it was to be flooded by a hydroelectric project. The land would then be sold back to the government for an enormous profit.

"Some men have all the luck," Quinn quipped.

As they strolled through the Saturday-morning markets of San Telmo, Mike pointed out that there was still the matter of Zanetti getting the president his cut without raising suspicions. Fortuitously, the president's family owned several hotels in Santa Cruz, despite the province's humble tourism offering. It was reported that every day for the last three years, Electroingenieria Ltd. had maintained the occupancy levels at the president's hotels at one hundred percent, booking and paying for rooms that were never used, providing a comfortable, discreet, possibly legal, flow of cash back to the president.

"So why," Quinn asked, "if this is all over the papers and the news, is no one in jail?"

Mike turned over an antique in his hands. An old German soldier's helmet. Probably Second World War. Mike considered buying it. A helmet might prove be useful for the taxi ride home. He put it back on the dusty shelf and looked at Quinn with the patience of a father explaining something to his son for the fourth time.

"Because they are too busy investigating Alberto Sanz."

Alberto Sanz, Mike elaborated, as they strolled the smooth cobblestones of San Telmo, was another of the president's inner circle from Santa Cruz who had been brought to the Pink House when the president assumed power. A low-level political operator, over the years Sanz had made himself indispensable to the president as a procurer of warm bodies and disappearer of cold ones. The former female, the latter male. As the future-president rose so did Sanz.

Once installed in the Pink House, the president, in acknowledgment of Sanz's exemplary services of supply and demand, had named him minister for transport. Lacking the glamour of other ministerial remits, the Ministry of Transport was still lucrative for those so inclined and Sanz showed himself to be more inclined than a hike up Aconcagua.

Public transport was subsidized and the budget for those subsidies was controlled by Sanz at the Ministry of Transport. His diligence had earned him the nickname "Lord of the Subsidies". He wielded the government's financial assistance without mercy, doling out fear and favor, rewarding some, castigating others, and all in return for personal gain.

When Sanz was arrested earlier in the year the column inches on the front page of *La Nacion* recited Sanz's criminal curriculum vitae: embezzlement, irregularities in awarding subsidies, abuse of authority, misappropriation of public funds, conspiracy, concealment of evidence. Above it all a photo of a handcuffed and sheepish-looking Sanz.

"His case is still before the court now," Mike said. "He's been sacrificed. A pawn thrown to the pack, to satisfy, rather than save, the King."

With the sun offering a bite that they hadn't felt for months, Quinn insisted on stopping for a while. They sat on three-legged wooden stools on a street corner, backs against a wall, the mass of Saturday-morning antique shoppers molding past them. Two uniformed policemen made their way up the street, entered the café, and a short time later, despite the long lines of waiting customers, remerged with replenishments, or at least a brown paper bag with the week's take. Mike ordered Quilmes, a tall bottle, and two frosted glasses.

"Why doesn't Sanz just roll over? Tell everything he knows and save himself?" asked Quinn.

"He's playing a long game. This president won't be around forever. There might be a place for Sanz in the next government. That's what he'll be thinking. There is always a place in government for someone who knows how to keep their mouth shut."

CHAPTER 23

"It's Finklestein," said Andrea, holding the telephone away from her ear as if even telecommunication with Finklestein carried a risk.

"Ask him if it is done," said Mike from his computer where he had positioned the Google Earth camera over a small stream running through a Sicilian valley. It looked like you could walk in from a dirt road. It was promising.

"Is it done?" Andrea repeated into the telephone, still looking at Mike. She relayed Finklestein's answer with a shake of the head.

"He can call back when he has some information. Or he can return my fifteen grand. I don't want to hear any more excuses. I've heard enough shit to fill a thousand ears," he said and returned his full attention back to the trout stream on his screen, a welcome distraction from the streets outside his window.

The continual churn of revelations and scandal had begun to depress Mike and he struggled to explain to Quinn their meaning or even follow each scandal through to any kind of conclusion. Impunity was the only constant.

Today it was news of the suspicious purchase by navy officials, unnamed yet, of inoperable submarines from China. The subs were stagnating in dry dock at the Comodoro Rivadavia Naval Base, the local operators unfamiliar with the systems and unable to make head nor tail of the Chinese-language operating manuals. When government representatives were quoted as complaining that the purchase price of the submarines was two to three times the quotes on similar submarines from France, further suspicions were raised.

"I can't keep up, Mike," Quinn complained, over a plate of *empanadas salteñas* later that night.

"That's the idea."

Mike walked home along the streets of Recoleta and studied the faces of those who passed him by, each one locked in their own battle for survival, too tired, too worn out to process the front pages of the papers that hung outside the kiosks, easier to read about the football than remember yesterday's front page or anticipate tomorrow's.

He arrived at his apartment and waited for the doorman to raise himself from behind his desk and waddle to the front door. Alvaro, a stooped gentleman from the north, had come to Buenos Aires looking for better times only to find that bad times had beaten him there. With a pistol holstered haphazardly from his hip, he unlocked the door, stood to the side, and allowed Mike through with a deferential good evening. Mike nodded and headed for the elevator.

Inside his apartment he opened the sliding door that led onto the small balcony that overlooked the street. The warm evening air rushed in. He could smell the city, a smell of decay yet somehow sweet. He eased himself onto the sofa, kicked off his shoes and swung his feet onto the coffee table. He looked over his shoulder and eyed the unopened bottle of Glenlivet.

From the open balcony door came sounds of a disturbance in the street. It came on with the breeze that slipped through the high-rise apartment blocks of Recoleta. He closed his eyes against the day, the news, the stories, the heat, and the city, and the noise grew louder.

He hefted himself from his sofa and hobbled out to the balcony. Grasping the rail in both hands and leaning out, he looked left down the street and saw a stream of people oozing their way towards his apartment like human lava; men, women, and children filled the width of the street with those at the edges forced to scrape along walls and shopfronts.

Each held a pot or pan that was percussed with the lid of the same or a spoon or another pot or pan. The noise was tremendous, filling the narrow streets, rising and penetrating every open window and balcony. The innocent could be forgiven for thinking that the city's chefs had gone on strike.

Back inside Mike turned on his television. The 24-hour news station was broadcasting pictures from around the city. The screen was split in four, each quadrant labelled with the name of a different suburb where the same protest was being replicated. The captions that scrolled below the images kept repeating the words *fondo de pensiones*, pension funds.

The noise from the street grew louder as the crowd slid beneath his balcony, the clamor from the street mixing with its recorded impression coming from his own television.

He stood staring at the television, remote control dangling from his hand. He did a mental inventory of his own kitchen. There was a spaghetti pot and a colander that would do the job. The mass of people crawled forward, an angry, discontented stream flowing through the city, the hammer of metal on metal an audible protest of years of frustration and impotence. He identified with the feeling if even for different reasons. The frustration of exclusion, of feeling that events were passing him by without the possibility of him influencing them, or at times even being aware of what was occurring. He sat back down on his sofa and turned the volume of the TV to full and allowed the recorded sounds of their own protest to feedback down to the crowd below, his own effective, if lazy, show of solidarity.

After the protests had passed and the kitchen sounds had deserted the streets and faded from the evening air, Mike lay on his bed. The evening procession had continued for over three hours. The television coverage had shown the same protests repeated all over the city of Buenos Aires and in the regional cities of Cordoba, Rosario, Mendoza, and Salta. The protests were a brief blip, a hot bubble that formed, expanded to bursting point, and left nothing behind. The excesses and the corruption of this government were unacceptable. For tonight. Tomorrow the long, slow rape of resources would continue.

Could that be the secret of survival? To expel the bubble of hot air from your system, to get it out and move forward without question? Could it be possible that understanding only came when the attempt to understand had ceased? At the bottom of the world it was a notion that made sense.

Mike drifted into sleep and dreamed he stood on a cliff overlooking a beach. Below he could see the postage stamp of towel on the yellow sand where Emily Parisi sat. Her head was turned towards the cliff to watch him. He dove off the cliff, arms arcing out in front of him to form his spearhead, moments before he broke the surface. When he emerged the cool ocean waters had transformed into leaves. He was breaststroking through a canopy of lush tropical forest. He ducked his head into the leaves and could see the ground far below. He raised his head, drew a lungful of air and glanced sideways towards the shore. He was alone.

CHAPTER 24

The news of the nationalization of the nation's pension funds had put Mike Costello in a good mood. For the first time in many weeks his first thought in the morning had not been of walking along mountain streams in search of a pool big enough to hold a brown trout. He had agreed to meet Simon at 10 a.m. in a coffee house on Corrientes and had chosen Café Orleans as a little surprise for his client, a reflection of his improving mood. He woke early with the idea of walking, taking advantage of the clear morning, and avoiding the heat that would no doubt arrive later in the day.

At the kiosk in front of his apartment he stopped and looked over the front pages of the morning's newspapers that were arranged on wires as if hung out to dry. *La Nacion*, *Clarin*, and *Pagina 12* all led with pictures of the previous evening's protests. The *Ambito Financiero*, a poor man's *Financial Times*, led with a picture of an Aerolineas 747 aircraft, overlaid with a picture of an irate-looking board of directors.

The kiosk owner, used to Mike's morning stopover, kept his head buried in his daily football paper, knowing that Mike would only require his commercial attention on the Saturday when he stopped by to purchase the *Buenos Aires Herald*.

By the time Mike turned left into Corrientes small patches of sweat were already beginning to expand from under his armpits and at other points on his body where skin and fabric met. Buenos Aires in summer was not a city for suits.

The city's garbage collectors were still on strike and the morning sun had an adverse effect on the piles of rubbish bags that had accumulated into large towers on the footpaths. Some had reached such a height that they had toppled into the streets. The smell of rubbish, rotting under the heat and humidity, penetrated his mouth and nostrils, growing stronger with each step closer to these fetid cairns, reaching a point where it was necessary to halt his breathing, only to be resumed when he had moved past.

When he had broken free of the last tendrils of stench from one pile he would step into the olfactory sphere of influence of the next, the effect being that his walk down Corrientes was a continual crescendo and fall of odors of the previous days', or maybe even weeks', filth, grime, and smut of Buenos Aires life.

Causing most offence were the piles that had been picked open by the city's stray dogs, or the drug addicted and downtrodden, whose scavenging, either by hand or paw, left gaping holes in the rubbish piles from which detritus oozed like an infected, pestilent sore. Clambering on one pile, a man, his shoeless feet blackened and hardened from walking the streets. Mike averted his eyes as he walked by and the smell of the man, a smell that was somehow human, overpowered even that of the rubbish in to which he was elbow deep, searching for something to eat or smoke or sniff. The man had long ago exited their shared mythos.

Mike grasped the top button of his shirt between thumb and forefinger and using it as a tiny handle, fanned himself, a futile attempt to create airflow around his body. He continued on Corrientes until he came to Café Orleans. He glanced at his watch. It was ten past ten. Still thirty minutes early by local time.

Inside the café Quinn sat at a table, his head buried in a folder. The café offered a welcome respite from the heat, smell, and noise of the street.

"Good morning, Simon," said Mike.

Simon did not lower the folder but bent the top half forward to allow his greeting to escape.

Mike smiled as if holding back a secret that he would soon enjoy revealing. Simon was halfway through the tea that he favored, so Mike called over the waiter and ordered an *americano* and three *media lunas*. Simon declined the offer for *media lunas* explaining that he had arrived forty-five minutes earlier. He had eaten whilst catching up on some work.

"Been here before?" Mike asked.

"No."

"I've been saving this one for you. Thought you might like it."

Quinn looked around the interior as if for the first time noticing where he was. Décor-wise it looked just like every other cafeteria. Non-descript table and chairs, bought for utility rather than comfort. Curtains drawn tight against the outside sun, natural light replaced by naked, yellow bulbs clinging to various wall spaces.

Though the other tables were occupied there was little chatter. In fact, no chatter came from the tables. Apart from Mike and Simon, the only human noises were coming from the kitchen and wait staff. Quinn's eyes swept the room again.

Mike watched, waiting for his client to make the realization that not only were they the sole talkers; they were the only men. Women, in groups of two, three, or four, occupied every table. They sat in silence. As Quinn now noticed, the women looked if not at him, in his direction. He averted his gaze and turned back to Mike.

"Don't shit yourself, Simon." Mike's eyes crinkled at the corners. "I thought you could do with a laugh. In Chile, they call this *café con piernas*, coffee with legs. In true Argentine fashion, they have outdone their Chilean neighbors. Here you can have the legs and the rest."

Quinn's face reddened as if he felt the eyes of the room on him. "Having coffee in a brothel is not how I imagined starting my day, Mike."

"It's not a brothel, Simon," Mike said in a hurt voice. "It's a coffee house. All above board. The owner has an accommodation with these ladies. They can come to offer their services, if wanted. Strictly no hustling. Businessmen can come in, have a coffee, and an ogle or more. That's up to them. We'll be left well alone if that is our wish. I understand that there are some rooms around the corner for those that want a little sugar with their coffee. I only brought you here to show you another side of Buenos Aires."

"Any more sides and I will begin to think it's a dodecahedron."

The waiter brought Mike his *americano*. Receiving it in both hands he followed Quinn's eyes to three ladies seated at the nearest table, careful not to signal any unintended interest. Nocturnal lighting conditions would have enhanced their business prospects.

"Is this why you are looking so smug this morning?" asked Quinn, turning back around.

Mike held up his hands. "I have long ago abandoned the pursuits of youth." He changed subject. "I've been doing some reading on the events of yesterday."

"I had crowds under my balcony half the night," said Quinn.

"Ah yes, the protests. No interest to me, Simon. What interests me is the nationalization of the pension funds. It's something I've been following for a while. I hadn't dared hope that it would happen.

"When Argentina defaulted on its bonds back in 2001 a lot of people—well, not people—funds, were left out of pocket. They have spent the intervening period chasing the government through the US courts, trying to recover what they consider their money. The ethics of it all, I ignore.

"You may be surprised to learn that I have other clients outside of you. A few years back I was hired to assist one of these funds to identify assets held by the Argentine government and make up a hit list, if you like, of assets held outside of Argentina that could be targeted with a Mareva Injunction, a freeze-and-seize order. We've had limited success. We got close a couple of times. A navy training ship that made the mistake of docking in Ghana. We slapped an injunction on it and we managed to hold the ship for a few months. Unfortunately, the

Argentines were able to provide the Ghanaians with the required paperwork to free it." At the mention of paperwork, Mike held up his hand and rubbed his thumb and forefinger together, indicating what kind of paperwork had been lodged with the Ghanaians.

"Then last year we almost got the presidential plane. It was scheduled to be sent up to London for repairs and maintenance. At the last minute, the trip was cancelled. I've no proof, but I suspect that the Argentines were tipped off from someone here in the British embassy." Mike raised his eyebrows, indicating that Quinn could join the dots on that one.

"How does that tie into the pension funds?"

"The pension funds, before yesterday, were one of the best-run investment programs in the country. They were managed by some savvy financial operators. Year on year they would outperform similar funds across the continent. Which is why they became such an attractive target for nationalization. What is of interest to me are the funds' investment mandates. Each fund was required to hold fifteen percent of its portfolio in Argentine assets, meaning that most of the capital were tied up in foreign equity and bonds. As of yesterday those holdings are owned by the Argentine government making them fair game for seizure. It's a monumental oversight on their part."

"They must have considered it," said Quinn un-impressed.

"You would think. But I will give you an example of the wisdom of this government. When I heard that this could happen I began to map the equity holdings of the funds. Not a difficult task as the positions were publicly distributed every quarter. One of the larger private equity holdings was in a company that I'm sure you are familiar with, BHP.

"I'm sure you are also aware that by operating its oil and gas business in the Falkland Islands, BHP, by law, cannot operate in Argentina. That is one of the ways Argentina is fighting Britain on the sovereignty of the islands. Any company operating in the Falklands or working with companies operating in the Falklands, is prohibited from doing business in Argentina. You now have the unusual case of the Argentine government being a shareholder of a company that, by its own laws, is illegally exploring for oil in, what it considers, Argentine territory."

It was the kind of story that Mike enjoyed telling Quinn, feeling a small sense of superiority in knowing more. None of it made sense, none of it seemed plausible. For some reason he enjoyed being the one to reveal it.

"Can shares be seized?" asked Quinn.

Mike shrugged. "That I do not know. I'm only retained to provide the targets. And this morning I fired off a list of all the foreign-based assets that the government now own. How they go about tracking them down and seizing them is a job of the lawyers. My part is done."

Quinn played with his napkin, using it to sweep some crumbs onto the floor. "If the assets are seized, the ones who will suffer are the mum-and-dad Argentines who have their pensions tied up in the funds."

The thought had already occurred to Mike. "I see it like this. The government only need the pension-fund money because they chose to default on their debt in the first place. If people lose their pensions maybe they will think again about voting them in at the next election. There are never any bloody consequences in this country, Simon.

"People say that corruption is the problem here, it's not. Corruption is everywhere. Watergate, HSBC, Enron. Corruption is not an Argentine problem; it is human. The difference is that in the US, people go to jail. Here they just get promoted or a seat in the senate. Impunity is the problem here. If I can bring about some real consequence, some tangible, grab-you-by-the-balls, punch-you-in-the-face consequences, maybe I am doing these people a favor."

Mike could hear the conviction in his own voice and it surprised him. Did he care what happened after he cashed his check? The tightness in his jaw told him he did.

"From what I saw last night those consequences are coming anyway. I doubt they will even get to the next election," said Quinn.

Mike doubted that Quinn knew when the next election was. He watched as Quinn leant forward and helped himself to the third and final *media luna* on Mike's plate. He considered defending it, the walk had made him hungry. He offered no resistance.

"You can't judge anything by that," said Mike. "Banging some pots and pans may scare a rat out of a kitchen. To force a pig to remove his snout from the trough? Rather ineffectual in my experience."

"It's not just the protests. Every day there's a new scandal. Are you telling me that that means nothing? That it's all just business as usual? I think people are fed up, I saw it with my own eyes. They want change. Thousands of people don't just take to the street one day then go home the next as if nothing has happened."

"They've had their say. They've been heard. This evening they will be in their homes, drinking their wine, and complaining about the government. These scandals, the ministers on trial, the fraud, suspicious campaign funding. I know what you're thinking, any one of them would be enough to bring a government down where you're from. Here? It's just part of doing business.

"These are not scandals. Not real ones. They're moves, plays and you need to read them as such. A minister goes on trial. Is he ever found guilty? Does he ever serve time? Is a crime solved? Victims compensated? Doubtful.

"We need to think why this is happening. What's the play? Are they executing one to educate a thousand? Are they repaying a debt? Are they disciplining someone? Are they currying favor? With who? Why? An investigation is never about solving something, it's about sending a message, achieving an objective in the great show of government. And the public respond to the show they are given.

"Think of last night as a hostile audience throwing tomatoes at a bad performance. That is all it is. A message back to the government: You've gone too far, I'm not liking this. Nobody is bringing down a government by walking through Recoleta in a fur coat, banging Nona's colander and singing the national anthem."

Mike sat back in his chair and brushed the crumbs from his hands with undue aggressiveness. The usual humor in his voice gone. He hated what he had just said, hated it because it was true.

"I can't believe it's just business as usual," said Quinn.

"I agree in part. There is an unusual amount of activity. The methods though are nothing unusual."

"Any guesses to why that is?" asked Quinn.

"It can only be about money. They are running out of money. They are subsidizing half the population. Electricity, transport, gas. It's expensive. They can't go to the international markets, so they need to find it locally. I think these scandals, as you say, are the visible result of deals that are being done behind closed doors to get their hands on funds.

"To get the votes needed to nationalize the pension funds they may have had to offer up a head, take a revenue stream from one union and give it to another, make a show of force to prove they are serious." Mike paused and inhaled, the breath whistling through his teeth. "The point is, Simon, you need to be careful. What all this activity tells me is that they are shaking a lot of trees, doing a lot of deals to get their hands on more cash. Under these circumstances, I would not want to be a man holding a hundred and fifty million dollars of what they consider to be their money. You need to be smart. I don't think you can keep this go-slow operation running much longer. They're going to want to see some cash coming out, which means you need to start work, even if it's just some minor stuff. I thought that maybe you could move forward with something small, inconsequential."

Simon shook his head. "My course is set. It's the right one. I can't see how this government can survive much longer."

"This government is going to serve out its term, and maybe the next term."

"Another fucking term?"

Mike let the question hang. He looked at a table across the room. A man in a grey suit, who he hadn't noticed come in was chatting, or more likely negotiating, with two ladies. The man ordered coffee for all three. Mike returned his attention to Quinn.

"Mike, you are the one who advised me to play the long game. To wait them out. They were your words. Now you are saying they're going to be around for another term?"

"I said play the long game. Same as I'm telling you now. They won't be kicked out. You must wait for the election cycle. It's only another four years. If there's one thing that they've learnt well, Simon, it is that you can do whatever you want in government, just do it within your election cycle and make damned sure you have a peaceful, democratic, handover of power. Nothing surer to get the international community interested than a coup or a president that doesn't want to go. Even Menem just packed up and left when it was his time."

A red tide rose in Quinn's face. He grabbed the edge of the table with both hands as if ready to flip it. Mike braced for the eventuality.

"Four fucking years, Mike? I can't wait four fucking years!"

"You're going to have to," Mike said. "Because unless MinEx has a small army that you haven't told me about, I can't see how you are going to dislodge an elected government from power."

"I meant I could wait six months, twelve maximum."

"Argentina moves in cycles; you need to work the cycle. What I said is do nothing in this cycle, you may get a better government in the next cycle. I'm sorry if I wasn't clear on that."

"What about your famous fucking flush rate?"

"That was never about a change of government, Simon. It was just a joke about how quickly the government was destroying the country."

The sentence hung over the table. Mike watched as Quinn tried to calm himself down. The meeting had begun to rot like the bags on Corrientes. He attempted to save it.

"Your plan is good, Simon. Play it long. All I am saying is that at this very moment, be careful. It may be wise to cede some ground, start a small piece of work, drip some money through, just until things cool down a bit."

"And then in four years I can get my teeth into things? Is that what you're saying?" said Quinn, the sarcasm bouncing around the room.

Mike ignored the emotion. "You need to get past that. The strategy is the right one. You just need to tweak it. Be patient."

Quinn stood up, his chair teetering backwards then hitting the floor. He made no attempt to pick it up. He grabbed his folder and walked out of Café Orleans.

Mike stayed sitting at his table. By any measure it had not gone well. But that was to be expected when he was tasked with the impossible. He started flipping through his mental files, searching for a client that he had advised to any kind of successful conclusion. There were only two categories; those that paid their way through and got results, and those that took the moral high ground and found that apart from the elevated view there was very little else in its favor.

Mike had had enough. Quinn was an idiot, but he could make his own bad decisions. Fuck him. Alex wouldn't be happy but fuck him too. He hadn't come through on his end of the bargain either. Mike didn't owe him anything. It was already November. Six months had passed since Mike decided to get out and he was no closer to Sicily. Fuck Simon Quinn. Fuck Alex Harper. Fuck Tomas fucking- Finklestein.

He took a sip from his *americano*. A scraping of chairs on the floor drew his attention. He watched the man in the grey suit who had come in earlier move to the door, holding it open for his female companions. As the ladies left Café Orleans, Mike reflected on the similarities between their immediate future and his own. At least they'd got a free coffee. He consoled himself by imagining that their names were Fortune and Destiny.

CHAPTER 25

On Sunday Mike Costello made his way north to keep an appointment. Alex Harper had phoned the previous evening to invite him to morning drinks at the beach. He had good news. Big news he had said. It could only be about Mike's apartment. The promise of good, big news was enough to convince Mike to brave the slow crawl of traffic up Libertador, one more in the exodus of people looking to escape the weekend's forecast heat.

At Palermo, opposite the Hippodrome, an ambulance, lights flashing, sirens wailing, forced his taxi to the side of the road. The driver allowed the ambulance to pass by. Then, like any driver deserving of the name, the cabbie pulled into the slip stream of the ambulance and hitched a ride through the morning traffic, a remora attached to a flashing, wailing hammerhead. Two motorcycles, in the style of presidential outriders, then attached themselves to Mike's cab, forming a procession of opportunists whose path opened along the length of Libertador. When the chaos, recklessness, and complete disregard for good manners of his adopted city worked in his favor, Mike Costello was at his happiest.

By the time he reached the suburb of Accassuso the cab had dropped off the back of the ambulance and the outriders had departed.

It had been too long since he had come north, not since he had cut relations with the Doctor, an episode that still caused a diminutive burr of unknown portent to form inside him. He made a mental note to return soon.

The cab found its turn off Libertador and moved through the residential area of Accassuso. Large gated houses populated by successful families whose children were more likely to play rugby and hockey than football. He was sure he would not find any Lanus fans this far north. Here expatriate embassy staff were housed so they could enjoy the sugar of Latin America. The local staff were left in the salt further south.

Mike's ride ended at Peru Beach. He had never tracked down the origin of the name, another of his investigative failings. For a city that had turned its back on the ocean, Peru Beach served as the substitute. If you sat at one of the many outside bars that populated the strip, on a raised wooden deck, protected from the sun by a plastic Coca-Cola-branded parasol, with the water at your back, you could almost forget that you were on the River Plate, and across those muddy, silted waters, only made visible by squinting, and only then on a clear day, sat Uruguay, a country blessed with golden beaches.

Brazilian music pulsed out of speakers that had been stacked up outside the bars. Every few meters a different set of speakers and a different song. The result was confused noise with a samba beat.

A decent crowd was already in at this early hour. They were a young crowd who came to kitesurf or to loll around in the sun. Black wetsuits were stripped back to well-toned waists, the intended impression being that they had just emerged from or were about to go for a surf. It left them looking like half-peeled, overripe bananas.

If he had the time to stop and observe them for long enough Mike was confident he would find that they never did much else but drink and discuss their exploits, most likely invented. The behavior justified by the pretty young girls that sat around these itinerant kitesurfers, hanging on their every word. It served to remind Mike why he no longer came here. Peru Beach was a young man's game.

He found Alex Harper slouched at a red plastic table, a scrabble of names etched into the surface. A parasol offered some protection from the elements, though Alex had chosen to sit outside its sphere of protection, attempting to grill some color onto his body.

Alex was nowhere near done. Bare-chested, his lily-white torso exposed to the South American sun, Alex wore only a pair of sunglasses, his mistresses, judging by the wide plastic frames and the red-and-white color. A wide-brimmed hat that would be more at home in the Australian outback completed the unusual look. A shady man in a sunny place thought Mike, rehashing a favorite phrase of a Texan client who had neither the IQ nor the library to have credited the author.

By Alex's side in much more sensible, middle-American style, Mike was surprised to see Greg Stelton.

Alex's first public appearance in Buenos Aires was the US embassy ball and the incident had become diplomatic folklore. Whether due to the free-flowing liquor, the fresh pampas air after the clog and grime of London, or just the freedom of escaping a wife and children, Alex Harper had been in good spirits. It was well into the evening, but still early enough so that even the visa-section staff had not yet left. A statuesque woman, whose sequined dress clung to her body in a failing attempt to cover the results of long hours under the elective-surgeon's knife, made a tottering entrance in to the ball, balancing on heels that reached heights that her surgeon had not. In her hand, she clutched a bag so tiny that it could only have held her self-esteem. Alex had watched her remarkable entrance from across the room and for reasons that were never made clear, announced in a let's-get-ready-to-rumble-kind of voice, "The stripper's here!". Though her face had lost all ability for the expression of emotion, it was reported that a single teardrop of humiliation had formed, one that Greg Stelton dried as he rushed to comfort his wife.

Only some quick and contrite talking from Alex the next morning, in front of a hungover ambassador, had saved him from the ignominy of the shortest posting in Foreign Office history. That Stelton was an oily, as those in the oil and gas industry were known, and a yank to boot, no doubt helped.

Mike greeted both men and sat himself down. He looked around the nearby tables, confirming his suspicion that only if he had come ten years ago could he have said that he was old enough to be the father of most of the other drinkers. He was now well into grandfather territory. He ordered a beer from a passing waiter who lurched off to fetch it.

"Glad you could make it, Mike. Greg you already know, I presume?"

For a diplomat Alex had an awful memory, or at least pretended to.

"Greg, good to see you again. How are things?" The two men shook hands.

"Things are good, Mike," said Greg in that enthusiastic way that one American greets another outside of the States, not wanting, for an instant, to let the other think that his expat experience is superior. "Been back in town for a few days and head south again tonight. Thought I'd do a bit of kitesurfing on my last day."

Mike noted to himself that Stelton had neither the equipment nor the physique.

"The reason I have dragged you all the way up here, Mike, is that this is my farewell. I'm off," said Alex, with a finality that hinted at some relief. Then with a smile, "As they say, it has all gone to shit."

Mike wondered how this related to the big news but didn't press for confirmation. "The girlfriend?" guessed Mike, confident that whatever Alex had told him had already been shared with Stelton.

"Ex-girlfriend," corrected Alex. "Last week she came to me, beaming she was, great news, Alex! I'm pregnant! The little bitch."

"Did you share your medical history with her?"

"Of course not. If she knew I'd been lying to her she would have had my balls. My lie preceded hers so I could say nothing. We celebrated in fact, had a wonderful night. The next morning, I spoke with the Ambo, came clean, and asked to be reassigned. The Foreign Office is a bit like the Catholic Church in that respect. They don't mind what you do, if you confess. They don't like being caught unawares; not good for business. After I explained my situation and assured him that there was no way the child was mine, the Ambo agreed that it would be best if I made a discreet exit."

"When do you leave?" asked Mike.

"Tomorrow morning."

"Back to London?"

Alex leant forward, a sucking, liquid sound audible as he unstuck his back from the plastic chair. "No. I'm afraid not. Wouldn't be welcome there."

"Wife?" asked Mike, guessing again.

"Ex-wife."

"So you told her?"

"Do we ever need to, Mike? They sense these things. I can see you've never married." A comment that perhaps wasn't meant to hurt but found a mark anyway. "If you need me, I'll be in Iraq."

"Iraq?" asked Mike, finding it hard to believe, despite his lack of experience, that any matrimonial danger could justify the move.

"I'll be safe out there. Compound life. Nothing gets in, nothing gets out."

Mike wasn't sure if Alex was referring to his wife or Al Qaeda. He had always seemed to have an irrational fear of his wife.

Greg Stelton who had sat half-listening, eyes fixed on the river, got to his feet and shook off the morning's drinking. He raised his wrist to within inches of his face to look at his watch. "Right, that's me. Class time. You guys going to hang around?" He looked at Alex, who made no signs of moving. "Of course. Wish me luck."

No one did and he moved off towards the waterfront where young instructors with bodies that looked nothing like Greg Stelton's readied enormous kites and strapped frightened-looking people into harnesses, ready to be flung into the River Plate.

"You've seen the papers this morning," Alex stated as fact.

Mike had seen the papers. He had also heard the news on the radio on the drive up. The Ministry of Planning had been doing the press rounds, defending their decision to suspend MinEx's project for an indefinite period of time. He'd told Simon that he should have started some work. On hearing the news Mike had felt the satisfaction of being due an "I told you so."

"I spoke with Simon, yesterday afternoon. He'd just come back from Planning."

"Anything else to add?"

Mike considered the question. Unsure how much Alex knew, unsure how much to tell him.

"The official line is what you've seen in the papers. MinEx have technically failed to employ any locals so they are in breach of their contract. There is a requirement for seventy-five percent of the workforce to be Cordobes.

"Planning's view is that as work hasn't begun and nobody is getting paid then nobody is employed. Worse still, the Ministry of Work is now taking an interest and has ordered MinEx into a forced conciliation process with the Ministry of Planning."

"What does that entail?" asked Alex, his disdain for detail evident in his voice.

Mike tried anyway. "Forced conciliation is an instrument used to solve industrial disputes. It's a bit of a misnomer. The conciliation itself isn't enforced, the payment of wages to the affected workers is. And for the duration of the dispute. You can imagine how it plays out.

Courts are underfunded, understaffed, and the judges prefer a blind eye to blind justice. Disputes can run for years."

Alex nodded and smiled his thin, watery smile. "I'm none the wiser."

No, but you are better informed, thought Mike.

Alex proffered his own summary. "The Planning Ministry has suspended the project because MinEx stopped work on the project. And they're getting paid for doing it." He laughed at the absurdity of it.

"To be fair, the project was never stopped, Alex. It was going through due process."

"A game, Mike. It's all just a game. And I warn you that you are playing against the masters." Alex looked out over the River Plate. A small rivulet of sweat made its way down his chest. Red creases scored his stomach and folds of loose skin were beginning to turn a newborn pink.

"I'm going to miss these bastards, Mike. We should be thankful that they do spend all their time at the psychologists trying to work out if they're Italians or French or British; that their vision is always inward, fixed on the pampas and not on foreign shores. For if it wasn't so, believe me, they'd create like the Italians, philosophize like the French, and pillage like the English. They'd be the end of us all."

He turned his attention back to Mike. "What has Quinn had to say about all this?"

Incandescent with rage, was the phrase that Mike considered using. When he opened his mouth, a more reserved "perturbed" escaped. It sounded ridiculous even to him.

"Perturbed? I didn't think anyone got perturbed any more. I can imagine he was fucking furious." A sharp inward suck of breath caught the laugh that followed his words. "Though he shouldn't be, what did he expect? I told you before. I don't know how they pick these people. No fucking idea at all. They get down here, cock it all up, and then get sent home."

Mike chose not to point out the similarities with the speaker's own situation.

Alex looked back out over the water. Mike followed his gaze to where a Greg Stelton-shaped figure struggled against a giant kite, suffering the indignity of being lifted and dumped into the River Plate, like an oversized and reluctant teabag.

"Have you spoken to Planning?" asked Mike.

"I'm in contact with them on a few issues. During those conversations, they did raise their concerns about MinEx's behavior."

"There's nothing you can do, from your side? I think I have done about all I can."

"Believe me, that MinEx are even still here is testament to the fact that I have done all I can do." The kind of statement that diplomats threw out, grandiose, self-important, impossible to verify, and pointless to dispute.

"What about your guys in Trade? Don't they have someone here in the embassy?" Mike recalled meeting someone a few years back whose face and name had managed to erase itself. A forgettable figure lost among the bland faces of the diplomatic cocktail circuit.

Alex let out a laugh of disdain, the contempt of one public service for another. "If I thought it would have done any good I would have introduced Quinn to the esteemed trade commissioner a long time ago and let him deal with it."

"No good?" asked Mike.

"Never have I met a man who knew so little about so much," Alex said in his usual charitable way. "The kind of man who expects to find a conundrum in the percussion section."

"What would you do if you were in Simon's position?"

Alex leant forward, ever the diplomat, eager to give his opinion oblivious to the disinterestedness of his audience. Mike couldn't give a fuck about Simon Quinn or MinEx. But he was quite happy to lead Harper further away from the fact that Mike was no longer willing to be their chaperone, wiping their ass every time they shit themselves.

Alex took off his glasses and used the heel of his hand to rub away the rings of sweat that had formed around his eyes.

"I would have found a better country in which to dig a hole."

Mike conceded it was a fair point. But that was not Simon's decision to make.

"And I would not have taken a hundred and fifty million off a government that is desperate for money."

"That's what I don't understand," said Mike, giving voice to a misgiving that had been circling his mind, increasing in volume with each circuit. "Why is the government so keen to get their hands on this money? What do they need it for?"

Alex laughed. "That's what I like about you, Mike. You've made your home around the edges, dipping in and out but never diving in. I respect that. You know where to draw the line. Of course, it means that you never see the big picture. But I envy you that. Who would want to see the big picture? The big picture is just a stinking, rotten carcass that you can never unsee."

Mike sat and filled his eyes with the river. He had been coming to the same conclusion himself. But Alex was wrong to think there was anything enviable in this. Mike was tired of being peripheral to events, to seeing movements from the corner of his eye, to be dealing with shadows, to having the shit beaten out of him and no clue by who or why. That was the real reason he was leaving. He drew a long breath and pursued his original line of questioning.

"What would you do in MinEx's place, now, with all that has already happened?"

"I'd find myself a nice Chinese partner. Sell them forty-nine percent and let them earn it by dealing with the locals, let them get their hands dirty. I'd concentrate on building the bloody thing or running it or whatever it is that MinEx does."

Stelton's class had finished and he dragged himself up the beach, back towards the bars. Mike had to take a second look to confirm that Stelton wasn't still attached to his kite such was his slow progress.

"Tell Quinn to be careful. He has no idea how far he's in. If he did, he wouldn't be here."

To Mike's ears the words sounded liked the first true sentence that Alex had ever spoken to him. He almost sounded concerned for Quinn. He would relay the message though he suspected that Alex's expressed humanity came more from an interest in avoiding the last-minute workload that a diplomatic issue would create rather than any real concern for Simon's well-being.

"Alex, what about our deal? That is why I thought you called me up here."

"Ah that. Yes, our request has gone in to the Argentines. I have left a note for my successor. I am sure he will follow it up for you. As for Quinn. No longer my problem. Advise him as you wish."

Mike stared out over the river. There was nothing to say. His utility to Alex Harper had reached its limit. Mike was someone else's problem now. He wondered what it would feel like to take the empty beer bottle from the table and smash it into Alex's face. Could he first grab the bottle by the neck and smash off the bottom on the edge of the table? He was unsure if the plastic table was up to leaving a nice jagged, face-cutting edge. He closed his eyes and savored the fantasy.

"It has all worked out well for you hasn't it, Alex? You're out of here tomorrow, the Falklands are still British, you got what you wanted."

"Yes, that has worked out quite well for me, the Malvinas," said Alex, oblivious to the threat circulating through Mike but still alert to any opportunity to turn the conversation to self-praise. "The navy's left with inoperable submarines, the leadership removed. I almost feel like the president has done my job for me. My only regret is that I won't be around for the navy's riposte." Alex squinted into the sun.

Mike stood, fixed his eyes on Alex Harper, his back to the river. "You're a cunt, Alex."

On the street Mike hailed a taxi and joined the flow of traffic back to the city. He chewed on his conversation with Alex Harper, rolling it around in his mouth, his jaw tensed. He thought about Alex Harper burning on the outside, pickling on the inside. He hoped he'd meet a mortar in Iraq. Somehow he knew he wouldn't. He would be the same Alex in Iraq as he was here; lying, cajoling, manipulating, and always moving forward.

As he passed the hippodrome for the second time that day Mike's thoughts settled on Simon Quinn. Alex was right, Simon was in over his head and he didn't know it. He would work that out for himself soon enough.

Nothing more could be done today; it would have to wait until tomorrow. Quinn had calmed down and wanted to meet to discuss Marcelo Decoud. Dealing with Decoud while the standoff with Planning continued was the equivalent of watering your garden while the house burned. Nothing good would come of talking. The only solution would be money. That had been Mike's experience and he was yet to find a convincing argument against it. Talk was cheap and solutions were often expensive. There was no way around that. The problem was that Quinn never listened. After tomorrow it would no longer be Mike's problem. He would tell Quinn he was on his own from now.

Mike tried to conjure the image of the Limay River in his mind but he couldn't bring it forth. The cab turned off Libertador and wound its way through Recoleta. The pull of the Oak Bar was strong, challenging Mike's determination to go straight home, but an early night would be a good thing.

CHAPTER 26

When Mike Costello woke the next morning, his skin tingled with the burn of the previous day's sun. His determination to avoid the Oak bar had come to nothing. After exiting the taxi instead of turning left on to Alvear as he had promised himself, he had turned right onto Posadas, a trajectory that led him to the Oak Bar. Just one, he said as he settled into the familiar chair by the fireplace.

Now, as he examined his face in the bathroom mirror, he saw that his forehead had turned an attractive hue of pink. A scalp peel was inevitable. He doused his face in cold water and washed away the internal scratchiness left by too many fingers of whiskey. He shouldn't have mixed though it was never the mixing, always the quantity. One beer followed by one whiskey was fine. Three beers followed by three whiskies, four if he counted the one for the road, which being on the house he never did, and he was in trouble. Once again, he made a mental note to remember this.

Washed and dressed, Mike felt eighty percent again, as much as he dared hope for these days. He made his way down to Dos Escudos. He greeted the waitresses and took a seat at the table located in the back, the rest of the room, and most importantly the entrance, in full view. The morning crowd was quiet, tables occupied by individuals, the sound of newspaper pages being turned scratched the air. A television set was wedged high in the back corner, sound turned down. An attractive female presenter spoke to camera, a 24-hour news ticker crawled across the bottom of the screen.

Mike awaited the arrival of his *media lunas* and coffee and checked his phone. Three missed calls from Julian Martinelli was unusual though not irregular these days. It had been months since he had spoken with Julian, periods of silence broken by a message asking if there was any work for him. It annoyed Mike that Julian still signed off his messages with "The Doctor", the affectionate nickname that he had lost all rights to use. As he stared at the screen a text message from Julian arrived: *Please call me.* Mike deleted the message.

His order arrived and he delivered a *media luna* to his mouth and glanced at the television screen above him. Before his hand could reach his coffee cup the shock of realization dried his throat; the light, buttery pastry stuck to the roof of his mouth; a leaden weight thumped to the pit of his stomach.

He stared at the screen, his mouth open, frozen mid chew, flakes of pastry clinging to his lips. On the television, two men wheeled a body out of an apartment in what looked like the early hours of morning. Yellow-and-black police tape lined the path of the stretcher. The ticker below the images merged into a conga line of letters, with the one word, "Suicide", forming, blurring, and reforming in Mike's vision.

A still image overlaid the footage. The type of photo provided by a family member who hoped to show the deceased in happier times, as the family would have them remembered, a counterpoint to the lifeless skin and bone being trolleyed out in the images. Mike stared in disbelief at the familiar face. Simon Quinn's 9.30 a.m. meeting would be an apology. Marcelo Decoud was dead.

Mike's mind creaked into gear. He rinsed his mouth with coffee, registering neither taste nor temperature. Julian's missed calls now made sense. He retrieved his phone from his shoulder bag and dialed, his sense of survival overriding his sense of betrayal. He skipped the niceties; Julian could only be calling for one reason.

"I saw. Yes. Where? OK."

Mike hung up and was halfway to the counter to settle his bill. He overpaid, even more than usual, and made for the street. He flagged the first taxi that passed. The driver pulled over to the curb and leaned his head towards the passenger side, his hand flapped over the steering wheel, a toothpick hung from his lips. Through the open window he asked for the destination. At Mike's response, he shook his head, the toothpick moved back and forth like the hand of a tiny compass unable to settle on north. Mike punched the door, swore, and stalked off, glancing over his shoulder for approaching taxis as he went. On the third attempt he found a driver willing to work. He settled into the back, accommodated his bag on the worn, leather seat beside him and asked for the radio.

The first bulletin led with the government's decision to proceed with the nationalization of another Spanish company, this one in the oil and gas sector. That was followed by the trial of the ousted transport minister, a daily update required to communicate the litany of abuses that were being investigated. An interview with a local author who was about to set off on a cultural tour of China preceded the story of the suicide. The bulletin failed to provide any further information than that which Mike had gathered from the muted images he had witnessed in the café.

The second bulletin carried the same information, though the item of interest had moved up the priority line and now came before the news of the embattled former transport minister, a jump that could be ascribed to the addition of a quote from the president. The China-bound author was bumped all together.

The president, employing that sincere tone reserved for death and tax hikes, lamented the suicide of a man who had dedicated his life to defending the resources of the country he loved, expressing a sentiment that his death was a tragedy for all those who desired the progress and development of the nation. It was hoped that the unfortunate death of Decoud would not be used as a weapon to further undermine the government by those that did not wish the country to progress, by those that worked day and night to destabilize rather than develop, to destroy rather than construct. The president's intervention confirmed Mike's initial instinct. Events had escalated.

When Mike arrived at his destination he found Julian Martinelli standing on the pavement in the impatient pose of a man who had been waiting quite a while. On sighting Julian his former anger at the man returned. He breathed in, stuffing the anger deep inside, and disembarked from the taxi.

"Good morning, Julian," he said, his voice devoid of any emotion that could be misconstrued as forgiveness.

"Good morning, Mike, thank you for coming," returned Julian with a warm smile, as if Mike had arrived to enjoy a day out on the river.

Julian showed no hint of uneasiness; the way that some men can have coffee with a colleague in the morning then fuck his wife that evening. "Let's walk and talk. Much safer to do so until we get a handle on what's happening."

The two men strolled along cracked footpaths, no set direction, passing the well-manicured lawns and high-walled residences of the city's affluent. Julian was a picture of calm. The casual observer would have had no reason to connect him to the events of the early morning. Mike though noticed the occasional glance over a shoulder or the hesitation and second look at a parked car and its occupants.

"What have you learnt?" Mike asked.

"Not much. They took the body to the Palermo Clinic this morning. Naturally, I reached out to my guy there to see what he might know. The prostate guy," he added for unneeded clarity.

"You're still in contact with him?"

"After the effort I put into him I was never going to just throw him back. Once compromised, Mike, with the right handling, they're yours forever. You never know when you might need them."

"And you've spoken to him?" asked Mike, ignoring Julian's gentle lecturing.

"Briefly. He'll see us tonight. Late. And he wants to be paid. He's running a considerable risk. You'll have to do it. I swore I'd never pay that man another cent. I am nothing if not a man of my word."

Mike wondered what his word might be. It wasn't honesty. Mike suspected it started with C and rhymed with bunt.

The two men finalized their plans for the evening and walked back to where they had begun. Julian stopped to pick some flowers for his wife. Her favorites, he explained, he would never be forgiven if he didn't collect a few for her, seeing as they bloom so rarely in these climes.

At the appointed hour, long after the sun had set and at a time when the city's residents were preparing to venture forth for an evening meal, Mike waited on the pre-appointed curbside. He had taken the train from Central station and had alighted at Lisandro de la Torre. He had attempted to make sure he wasn't followed but had no real way of telling. He saw the small red Golf approach, Julian perched behind the wheel like a bantam rooster. He flashed the headlights.

Mike got in and they drove to their rendezvous in silence, the overhead street lights—the ones that were functioning—scanned over their faces as they passed beneath as if they were bar codes. Mike switched on the radio. Carlos Gardel was lamenting the difficulties of distinguishing between a thief from a gentleman. Mike agreed. It was a difficult task.

• • •

"He was suicided," said the man in the blue scrubs, his surgical mask crumpled around his neck. His ears were pricked forward, an effect of the mask's elastic straps that were stretched back behind his ears. It gave the impression that he was on high alert.

Mike Costello looked at the man, wondering if he should correct him. He expected greater precision from a medical practitioner. Even in times like this grammar was important.

He looked around the empty parking lot. The red Golf they had arrived in was parked three blocks away to avoid suspicion. Through the trees to his right he could see the sparkle of the hospital lights and he imagined Decoud, the victim, as he had just been described, lying up there, a sheet pulled over his face. Mike shook his head to remove the image.

Mike could not resist. "Committed suicide," he said, at the same time regretting the impulse to correct the man in his own language.

The man in blue shook his head and repeated the phrase. "He was suicided. If you commit suicide, or you suicide," he said, imitating Mike's own accent, "you don't cave in your own ribs and kick in your own kidneys before placing a bullet in your brain."

Mike looked at Julian for direction and received none.

"We have proof of this?"

"Only what I saw. There will be no file. The body has been taken away for cremation."

"Already?"

"Normal procedure, I'm afraid," offered Julian. "In the case of government-assisted suicides."

"There's nothing more," the nurse said, indicating that the meeting had finished.

He extended an open hand. Unsure if the informant was asking for the prearranged envelope or saying goodbye, Mike fumbled in his jacket. He grabbed hold of the envelope and passed it over. Without opening it the man turned and walked away.

Mike watched him make his way down the path that led back through the trees to the hospital, his blue uniform blending into the black of the night.

He turned to Julian. "Murdered," he said. "Another tragedy in a long history of tragedies."

Julian shook his head. "We don't have a long history of tragedies, Mike. We have just one tragedy that we insist on reliving every day. That's our tragedy."

CHAPTER 27

M ike stared straight ahead unblinking, the word *suicided* bouncing around his head. Julian Martinelli had both hands on the wheel, steering the red Golf through the late-night traffic with a minimalist's regard to the use of the indicator. Neither man spoke. Mike was going over the conversation with the nurse. After a while he broke the silence.

"I'd never heard that phrase before, 'he was suicided.' I thought he had misspoken."

Julian spoke without turning his head. "I'm afraid it has become a part of the local dialect. Mr. Decoud is just one more in a …" He paused to think. "What's the collective noun for a group of victims? A murder?"

"No, that's crows. Not sure."

Julian shrugged. "Let's say one more in a line of victims who, for whatever reason, are sacrificed in the name of something that they will never understand or even know about. Understanding is often beyond even us," he said, with no clarification of who "us" comprised. He nodded his head toward a street sign. "Libertador, 9 de Julio, Lisandro de la Torre, 25 de Mayo, San Martin, Arenales. Every street named after someone or something from history, stepping stones of the nation's progress. Or so they want us to believe." He grunted in disgust. "This country was built on the bodies of those who have tried to change it. There are no signs for them. Just obituaries, forgotten the next day. Their bodies are the shadows of objects being moved by those that we cannot see and for reasons that we cannot grasp.

"In this instance, our connection to the deceased places us in an uncomfortably close position. Dangerous even, Mike. When I heard the president speak this morning I had a sick feeling that this was not a suicide. Did you not think it strange that the president of the nation would pronounce on the suicide of an unknown activist from Cordoba from a prepared press release? Make no mistake, Mike, this is not the action of a rogue element, or a settling of provincial scores. This has been sanctioned at the highest level. That body is a message. For *us*," he said, leaving no doubt who he referred to this time.

Julian continued. "I spoke to Decoud last week. Thought he might still be useful at some point. He told me he was coming down to Buenos Aires to meet with MinEx. He seemed excited at the prospect. It didn't make any sense that he would come all this way to take his own life."

It didn't make sense to Mike that anyone would take their own life anywhere, regardless of the distance travelled. He had spent his life clinging to it. The closest he had come to death were a few funerals and even then, only the necessary ones. The others he had avoided where possible. The thought of not existing was a prospect too large and powerful to hold in his mind, like trying to hold a wave in the palm of his hand.

"What now?" asked Mike.

"We assume that they know or will soon know of our involvement with Mr. Decoud. I trust that there are no loose ends on your side?"

Mike assured him there weren't. He had destroyed all materials and all communication between himself and Julian and himself and Simon. No physical evidence that had been in his possession still existed.

Julian nodded in satisfaction. "Still, there may be evidence that we do not have. My ticket to Cordoba must be retrievable from a system somewhere, video of you and I meeting. Who knows? We need to take precautions. You need to stay close to Quinn. Make sure he doesn't panic and do anything to endanger us."

Mike had come to the same conclusion. If Decoud's lifeless body was a message then the biggest danger now was Quinn.

"What do you suggest I tell Quinn?"

"He can't be intimidated by this. If they sense weakness we're all fucked. If they accuse MinEx of this and Quinn caves to the pressure, cuts himself a deal, then the government will still need to fit someone for the murder. No guesses who that will be." Julian slowed for a red light but didn't stop and the Golf rolled through the intersection. "The president has called it a suicide. No mention of any investigation, no mention of any suspicious circumstances. That's a good sign. The door is open, for now." Julian turned and looked at Mike. "Your client must be proactive. He cannot allow the government to shape the narrative on this. If he is accused, he must fight back. They only respect strength. And Mike, I will say this now. If it comes to a situation of us or Quinn, you know what I will do."

"I know," said Mike. He would make the same decision. The difference was that he would feel some guilt.

The Golf crept along Posadas.

"I just realized I have no idea where you live."

It was no coincidence and Mike had no intention of rectifying the situation tonight.

"You can drop me out the front of the Duhau. I think I'll take a nightcap." The lack of invitation to join him was as audible as any spoken invitation would have been. Mike wanted to be alone. To think. Taking Julian's advice was just one option, he wanted time and whiskey to think through others.

As they pulled up to the curb Mike considered giving voice to what he had wanted to say to Julian since the day he had sat in Mickey Mouse's smoke-filled office. He had no doubt that Julian would have spoken to Mickey Mouse and pieced together what had caused Mike to sever relations. Rather than broaching the subject Julian was happy to play along, content to pretend that nothing had occurred. The ability to subjugate short-term personal emotion to the larger stakes at play was a key skill if one was to survive the murky world that Julian had inhabited all his life. That Julian played it so well angered Mike more than the initial betrayal.

"Good night," he said and got out of the car. He closed the door with a gentle click and watched the tail lights of the red Golf disappear around the corner of Alvear.

CHAPTER 28

M ike stared out over the waters of Puerto Madero as he waited for Simon Quinn. The wind ruffled the surface. Thoughts of sails came to mind. It occurred to him that during all the times he had visited the port not once had he seen a sail, or a ship, or a boat, or any port activity at all. The Puerto Madero seemed a port only in name, its commercial activity restricted to the bars and restaurants that dotted the shoreline.

A young couple strolled along the edge of the dock and stopped by the railing on the water's edge. He watched them until he felt uncomfortable at his own voyeurism.

When Quinn arrived the two men walked along the docks, side by side, in silence. The heat of the day slumped heavy on Mike's shoulders as if it were a physical object hanging from his body. Mike hauled behind him the weight of the heat plus the years he had lived, each multiplying the effects of the other.

The Doctor was right, as he so often was, when it came to the ways of the Argentine. Mike's future relied on Quinn making the right decisions. Mike would have felt more comfortable if his future hinged on the spin of a roulette wheel. The Doctor's confidence in Mike's ability to persuade Quinn to act in their interest was, at best, misplaced. The first step was to convince Quinn of what had happened. If he couldn't do that there would be no second step.

They stopped at a small café, taking a place at an outside table. They were alone except for the waiters and a few seagulls, neither would bother them unless called.

"The government?" Simon Quinn exclaimed from across the table. "You come here, you tell me Decoud has been murdered, with not a shred of evidence except for some shady meeting in a hospital parking lot with a doctor you've paid off, and you think this is going to be pinned on me?"

"I think he was a nurse actually. But I get your point."

It was the reaction that Mike had expected. He knew how crazy it would sound.

He had to accept that Simon was right, the physical evidence was not overwhelming. A deep understanding of Argentina was required to give meaning to the events as outlined by Mike. Would Mike even have believed what had happened and what it meant without the aid of the Doctor, his shadow cipher?

He changed tack. "Who knew you were meeting with Decoud?"

"Just you, and my assistant, Cecilia. She set the meeting up."

Mike pursed his lips. "I suggest you start restricting information to Cecilia. The leak could have been at Decoud's end. Nevertheless, I wouldn't be taking any chances."

"How am I supposed to proceed with my work if I can't share information with my assistant? How is that supposed to function? Or should I just have her rubbed out? Is that how things work here?"

Mike ignored the petulance. "Proceed? I told you how to proceed. I told you to start the work. You chose to ignore that advice."

"You are blaming me for Decoud's death?" asked Quinn, his voice rising in pitch.

"Of course not, I'm only saying, it is quite clear how you must proceed. If you are unable to do so or are uncomfortable doing so, then my advice is for you to leave the country. Whatever consequences await you back home cannot be worse than what lies ahead here. I don't understand how you can be asking me about the future of the project when what I am telling you is that your life is in danger. This was a warning. They were prepared to kill a man just to send a warning. Do you get that?" Mike paused to allow his interpretation of Decoud's death to sink in.

Simon's head bowed and he studied a stain on the table, rubbing it with his thumb. He took a deep breath and looked out over the water. It appeared that Mike's message had found its mark.

"You know what I think, Mike? If these people are prepared to kill someone, an innocent man, to send a message to me, then I think they're desperate. They know their time is running out. And when it does, when they are thrown out, I will still be here and I will build this fucking railway if it is the last thing I do." He slapped the table hard with a force that startled Mike.

"You're wrong, Simon. They're not going anywhere. They're going to come to you to make a deal. If your number-one priority is to finish the project, which given the circumstance appears to me quite fucking ridiculous, then my advice is that you take that deal. Pay them whatever the fuck they want. On their terms." Free of the shadow of Alex Harper it felt good to give some good honest, unencumbered advice.

"It was also your advice to play the long game, wait them out. How did that go? I'll tell you how. I am in a forced conciliation. I am being forced to pay those bastards for doing nothing while the courts consider our case! Forgive me if I am a little reluctant to be receiving more advice."

Mike had no desire to defend himself. Like a man lost in a forest he saw no utility in wondering how he got there or attempting to justify why he went left or right, only an urgency to find the right path out. It was curious how priorities can change in an instant, like a wind change on the water. His thoughts were no longer preoccupied with planning the next twenty years of his life, finding the perfect trout stream, imagining the coarseness of Mediterranean sand beneath his feet, the color schemes of kitchen and patio, wondering if he would have to rent a parasol or could take his own to the beach that he imagined in front of his villa. It was as if his imagination had retracted from a panoramic wide shot of the future to zoom in on nothing more than the next twenty-four hours. He had lost all right to look farther ahead than that.

He returned his focus to Quinn. "I gave you the best advice I could at the time. I didn't expect dead bodies to start turning up. I can only advise you based on the information I have to hand and in light of yesterday's events this is now my advice."

Simon got up from the table. "I think I might just follow my own instinct for a change on this one. I'll call you if I need you."

Mike watched his client walk off down the docks. You can lead a horse to water but you can't make him think.

CHAPTER 29

Mike stood on the pavement in front of his office waiting for the Doctor. He preferred to meet him on the footpath than receive him in the office and play intermediary between the Doctor and Andrea. Both seemed to want to protect Mike from the other. Mike had never bothered to share with Andrea the news that her suspicions of the Doctor had proved correct. It was a "told you so" that he didn't need. Her face had brightened when she asked why Mike had stopped making the monthly payments to the Doctor and received a grunt for a reply.

The Doctor had called ahead saying he was five minutes away and Mike had come downstairs. That had been fifteen minutes ago. Accepting the Doctor's help, deferring to his decision-making, still didn't sit well with Mike but it was better than jail. For now he was able to swallow his pride.

He folded his arms and leant against the window of the stationery shop, taking his weight on the sole of one shoe that he had cocked behind him, careful to keep his clothes from contacting the dusty window. A security guard from the building next door, shotgun slung over his shoulder, patrolled the footpath, keeping a watchful eye on Mike. The shotgun seemed out of place with the urban street populated by suited workers. Alerted by a greeting behind him, Mike turned his head. The Doctor was ejecting himself from the back seat of a taxi.

"Sorry, sorry, sorry," the Doctor apologized, extending his hand for Mike to shake. "One of those days."

"There's a little place around the corner. Shall we?"

The Doctor extended his hand, indicating that Mike should lead the way.

The door of the small café on Arenales rattled as the men pushed through it. They moved to a table at the back of the room. On the television a replay of last night's game was showing. Lanus were down 0–3. Mike took the seat facing away from the television.

"Again, sorry for leaving you on the footpath. I have had some excitement this morning. They've published my article!"

The blank look on Mike's face demanded an explanation.

"*Environment and Modern Man*. They published my article on Decoud." The Doctor seemed rapt with his publishing success. "A kind of posthumous homage. It's on their website."

Mike nodded as he thought he should in the presence of a writer but made no move. The Doctor insisted. "You can see for yourself on your phone."

Reluctantly Mike drew his phone from his pocket. "How do I find it?" he asked.

The Doctor grabbed his phone and began interrogating the buttons.

"Good morning, gentlemen. Mind if I join you?"

The voice was recognizable, but Mike swung around for visual confirmation. Luis Lopez stood over the table. Through the front window of the café Mike could see a man dressed in a dark suit, white earpiece snaking from his ear, standing beside the passenger door of a parked vehicle. The driver remained behind the wheel. Luis followed Mike's eyes back to the car.

"Nothing to worry about, Mr. Costello. Just a couple of friends. Can we talk?"

Not waiting for an answer, Luis sat down.

"Not very smart for us all to be seen together," Mike observed.

Luis smiled. "All that exists is what history records. I doubt very much that history will bother to record this little meeting. Just a chat between allies."

"What do you want?"

"I was briefed by the minister this morning, who himself had been briefed by the president. The investigators have turned up," Luis paused for effect, letting his words hang in the morning air, "certain inconsistencies around Decoud's death."

Mike shot a glance at the Doctor, willing him to intervene. Surely this was his territory to navigate.

"You see, it has come to our attention that a certain ex-naval intelligence officer was in contact with Decoud." He nodded at the Doctor who remained statue still. "We have reason to believe that that was done on your behalf, Mr. Costello. We did a little more digging and it appears that you had taken quite the interest in Mr. Decoud. It was revealed that he was to meet with your client here in Buenos Aires, a meeting which we now know he never made it to." Luis clicked his tongue in mock disappointment and looked at Mike, awaiting an objection that was not forthcoming.

"Two theories are being pursued. The first, and I hope that this is the case, is that Marcelo Decoud had become an irritant to the MinEx project. Understandably, you wanted to find out what made the man tick, what was his price, or how you could make him go away. You hired one of our *ex*-spies—" another glance at the Doctor, not so deferential "—to do some checking for you, ask a few questions, get a measure of the man. No harm in that. Indeed, it keeps our retired intelligence officers occupied. God knows there hasn't been much for them to do since the eighties and we'd much rather have them running around looking at activists on your behalf than sticking their noses into politics. We saw how that ended last time." Luis gave a humorless chuckle at his own joke. Mike looked at the Doctor expecting a reaction but saw only the tic of a blue vein above his temple.

"Having got a handle on the problem, or should I say the man—and let's be honest, gentlemen, the problem is always the man—you make him an offer, he accepts, and you invite him down to Buenos Aires to finalize the details. The night before you meet, he has the classic ideologue's crisis. Alone in his apartment with just the betrayal of his colleagues, the betrayal of his ideals for companionship, he takes the only noble path left and places a bullet in his brain."

Luis waited as if in expectation of applause at the theatre he had laid out.

Mike expressed no opinion.

The Doctor asked, "And the second theory?"

"Ah, the second theory, I am afraid is a little more complicated. For you two, that is. The second theory begins much like the first. Marcelo Decoud made the mistake of becoming an irritant to the advancement of MinEx's interests in Argentina. An honest man, whose only intention was to defend his lands against foreign predators. You could not abide that; you could not understand a man who placed passion and ideals above money and profit.

"So you send your spy to investigate the man. You discover that Decoud has information that proves that MinEx has been engaging in corrupt practices, forcing companies to inflate their prices and pay the excesses back to your client. Maybe to an offshore account in Uruguay. You pressure Decoud to stay quiet, but he does not buckle. His resolve only strengthens. He threatens to go to the press. He sets fire to the MinEx offices in Cordoba.

"Desperate, you hatch a plot to lure him to Buenos Aires. You tell him that you are ready to make a deal. He agrees to meet with you, unaware of the trap that has been set for him. In his apartment, he has one last chance to cooperate. He doesn't, he holds tight. So you give the only order left to give: Dispatch him and make it look like a suicide"

The Doctor looked not at Luis but through the front window and Mike followed his stare. The man with the earpiece was speaking into his sleeve.

Listening to Luis, Mike realized that he was in the presence of organized crime dressed up as government.

"I have a theory of my own, Luis," Mike said. "I think your transport minister is about to go to jail. Your top navy officials are off to jail. Your union mates are about to be thrown in jail. Your finance secretary is under investigation. Your president's election campaign financing is under the microscope and when it comes into focus I think they are going to find that a hell of a lot of drug money went into getting elected."

Luis made no sign of interrupting, content to listen.

Mike continued. "Sorry if I'm a little skeptical or a little reluctant to cooperate with your schemes. What I see is a desperate man. An emissary of a money-grubbing government on its last legs. I can smell it on you," he added, trying to provoke a response. "Why go to all this trouble? You said yourself, if you wanted to you could just nationalize MinEx."

"You are right, of course we could. But it takes time. Law changes, debates, approvals. Even applying the veneer of due process on such a maneuver takes time. And that we don't have."

"My message to you, or to the minister, or to the president, you can tell them all. MinEx came here to build that fucking railway and that is what they're going to do. And you are not going to see another cent of their budget. You think you've got this special way of doing things down here, Luis. It's not special. You're just like every other government prick I've had to deal with from every other tin-pot country I've ever had the misfortune to set foot in."

Luis arched his back in his chair, stretching, appearing to enjoy the time out of the office. "I came here today as a friend, Mr. Costello, to advise you of your true situation. You don't seem to grasp the desperation of your position."

"You forget, Luis, that the president has already declared it a suicide."

Luis laughed, indicating the importance he placed on that. "Even presidents can be misinformed. I can assure you that the president's next announcement will be much better informed. I am not here to debate you, Mr. Costello, or even explain the way of the world to you. I am here to deliver a simple message which I think I have done. For your benefit, I will repeat it: Ensure your client stops fucking around. Start building and start paying the contractors and you will have no problems with us. If you don't, Mr. Costello, you have seen what we have done with Decoud. You will be next."

The words carried a threat disproportionate to the physicality of the speaker. Luis stood and left the café. Mike and the Doctor watched as the man with the earpiece held the back door of the car open while Luis slid inside. The bodyguard closed the door, looked left and right, and entered the car. The car slipped from sight, lost to the morning traffic.

Mike turned on the Doctor, a burning in his chest. "Thanks a fucking lot," he said. "I appreciate the support. You may not have noticed but that was directed against you too!"

A heavy, humid breath escaped the Doctor. He reached into his shirt pocket and retrieved Mike's telephone. He peered at the screen, ignoring Mike's tantrum.

"Do not show me your fucking article!"

The Doctor placed the phone on the table and pressed a button. From the little device, words muffled by background noise but still audible began to float upwards:

If you don't, Mr. Costello, you have seen what we have done with Decoud. You will be next.

Simultaneous grins broke out on the two men's faces.

"Gotcha," said the Doctor in English.

CHAPTER 30

"What have you got for me?" Mike asked Andrea as he came into the office.

Andrea had emerged from behind her desk and positioned herself in front of Mike as soon as he had entered. Her relocation was a bad omen. He didn't care. The morning was impossible to ruin. The Doctor's recording skills had swung events in his favor.

"The Ministry of Planning has just issued a press release."

"Let me guess, the courts have considered MinEx's appeal of the forced conciliation and found that the claim has no merit and that MinEx is hereby instructed to continue paying its legally contracted suppliers until a full and satisfactory mediation can take place? Close?"

"No," said Andrea, her face serious. "I have it here, shall I read it for you?" She held up some pages, her red fingernails, little flags of warning, dotted the pages. Above the nails, Mike could make out the shields and symbols on the paper that conveyed a certain, though limited, amount of seriousness to the official materials from government.

"Go ahead," said Mike, rocking back and closing his eyes.

"Announcement of the Investigation into the Suspicious Death of Mr. Marcelo Decoud," began Andrea.

Mike remained unmoved in his chair. The ministry had acted quicker than he could have expected.

"The Honorable Minister for Planning has this morning instructed Federal Prosecutor Mr. Alberto Roncaglia, to open an investigation into the suspicious death of Mr. Marcelo Decoud. Initial investigations led to the conclusion that Mr. Decoud's death was a result of suicide. However, a detailed review of the crime scene and searches of the deceased's property in Cordoba, from where the victim is from, have given cause to suspect foul play."

Andrea paused, allowing Mike a chance to comment or react. None came. He remained still, only a slight nod of the head indicating that Andrea should continue.

"Yesterday, police officers completed a review of a trove of documents that were recovered from Mr. Decoud's home. The review uncovered several files that contained information that gave the investigating officers cause to believe that Mr. Decoud may have been in possession of information relating to acts of corruption that were being perpetrated by the multinational firm MinEx, a company with business interests in the province of Cordoba.

"Mr. Decoud was known as an outspoken advocate for better controls to be placed on the activities of MinEx. It is also known that Mr. Decoud was in Buenos Aires to meet with executives from MinEx. Mr. Decoud died before this meeting could take place. At this stage, it is unknown for what purpose that meeting was for.

"Upon review of the files, and considering this new information, investigators asked that a second autopsy be performed on the victim. This second autopsy revealed that prior to receiving the fatal wound to the temple, the victim had received numerous blows to the head. The initial autopsy had attributed these blows to the victim falling after the fatal wound was suffered."

"Second autopsy? There is no fucking body! They burnt it the same day."

Andrea looked up from her reading but decided against asking for an explanation as to how Mike knew this. She continued reading.

"It would now appear that in his last minutes Mr. Decoud was subjected to a severe physical beating at the hands of his assassins. The minister considers that there is enough evidence to suggest that Mr. Decoud's death cannot be ruled as suicide, hence him taking the formal step of instructing Prosecutor Roncaglia to open the investigation.

"While respecting the jurisdiction of the Prosecutor, the minister has asked that the investigation look at the links between MinEx and Mr. Decoud and potentially corrupt relations between MinEx and local contracting companies. Pending the outcome of the investigation the government has taken the decision to suspend all activities being undertaken by MinEx in the Republic of Argentina. This decision however will not apply to the enforced conciliation process, the terms of which will remain in effect for the duration of the investigation or until a satisfactory resolution has been reached.

"Upon conclusion of the investigation the government will review its existing contracts and obligations with MinEx. No decision will be taken until such a time as the results of the investigation are known." Andrea paused again. "Then follows a quote from the minister."

She waited for a sign to continue.

"Argentina is a developing country. We are also a country that respects the rule of law. These are not mutually exclusive concepts. We cannot, and we will not, allow the sanctity of life, the rights of the Argentine people, to be pushed aside by foreign firms whose motives are driven by profit, whose balance sheets have no space for empathy, tolerance, and respect. I have asked the prosecutor to conduct this investigation as if he were investigating the death of a thousand patriots. For Mr. Decoud represents us all, every Argentine man, woman, and child. If we allow his death to go unpunished, if his killers are not brought to justice, then we have failed the man himself, his family, and the Argentine people."

Mike leant forward, blinking his eyes open as if waking from sleep.

"You know what I don't understand, Andrea? How could they retrieve the files from his home, bring them back from Cordoba, analyze them, and draw conclusions in less than twenty-four hours? I can't even get someone to come and fix the tap in my bathroom!"

Andrea glowered. "This is not a time for jokes, Mike. Do you know what this means? This is a murder enquiry. And it is a very short leap from MinEx to you."

Andrea had no idea just how short a leap. "I can handle this from here, Andrea. Thank you," said Mike feigning the recovery of control.

Andrea didn't move. "MinEx should make a statement. They can't leave this unanswered."

"Let me think about it," said Mike.

Andrea gathered her papers and made to return to her desk. She stopped and turned back to Mike, looking at him as though at a madman. She decided against saying anything and stalked into the kitchen.

Mike read the press release that Andrea had left on the desk. He skimmed through the Spanish text, *investigacion*, *homicidio*, MinEx. It was difficult to imagine that this official-looking document was not only all about him, it was written for him.

He reached for his phone. He scrolled through the saved downloads and came to the recording that the Doctor had made of his conversation with Luis Lopez. He pressed play, satisfied himself that the recording was still there, and put his phone away again. The recording was an asset whose value had appreciated. The Doctor argued for releasing it immediately. Mike was more circumspect. Yes, it was a grenade but grenades still needed to be thrown at the right time. And the right time would be when he was far from Argentina.

CHAPTER 31

The street blurred past Mike as he stalked down Cerrito. People stepped out of his way and stared as he went past, as if watching a man fleeing a crime, fascinated to watch but unwilling to stop him. Those who didn't see him coming received a slight bump as he passed. The usual joys of street life held nothing for him, his attention retained within his own mind as he went over again the news of the investigation. He should have never taken on MinEx as a client. That much was clear. It was clear before but he just hadn't looked. Harper was right. He never looked. It was all there. All in front of him. How did he keep missing it? And now it had all caught up to him.

He turned off the street and into the familiar run-down building that held Finklestein's office. He would pay whatever he had to pay Finklestein to make this mess go away, sell the apartment and go. No, he wouldn't even wait. He would let Finklestein sell the apartment and he would go. No point hanging around in Buenos Aires. He would get Simon to release the tape recording and be on the next plane.

Mike stood in front of Finklestein's office. He noticed that the brass plaque had been polished, the green tarnish removed. It was a small act of rebellion against the general decay that dominated the rest of the building. The door was closed and Mike knocked, louder than he intended too. He was in his lawyer's hands now, he realized. Mike would have to give him free reign to extricate him out of this impasse. Free reign would be expensive.

He had often thought that Argentina was a country invented by lawyers to ensure that they would always be in business. It was common knowledge that there were more lawyers in Argentina than psychologists. Mike was sure there was a connection between the two facts, a connection he was attempting to make in his mind when the door to the office opened and half of the grim face of Tomas Finklestein appeared. Finklestein craned his neck into the corridor and looked left and right before taking a step back and allowing Mike to enter the office. It seemed to have grown smaller since Mike's last visit, a fact attributable to more stalagmites of paper files forming from the office floor.

Finklestein looked nervous. His combover hung looser than usual, in need of a gentle pat, a sure sign that he was distracted. He kept a mirror on his desk for combover inspection, a duty he performed at regular intervals, mid-conversation included.

The leather-bound seat squeaked in protest as Mike lowered himself into it. He could hear Finklestein behind him locking the door. The office secured he returned to his seat opposite Mike.

"Extra precautions," he said as way of explanation.

"What's going on?" Mike asked.

"You, Mr. Costello. You are going on," said Finklestein. One hand brushed his hair across the top of his head then settled it with a familiar pat.

"I will be out of your hair soon enough."

"So, you still plan on abandoning us? I thought that come the first of January you would give up on this Sicilian dream. Much like the Mexican dream before that."

Mike looked around the little office. He should have been in Sicily, replacing glass in windows, laying floorboards, drinking early-morning espressos and going over maps of the next stream to be explored. The time had slipped away, or more accurately been eaten away. Eaten away by lies, bureaucracy, delays, and all the other bullshit that accumulates on a man when he spends ten years in a place that doesn't want him. There would be no free house waiting for him in Sicily but he was still determined to go.

"I need to get out of here. Now more so than ever. And don't remind me about Sicily. If you were any good at what you do, Finklestein, I would already be in Sicily claiming that free house." Mike stopped himself before he went further down the path of recrimination, regardless of how attractive that journey seemed. "What do we need to do to clear up this apartment business, Tomas? Just name a price to make it go away for me. Talk to whoever you have to, pay whatever you need to." Mike realized the economic recklessness of such an arrangement but his situation demanded it.

Finklestein sighed, the usual air of confidence about him absent. He looked around his piles of paper before laying his hands on the document he was looking for.

"I am not sure that will be possible, Mr. Costello. It seems you have some very powerful interests after you."

Like a man who had been beaten without respite, this final punch had no effect on Mike. He was past feeling the impacts.

"I have news on the Mareva Injunction. As we already knew, the AFIP has implemented the injunction. The question you had left with me was at who's request. I now have that answer."

Mike stayed silent.

"The British government requested the Mareva Injunction. Through their embassy here in Buenos Aires. I have managed to obtain a copy of the original order." Finklestein took off his glasses and leant across the desk to hand Mike the document. Mike accepted it numbly, nothing making sense.

He read through the document, recognizing his own name, his address, his telephone number. He placed his eyes lightly on a few neat paragraphs of prose, as if to give the full weight of his vision to the document was too dangerous. According to the paper he held, which looked official enough, his assets had been frozen at the request of the government of the United Kingdom to recover monies owing to the Crown in relation to ongoing criminal procedures in the United Kingdom against the United States citizen, Michael Salvatore Costello passport number 112819808 who is alleged to be involved in an international money-laundering organization. First murder, now money laundering. A gold-plated day. None of it made sense. His eyes skipped down the bottom of the document to a scrawled squiggle that completed the page. Below the squiggle, typed in official-looking font, was the name of the requesting party: Mr. Alexander Harper, Second Secretary, British Embassy, Buenos Aires.

"Mike, there is one more thing. I can no longer represent you in this matter. I can't put at risk my other British clientele, not to mention my membership at the Chamber of Commerce. I have helped you on a lot of things over the years, Mike, but money laundering? I can't be a part of this."

"Can't be a part of this? For fuck's sake, Finklestein, you bribed the AFIP to get me this information!"

"Facilitation payments, Mike. I already told you that." Finklestein's eyes darted to the closed door. "And keep your voice down. These walls are paper-thin."

Mike sighed and stood up. He retrieved the last words he had spoken to Alex Harper, polished them off, and gave them to Tomas Finklestein.

CHAPTER 32

M ike spent the morning in the office with Andrea. She typed away with a rhythm he could have danced to if he could dance. He dictated a few words at a time, making sure to include everything he needed to commit to record. Andrea printed off the document and gave it to Mike to re-read. Satisfied he laid it on his desk. He then retrieved his phone and with Andrea's help transferred the voice recording of Luis Lopez to a memory stick. He sat back at his desk and watched as Andrea placed the typed document and memory stick in a yellow envelope and sealed it.

Mike sat behind his desk, computer switched off, brooding. He blinked hard to get the face of Alex Harper from his head. Those drooping eyelids and that ridiculous shit-eating grin. Andrea, perhaps tired of observing his long face ordered him out of the office, sending him to pick up some coffee and milk from the supermarket.

He was grateful for the distraction. He wandered the aisles but was unable to locate his usual brand of milk. A shop assistant explained that a truck-driver's strike meant that their order had not been received that week. Another reason to hate organized labor.

Mike's hatred towards worker's unions was not some deep-seated political conviction. It was borne from the unsavory experience of eating a local variety of farmed fish after his supply of wild-caught Chilean salmon had been interrupted by the striking truck drivers' union who had refused to bring the piscatorial prize across the Andean ranges.

The chilled supermarket aisles were a welcome oasis of cool, a respite from the soaring January temperatures outside. A key supporter of the president owned the supermarket chain, guaranteeing that Mike could enjoy the cool with the knowledge that the blackouts that were affecting non-aligned business owners would not be of concern among the fish and frozen peas of Supermercados Disco.

Mike made his way to the checkout line and waited with the patience of a dead man as the single line to the one open checkout moved along at glacial pace. The old woman ahead of him paid for her items, counting out the exact amount in coins with a precision and care peculiar to the older specimens of the race, and proceeded to pack the floral-patterned, natty bags that she had brought from home. Mike joined the checkout girl in watching on as jars of *dulce de leche*, bags of *mate* tea, shortbread biscuits, Bimbo brand bread, and several enormous cuts of steak, the national staples, were packed away in precise order and with fastidious care.

Mike approached the register and unpacked his basket. The girl may have grunted a greeting; Mike wasn't sure, it could have been a cough. She swiped through his items with a disinterested, horizon-seeking stare. When finished, she extended her hand towards Mike, palm up, dispensing of all niceties or social etiquette that one expects to accompany a purchase. Mike placed a twenty-peso note in her hand.

The eyes came alive.

"I can't accept that. There's no change."

Mike bent his knees, gripped the edge of the counter and leaned back to check the total of his purchases on the register's small screen: 15.40, lit up in digital green.

"It's only 4.60 in change," he said. "In the whole store you don't have 4.60 in change?"

The girl was unmoved. "We don't have any change," she repeated.

Mike pointed to the woman who still had not made it to the sliding exit doors. "That woman paid in coins, I saw her! You must have her coins."

"If I give them to you I'll have none left."

"Left for who? Customers? What am I? This doesn't make any fucking sense!"

Mike closed his eyes and gripped the counter. Inside his head he imagined himself taking the girl by her blonde braids and smashing her head against the cash register as he used her pretty, button nose to ring up his shopping. Wrong brand of milk—smash! English breakfast teabags—smash! Nescafe instant coffee—smash! His murderous thoughts must have been noted.

"Look, *viejo*," the girl said, using the affectionate term for old man. "Take your note to the kiosk outside, they might have some change. I can hold your things here at the counter."

Mike opened his eyes, in control again, for now. "Thank you."

"You'll have to line up again when you come back. I can't let you cut the line."

Mike looked back at the long line snaking into the depths of the aisles and disappearing somewhere back near the shelves of pasta.

"Not a problem," he said through a grimace tighter than a trout's ass.

With hands and forearms he herded his items into a small grouping at the end of the counter and headed for the door. The sliding doors opened and he was hit by the heat of the day. From afar, he could hear what sounded like fireworks coming from the direction of the 9 de Julio. The sounds could just as well be tear-gas canisters, rubber bullets, assassin's bullets, or football fans rioting or celebrating.

He approached the kiosk and received a shake of the head when he produced his twenty-peso note. He walked a little further along the street to a second kiosk. There the man said that he could provide change on the condition that Mike make a purchase, minimum five pesos. Mike explained that that would then leave him with insufficient money to pay for what he needed the change for. His reasoning fell on large and unsympathetic ears.

He continued down the street, the walk back to the supermarket increasing in distance to a point that meant a return for his abandoned items was unlikely. He approached a third kiosk and felt the vibration of his cell phone against his breast. He spied some shade and flattened himself against a doorway, protected from both sun and theft. He had already had two phones plucked from his hand by opportunist thieves whilst speaking unguarded.

"This is a surprise. Yes, just finished up a meeting. I'm heading to the Officers' Club for lunch," Mike lied. "Would you like to join me? Know where it is? Great, see you there."

As all Argentines do, Mike abandoned his quest for change. He was by now a few blocks from the Officers' Club and, though the heat was increasing, the thought of a cold beer awaiting him at his destination justified the exertion. On his way he stopped by his office, apologized to Andrea for his shopping failure and picked up the yellow envelope from his desk.

Entering the Palacio Balcarce he exchanged pleasantries with the doorman. The ground floor of the building had been sold off to an art gallery, the rest remained in the hands of the Centre for Argentine Officials. The result of this opportunistic business deal was that the reception area became an odd meeting ground where the city's artistic types would pass retired military officers, skeptical glances ricocheting around the room as they crossed paths.

Mike climbed the ancient wooden staircase, a symphony of creaks and groans marking the slow progress of his climb. Straight ahead, down the length of the second-floor corridor, he could see the activity in the kitchen, which was to say he could see the cooks gossiping with the waiters, flying hands accompanying every word. From a distance, the agitated limbs gave the impression that the kitchen had been invaded by bees.

The doorway to his left opened into a large dining room, populated by a few unoccupied tables, set from habit rather than any expectation of lunchtime clientele. Mike had never known the club to hold more than a handful of diners even at the busiest of lunch hours; the empty tables a symbol of a country that had left its military establishment behind, banished into the corners of a dark and shameful history. Mike's only rule at the Military Officers' club: Don't mention the military.

He took his seat and a short while later Simon Quinn's head appeared around the corner. Mike raised his napkin signaling his presence, an unnecessary gesture as he was the sole diner.

Mike had chosen a seat at a table for four, adjacent to the windows that provided an unobstructed view over the manicured interior courtyard garden. In the center of the garden a white table was marooned on an island of green grass, with just two unoccupied seats for company and a dry, grey, cement fountain. A sparrow perched on the rim, head cocked to the side. It was, to Mike's mind, a classic English garden scene, rendered absurd by the 38-degree temperatures that caused little bars of heat to radiate from the garden furniture.

Simon took his place opposite Mike. He fussed with his napkin before laying it on his lap. Mike observed his lunch companion in silence. Now settled, Simon scanned the room.

"Lucky you made a reservation," he said.

"One of the last true retreats of Buenos Aires, Simon. I often come here when I want to be alone. The beer is cold and the steaks are large. I joined back when they were obliged to open the membership to officers from any country, just to keep the doors open." He added, "Except the Chileans of course. Even though Operation Condor is still one of the only successful instances of Argentine–Chilean cooperation. Nasty business and not one that people wish to remember," said Mike, breaking his own rule.

A suited waiter had broken away from the heated discussions that could still be heard through the door to the kitchen and took their drinks order. Both men ordered beers.

Mike said, 'Very few people come here now. Civil–military relations were strained to say the least following the dictatorship and this president has made sure that it would not be wise for most officials to be seen here."

The waiter reappeared with two frosted glasses, filled with beer, skinny streams of froth escaping over the rims. Mike ran his hand up his glass, from bottom to top, and sucked the froth from his finger.

"There is an understandable …" Mike searched for the right word, "… anti-presidential feeling, among the members. They feel a certain hypocrisy in the president's pursuit of crimes committed during the dictatorship. They question the president's own actions during this period, a period in which the fortunate few, the President included, accrued great personal wealth."

Mike picked up the menu. "We had better order. Don't be fooled by the rush hour, service can be a little slow here."

Alerted by the raised menus, a waiter approached.

"Gentlemen, I am afraid the menu is somewhat limited today. We are without electricity. With the extreme temperatures that we have been experiencing …" he trailed off, as if that were explanation enough. "However, we can still do most things, like the steak for example, which is cooked in the traditional style, over coals."

A culinary tradition, wondered Mike, or the traditional way of avoiding the government's capricious distribution of energy.

"Happy with steak?" asked Mike, not bothering to translate the waiter's comments.

"Sounds good," said Simon.

Mike closed the menus and handed them back to the waiter. "Two steaks please, and another two beers. If you have them cold."

"Yes sir, we have the beers in the ice box. We're always prepared," he said with the typical Argentine air of being surprised by nothing and ready for everything.

A thin, grey-haired couple came teetering in, arm in arm. It was difficult to determine who was supporting who. Short, shuffles of the feet polished the floor, whilst a waiter hovered close by, as if accompanying an over-stacked plate of pancakes, hands poised at the ready in anticipation of a messy fall. They took their seats in the opposite corner of the dining room.

Simon's eyes darted around the room, a sigh escaping his lips. "I take it you have seen the news."

"Yes."

"No concerns about having lunch with a man under investigation?"

"We're in the same boat, Simon, you at the stern and I at the bow." He saw no reason to inform Simon that he was also under investigation from the British government. Best to focus on the more immediate problem.

"If they pin this on you, it will be as the intellectual author. They will still need to have the actual murderers. I presume that that is where I would come in. A one-man play would interest nobody." He said it with an air of matter of factness that he didn't feel as he recalled Luis Lopez's reptilian voice in his ear.

"You believe this could come back on you?"

"It had crossed my mind," said Mike. It hadn't just crossed his mind. It had invaded his mind and made camp, like the Mongol hordes on the banks of the Sajo.

Mike handed his empty glass to the waiter who had approached and placed two fresh beers on the table. He watched the waiter return to the kitchen. Through the circular window cut into the door he could see the kitchen staff had still not resolved their argument. He hoped that someone in there had one eye on their lunch.

"It's the money they're after. The bodies are incidental, Decoud's, yours, mine," said Mike. "They are fucking animals." Mike looked over his beer at his client. "Are you now willing to take on board my advice?"

"Let's hear it."

Mike reached under the table and produced the yellow envelope that had been sitting on the chair beside him. The words Simon Quinn were scrawled across the envelope in blue ink in Andrea's distinctive handwriting. The envelope sealed with tape. He handed the envelope to Simon.

"Shall I open it?" asked Simon, turning it over in his hands.

"It's got your name on it. But I can tell you what it contains. A couple of days ago Luis Lopez paid me a visit." He left out the presence of the Doctor. "The message was the same as last time, start playing ball or else, though the tone was more hostile, if that's possible. And he wasn't alone. I thought it would be wise to take some precautions." With one hand Mike pointed at the envelope, while the other rubbed his chin. "In your hands you are holding a document that outlines everything that has happened since we started this project."

Mike had begun writing it himself until Andrea suggested that she do it in Spanish. "It details every interaction you've had with Planning. Them forcing you to qualify one company for the tender process, the inflated bid, the forced conciliation, the suspension of the project. Every threat, every misdirection. It's all in there. I've tried to keep it to the facts. Even so it reads like a work of fiction."

"Everything?" asked Simon, concern in his voice.

"Everything." Mike knew that Simon would not want any record of his fudged tender process to be committed to paper but it was the least of his worries. At least by getting ahead of it he could blame the government.

"What good will it do, Mike?" asked Simon, fanning himself with the envelope.

"None. Not by itself. But in the envelope, you'll find a memory stick."

Simon's fingers probed around the envelope, as if trying to guess a Christmas present, until he located the pen drive.

"On that memory stick you will find a recording of my last conversation with Lopez. He said enough to implicate the Planning Ministry in the death of Decoud."

Simon let out a low whistle. "How did you record it?"

"On my phone," lied Mike.

Simon looked impressed with the initiative. "What would you like me to do with this?"

"Have your office issue a press release in response to the government's announcement of the investigation." Mike pulled a piece of paper from his pocket and unfolded it. "The press release should say …" and he began to read from the paper that Andrea had given him. "We reject the accusations that have been levelled against MinEx and ask that, with immediate effect, the investigation into MinEx be dropped, that all of MinEx's legally acquired rights in Argentina be reinstated, that the forced conciliation process be suspended, and that MinEx be allowed to continue the development of its project of national importance, unfettered and unencumbered by government meddling." These were Andrea's words. They sounded official, the words of a lawyer.

Mike continued. "If these actions are not implemented, MinEx will make available to the press, documents and information that detail the unethical, irresponsible, and criminal actions that have characterized the Ministry of Planning's actions since MinEx's arrival in Argentina."

The reading finished with an elaborate sweep of the hand as if Mike had just unveiled a new car that Simon, as the lucky contestant, stood a chance of winning.

"Fuck me, Mike," said Simon, lowering his head. "Fuck me," drawing out each word. He tapped the envelope. "Is this the right way?"

"It's the only way. Give them a week to act. In the meantime, you'll need to keep the envelope someplace safe. If you don't see or hear anything by Wednesday evening, make the contents of that envelope public." He spoke with a certainty he didn't feel. But the Doctor was right, they had to respond with what the government would understand: fear, threats, power.

Simon sat still. The flick and flash of his eyes showed that he was playing through all the possible ways that his life would turn out if he walked out of this lunch and made public the press release.

"Should this come from me?" he asked, perhaps searching for a loophole. "Couldn't this come from the embassy? Government to government? In private? What if I asked Alex Harper to do it?"

"He's gone," said Mike, closing off that avenue of escape.

"Gone? Where?"

"Iraq. He left the same day Decoud was found."

"The prick didn't even say goodbye."

"An occupational necessity. People are like Lego to diplomats. They're dropped into a country and start clicking relationships on to themselves. When it's time to go, they unclick them. Him being here or not won't change much. He wouldn't have done it anyway."

"What if we just wait, Mike? I wouldn't be surprised if by next week we have a new government. They're planning another one of those marches tonight. What did you call it? A cacerola?"

"*Cacerolazo*," corrected Mike.

"Yes, and not just here in Buenos Aires, all over the country. These guys are not going to survive."

"You might be right," lied Mike again, using Simon's suggestive momentum for his own advantage. "The contents of that envelope might tip the whole thing over the edge. You'd be doing the country a favor." He didn't feel good about it but thoughts of Decoud lying cold on a morgue table seemed to justify all ethical gymnastics.

And he was saving Simon from himself. He'd thank him for it one day.

The waiter interrupted and placed two dinosaur-sized steaks on the table. The smell of the grilled meat and the caramelized fat filled Mike's nostrils, derailing his train of thought. He had forgotten how hungry he was.

They finished their meals in silence. Mike going over in his head all the ways his plan would go wrong. They argued over the bill, Mike insisting that he should pay, Simon promising to get the next one, and Mike hoping that there would be a next one.

"I'll be at the Oak Bar tonight. Why don't you drop by for a quiet one?"

"I think I will," said Simon with a procedural tone that left Mike unsure if he would see him later or not. Simon thanked him for lunch and made for the door.

Mike watched him leave the dining room. Maybe it was a combination of the heat and the beef that caused his mind to drift back to a distant summer in Madrid where he had attended the San Isidro bullfights. At the time, he had debated whether to pay the extra pesos for the *sombra* tickets, decided against it, and spent the afternoon roasting in the *sol* section. He had sat next to a Spaniard who was gracious enough to share his wine skin with him. In exchange, he only wanted to show off his English and his knowledge of bullfighting.

The stranger took the time to explain the intricacies of the ritual slaughter they were witnessing. He encouraged Mike to ignore the pomp, the flags, the cheers, the danger, the suit of lights, and focus only on the bull's front feet. He had explained that only when the bull's feet were in the perfect position, not too close together, not too far apart, would the shoulder blades part in such a way as to allow the clean entry of the killing blow. All the rest was just show until the matador had used all his tricks and talents to maneuver the front feet right where he wanted them.

As Mike stared out the window now, the sound of Simon's feet faded on the staircase and below the table Mike's own feet shifted, ever so slightly, apart.

CHAPTER 33

Mike departed the Officers' Club and emerged on to Quintana. Looking left he could see ribbons of smoke snaking skywards above the trees and buildings that stood between himself and the 9 de Julio Avenue. He turned right, heading down Quintana towards the Palacio Duhau.

He could smell the beginnings of a storm on the afternoon breeze. A gap in the buildings allowed him to look north, towards an unseen Uruguay, where a battalion of dark clouds were gathering. It would be a few hours away. The heatwave would break with a torrential downpour that would leave the ill-equipped streets flooded, cars rearranged by rising waters, pedestrians stranded, and the mayor promising, after blaming the president—though Mike was unsure how much influence the president had over the weather—that it will never be allowed to happen again. A pattern that would be repeated for the remaining days of summer.

Mike spied a group of shirtless youths making their way towards him. Two of them held large sticks in their hands. Others sniffed from plastic bottles half-filled with a clear liquid. They held their line of march, forcing other pedestrians to go around them or be bumped out of the way. They were the remnants of the afternoon's disturbances on 9 de Julio, taking a quick pass through Recoleta to see if there was anything they could take back with them to their *barrios*. Part of their fee for turning out on such a hot day. They would appear on cue, when and where needed, and their political paymasters would turn a blind eye to any mementoes they took with them.

Mike ducked into a jewelry shop and pretended to examine a diamond necklace, one eye on the street, making sure the group passed without incident. He had expected the protest to continue into the night and suspected that the approaching storm was reason enough for them to abandon their ideological positions earlier than expected. A lady stood at the glass cabinet, the shop assistant showing her a number of diamond earrings. A second lady approached the glass, a fine chain of gold draped over her fingers. "I'd like to purchase this please." The accent was unmistakably Brazilian.

"Excuse me," the lady who had been examining the earrings said, turning to the Brazilian interloper, "but as you can see, this young man is serving me."

"Yes, but I can actually afford to purchase this," the Brazilian said holding aloft the chain. Deciding it was probably safer outside, Mike slipped out of the shop.

Mike continued along Quintana. At the corner of Montevideo he waited for the traffic. As a boy, he had been taught to look left, then right, and then left again. When he was sure the street was empty, only then could he cross. Now, he waited until the street filled with cars, bumper to bumper, horns blaring. Once they were all locked in place, an automotive game of Tetris, he could

292

make his way through the stationary cars, safe in the knowledge that none would be moving any time soon. In this way, he crossed Montevideo and proceeded to the Palacio Duhau.

Inside the Oak Bar he found his favorite summertime seat unoccupied, away from the fireplace and in line with the stream of cool air pouring from the internal cooling system. He decided that one more beer wouldn't hurt. In this heat, he would sweat it out.

He pulled out his cell phone. He had several calls to make. He tried to reach Alex Harper's replacement at the British embassy but couldn't get past an officious secretary. He would have to go down there himself.

The afternoon ebbed by at a sluggish pace inside the Oak Bar. At one point the carnivorous lunch and the beers overtook him and for a moment his eyes closed and his head lolled backwards into the wingback chair. He awoke with a jerk, his arm flinging up to set the hook. Micro-naps were the closest he got to the river these days.

He checked the time on his phone as the bar manager stopped by to close Mike's account, letting him know that the evening manager would open a new one. He was surprised to see two beers on the account. Something a bit sharper would be required to chase away the cobwebs of his unplanned siesta.

When Simon arrived, Mike was on his second whiskey.

"It's done," Simon said.

Mike didn't feel relief, just a sensation that a giant ball had been set rolling down a hillside that had no bottom in sight. Simon seemed triumphant as if he had spent the intervening time analyzing his course of action and finding it satisfying. Mike longed for the younger man's confidence.

"*Que será, será*," said Mike, raising his glass. "What can I get you?"

"I think a beer will do nicely. A celebratory beer."

The beer arrived for Simon, Mike content to sit on his whiskey.

"You should get out of here, Mike."

Mike fixed his eyes on the oak paneling trying to relocate the carved tiger he had spotted earlier in the afternoon. He waited for Simon's words to fade. A warm gust came bustling through the open doors of the terrace, the vanguard of the approaching storm. It swirled around the Oak Bar. A waiter moved to close the terrace doors.

Simon again attempted to bridge the silence. "What's keeping you here?"

Mike sniffed and pondered the question. He could feel the whiskey mixing with the beers from the early afternoon. It was a question he had often asked himself. Even at his happiest moments he could never settle on a definitive answer. Even now, when he had decided he would leave Buenos Aires he could still see the positives. Breaking up is difficult because it is easy to remember all the tough times but it's impossible to forget the great ones.

"There's a realism here that's attractive. You and I are sold this dream that we're equal, can be whatever we want. No matter if you're dealt a two and a seven, off suit, you work hard enough and some day you can be holding a pair of aces. Down here, you're dealt shit and told to play with what you have. That's your lot. If someone isn't looking you can steal an ace and good on you." He raised his glass to that.

"Sounds like chaos, Mike."

"It is. Beautiful, natural, chaos. No point loving something for what it isn't." An empty smile hung on his face, like a sign left at the front of a store while he was out back taking inventory. He had loved it but it was unrequited love.

A flash of lightning lit the windows. Mike counted in his head like his father had taught him as a boy. One thousand, two thousand, three thousand, then the baritone of a thunderclap that seemed to emerge from the fireplace and shake the floorboards. Still out over the river, Mike calculated.

"That's how I got my apartment in Recoleta," he confided unprompted. "Took an ace when I could. Was working for a banker, Executive Risk Adviser they called me. He wanted someone to boast of his exploits to. For some men, the fucking means nothing if they don't have anyone to tell.

"This guy had all the tricks. Kept a small bottle of gas in the trunk so he could splash his hands with it after a tryst. He was convinced that it was the only way he could get the smell of sex off him." Mike laughed at the memory. "His wife always asked if we couldn't get a better car, she was concerned about the fuel consumption.

"He was out one night, right in the middle of the troubles. Shouldn't have been out, and not in the Mercedes. Down to this girl he liked to visit. On his way home he runs into a mob, they see the car and try to stop him. He accelerates through and received a spray of bullets. Gets one in the gut. Managed to get to a clinic and called me. I get over there and he's in the hallway on a trolley, bleeding out, trying to tell the nurses who he is."

Another flash of lighting. One thousand, two thousand, a rolling growl that turned well-groomed heads towards the windows. The door to the terrace slid open and the remaining customers came indoors, squeezing into spaces at the bar.

"The nurses don't care who he is, they've got another thirty people to deal with. I talked the triage nurse into bumping him up the line. He survived and his first day back at work I went in and asked for a loan for an apartment I'd been looking at. Zero interest.."

"Sounds fair. You saved his life."

"Yes, but not at the clinic. From his wife. When you get shot, time starts at the point that those bullets impact your body. The context is lost. The press never bothered to ask what he was even doing on the street that night, where he was going to, or coming from. Well, the wife did."

A lightning flash and simultaneous thunder clap that rumbled the bar signaled the arrival of the storm proper. Giant rain drops beat against the windows. Mike sat back, deep in his chair, content to let the sound of the rain mix with the whiskey in his head. It had felt good to talk, better than it should have. He knew the price of feeling like a million dollars tonight was feeling like a dollar tomorrow. As the voices of the bar swirled around him he felt as if he was holding pocket aces.

Identifying the time when he should be going, and for once translating that thought into footsteps, Mike said goodnight to Quinn and stepped out of the doorway of the Hyatt and onto Alvear. Torrents of water rushed down the street. Rippling puddles were lit from above by street lamps, the reflection creating the impression of giant, glowing orbs that dotted the sidewalk both left and right. Men and women emerged from taxis on the opposite side of the street, ran crouched across the road, before making ambitious leaps a meter out from the curb in the hope of clearing the worst of it. Success alluded them. Doormen from the Hyatt raced out to meet incoming guests halfway, umbrellas held aloft to shield them from the last few drops of rain. Their umbrellas could do nothing against the torrent of water that flowed at their feet.

Mike splashed his way down Alvear and turned right on Montevideo. The floodwaters, streaming downwards, were shallower here. Even so, before he had turned on to Posadas his socks were soaked through.

He approached his apartment and saw that the lobby was darkened. From the gloom, an unfamiliar silhouette appeared in the familiar uniform of the doorman. Mike waited as the man fumbled with the keys, tried one, then another before finding the right key and opening the door.

"Mr. Costello?"

Mike nodded. "Where's Alvaro?" he asked, stepping inside and drying his feet on the mat.

"Problems with the wife. I think she's sick. An operation maybe. Back soon. Ten days maybe?" he said. It was half a guess and half a desperate attempt to get out of a sentence that he didn't have the information complete.

"Send him my best, if you speak with him please," said Mike. He walked towards the elevator.

"Sorry, Mr. Costello. No elevator. No light." By light he meant electricity.

Mike swore under his breath. Just what he needed, a walk up unlit stairs.

The doorman shrugged an apology.

Mike made his way towards the staircase that was marked by the figure of a green man making a dash for it. He arrived at his apartment with his legs fatigued. He could feel the alcohol in his system. Hadn't he been told never to exercise after drinking? He wondered if that applied to stair climbing. He unlocked his door and went in.

It had the stuffy feel of the caravans he used to sleep in on summer holidays when his family would take him down the coast. After a day spent at the beach they would come back in the afternoon and he could still remember being hit by the wall of heat that had been baking all day long in the van. When the night cooled the caravan would groan as it shrunk back to its normal size. The noises had made sleeping difficult on those nights.

He moved to the balcony, unclipped the lock and slid back the glass door. He repeated the process with the gauze door. The rain had stopped now and he sucked in the cool, night air. Above him he could see the stars of the southern cross. By tomorrow morning the temperatures would begin to climb again.

He walked back inside and emptied his pockets onto the coffee table. He slumped into the sofa, not caring if he slept there and unbuttoned his shirt, happy just to take the weight off his legs and feel the night air blow across him.

CHAPTER 34

The morning dawned cool. A breeze rummaged through the tops of the trees outside Mike's balcony. The kind of day when it was good to be up early. It was only going to get hotter. The next cool change could come through tomorrow or next month.

He showered and got dressed in front of the oval, wood-framed mirror in his room. He leaned in close, studying his face for signs of aging. He had no baseline study to compare against, and there, an inch from the glass, he couldn't recall what wrinkles had appeared or when. No doubt life in Argentina had taken its toll, a glance at his hairline confirming the fact.

He still hadn't heard back from the British embassy. He had spent the first hours of the morning staring at his ceiling, approaching the problem from various angles. Even the most borderline jobs from the Doctor could never be considered money laundering. It didn't make any sense that Alex Harper would freeze his assets. He replayed in detail his relationship with Alex. Was Mike his target all along? How had they met? Mike had approached him, not the other way around. Alex always wanted something but Mike never got the feeling he was under investigation. He sometimes missed things but he was sure he wouldn't miss that.

Out on the street, he averted his eyes from the news-stands that would be carrying MinEx's press release of the day before splashed across the front pages of the morning papers. He would go through the press coverage at the office with Andrea who would be waiting for him with the newspapers piled on her desk.

He entered his office like a guilty man, knowing that Andrea would need only one look at him to deduce his whole night, even down to his poison of choice.

"Andrea, grab those papers and we'll go through them downstairs over coffee."

They found a quiet café with one or two other customers and they seated themselves near the front door. Andrea ordered two *americanos* without asking what Mike would like.

"Right," Mike said, hoisting aloft the first paper from the pile and handing it to Andrea. "What have we got?"

As expected, news out of Cordoba dominated the front page, though the news itself was not what Mike had expected.

Paula Saa, a wealthy socialite from the province of Cordoba, had been found murdered, sprawled naked across her teenage son's bed, the belt of a cotton bathrobe fastened around her neck, semen splashed across her legs. Andrea read the story aloud and her face flushed with the revelation of each new, sordid detail. There was speculation that it was a sadistic sex game gone wrong, a lover's revenge plot, or a straight rape and murder. The natural suspect, the well-to-do, playboy lifestyle-living husband was in Uruguay at the time of the murder, enjoying a golfing getaway with friends, one of whom was revealed as his wife's lover.

By the time Andrea had reached the final column of the front-page article she appeared to have forgotten where she was, who she was with, or the purpose of her reading. Her *americano* had sat untouched on the table, her eyes widening with each detail. A cough from Mike was enough to remind her. Her fascinated reaction told of the power of social scandal to captivate the local public.

"What about MinEx, Andrea? Anything?"

She abandoned the front page, blew a lock of hair from her brow—a clear sign of annoyance—and flicked through the paper. She reached the classifieds and returned to the front and repeated the process. She stopped two pages in.

"There's a piece here on the investigation."

"What's it say?"

Andrea read through the article. "The investigation into the death of Marcelo Decoud has led to more documents being recovered from the house of the deceased. These documents set out in detail a complex system of corruption between MinEx and the local contractor companies. It is believed that Mr. Decoud had been compiling a dossier on the activities of MinEx to be used to blackmail executives who were implicated in the scheme or turn it over to local police authorities. Either way, investigators speculate that it was the compilation of this dossier that got Mr. Decoud killed."

"Do they cite a source?"

"Anonymous source with knowledge of the investigation. There's more." Andrea looked up, waiting for a sign to continue. Mike nodded.

"A local contractor, again speaking on the condition of anonymity, has confirmed the details of the Decoud Dossier." She looked at Mike. "That's what they've dubbed the documents they've recovered, the Decoud Dossier."

She read on. "The source told this journalist that from the very start MinEx had placed pressure on contractors to cut corners and manipulate the bid process. By way of example, the contractor says that several companies were prevented from submitting bids.

"Furthermore, he says that MinEx executives told the winning bidder what numbers to inflate in their financial bids with the excess to be returned to the executives via offshore accounts in Uruguay. Specific instructions and bank accounts were provided. When the contractors pushed back they were threatened with expulsion from the project." Andrea stopped and looked across the table at Mike. "Shall I go on?"

"No." He had heard enough. "What about MinEx's press release?"

"I can't find it here."

"Look in the others."

Andrea grabbed the next paper from the pile. The smiling face of Paula Saa plastered the front page. Andrea skimmed the article and opened the paper. She flicked through a few pages and put it back on the pile. She picked up the next paper and repeated the process. She stopped a few pages in and shook the spine of the paper out.

"There's something here. Just a column."

"What's it say?"

Her eyes flicked over the article. "MinEx have threatened to release documents that could compromise the

Ministry of Planning. The documents relate to MinEx's flagship project in Cordoba that has been financed with a government loan. The loan scheme, a first of its kind in Argentina, has been held up as a prime example of public–private cooperation and heralded as a way forward for Argentina's construction sector as it continues to recover." Andrea stopped reading.

"That's it?"

"That's it."

Mike rubbed his face with his hand. Andrea watched him, the eagerness to return to the Paula Saa case oozing from her eyes.

Over the following days they repeated this scene with *americanos* for company. Paula Saa continued to dominate the front pages in a way that no political scandal had managed to do. The public were enthralled, as first the local handy man was accused and then released and then Paula's own son was arrested. Each morning Mike waited as Andrea updated him on the case's latest twist, taking for granted that Mike's fascination matched her own.

After he had sat through the explanation of how the semen that was found on Paula's legs had been tested and could only have come from her son or her doctor husband, who readers will remember was in Uruguay at the time of death, Andrea moved on, her disappointment evident to Mike, to more relevant matters.

The flow of leaks from the MinEx investigation continued, each juicier than the last, each painting a picture of MinEx as the foreign invader, sent to corrupt the innocent locals and make off with the loot. Their own version of the Spanish colonial tale written for the twenty-first-century mass-media consumer.

On Monday, an article appeared in *Clarin* carrying details of how MinEx had had Decoud followed by "an American spy" and intimidated before inviting him to Buenos Aires to meet and discuss a solution. It came as no surprise to Mike that the article provided no evidence, couched its revelations as allegations, and adorned the pseudo-facts with "supposedly" and "possibly" and all the usual journalistic ass-coverings.

Two days out from the MinEx deadline, the press release, which Mike had considered a political and journalistic bombshell, had garnered no more than the solitary column the day after its release. Buried. There had been no government reaction, no curious journalist had called for more details. There was no indication that any of MinEx's demands would be met. The last bullet in the chamber had been shot into the air as enemy forces approached their barricaded position. Mike was unsure of how to interpret the public silence. No news might be good news but it could just as easily be bad news.

As Mike sat behind his desk his mind wandered to a nature program that he had watched one night in his apartment when the heat would have made sleeping difficult if the whir of the ceiling fan had not made it impossible. With the television's sound turned down, the presenter, dressed in khaki shorts and outdoor boots, lay flat beside a snake that had coiled itself around a rat.

Being white in color, the rat must have been an unfortunate production extra. With every exhalation of his little rat lungs the snake's coils tightened, patiently and consistently. Mike had sat there willing the rat to do something, to resist. The camera zoomed in close on the rat's face. The eyes betrayed no sense of panic. Just a blank stare at its inevitable fate until finally the eyes were extinguished. He imagined Luis Lopez's face transposed onto the rodent and smiled.

CHAPTER 35

At midday, the dining room of Rodi Bar was filling up. Diners were back from their month on the beaches of Pinamar, Cariló, Mar del Plata and Santa Teresita; that is if they were above working class and below upper middle class. The wealthier classes had returned from further afield, most likely the Uruguayan playgrounds of Punta del Este or José Ignacio and it was unlikely that they would be eating at Rodi Bar. Those that occupied the tables would have been in their offices by ten in the morning and by twelve they were ready for a break.

Mike sat alone at his customary table, surveyor of all around him. Above him the ceiling fan chugged, mixing the summer heat and humidity of the room, like a lazy, wooden butter churn. The usual post-holiday buzz came from the tables as work colleagues raised both voices and hands to best each other with stories of lovers bedded and partners deceived, whilst the men talked mainly of football.

Mike checked his watch. Simon was late. Under normal circumstances he wouldn't care, he would enjoy sitting in this bar, watching his adopted compatriots go about their daily life, fascinated by their verve and spark that he once presumed he would one day possess as if by osmosis. Now he was just a resentful silent observer dreaming of other cultures. That had become his new normal.

But nothing about today was normal. This afternoon he had a flight to catch. He had been summoned to the British embassy in Montevideo, the Uruguayan capital Buenos Aires' charming little brother, an observation never to be made to a Uruguayan. Montevideo was a familiar destination for Mike. If he had time he would take the Buquebus, the oddly named ferry service that made two trips a day across the River Plate and which Mike often took when he needed to make use of Uruguay's open-arm banking arrangements, US dollars well-hidden in jacket pockets. The Buquebus was a useful service when speed was not essential and when the thought of taking the small propeller plane that ran the aerial route left him sweating.

The call from Montevideo clarified a few things in Mike's mind. Alex Harper must have been acting on a request from the British embassy out of Montevideo. Mike had no contacts in Montevideo so explaining his undeclared bank accounts there could prove difficult. He had considered not traveling but decided that more could be gained by going. After all, he had nothing to hide that had not already been hidden so well as to never be found. It had also crossed his mind that, under the present circumstance, a trip north would not be a bad thing, a chance to get out of Buenos Aires and to escape the heat in all its forms.

He looked at his watch. Still no Simon. He reached into his jacket and checked his phone. No messages.

When they had parted at the Oak Bar they had agreed that they should have no contact during the week, Mike had insisted, more for his own safety than Simon's, if he were being honest. They had agreed the lunch date in advance, a final synchronizing of strategy before releasing their dossier and voice recording the next day. They decided that if, for whatever reason, one couldn't make it they would send a simple, Mike considered it naïve, message: "Gone fishing". Mike had floated, "Gone to the polo", unwilling to involve such a noble pursuit as fishing in this business. When Simon had pointed out that the polo season had finished, Mike had accepted the piscatorial option.

The mere thought of fishing was enough for Mike's mind to cast off and start drifting down the Limay River on that yellow, inflatable raft, or was it red? He could no longer be sure. There had been so many days between that one and today that the color of the four-wheel drive that took him to the river and the raft on which he drifted down it, had mingled.

Never mind, he could still see the trout laying low against the pebbled bottom, fins fanning like the tail feathers of the small hawks that rose and stalled and dipped in the air streams above the river banks. The water so clear—snowmelt the guide had told him—that it was impossible to tell if he were in three feet or thirty feet of water. So clear, that Mike could count the spots on the browns, or so he told people when he had returned. Just thinking of that snowmelt river cooled him down.

By the time Simon arrived, Mike had packed away his five-weight rod and had his phone in his hand, ready to break protocol. The first thing that struck Mike was how good Simon looked. His memory, somewhat fuzzed, from the last time he saw him was of a tired man, kicking against the current and getting nowhere. Now he looked rejuvenated, light even. Mike imagined this is how he himself had looked that day on the Limay.

"Apologies, Mike."

"None needed. Though I was getting a little worried. I have a flight to catch this afternoon and I didn't want to leave without saying goodbye."

"Where are you off to?"

"Across the river. Montevideo," he announced, as if he were off to St. Tropez.

"Laying low for a while?"

"Work," Mike lied. "Though if I were laying low, I could think of no better place to do so," he said, returning to within touching distance of the truth.

"Glad to hear. I would hate to think I had driven you from your home."

"You may still achieve that. I'll only be gone the day. I'll be following the news and if I need to extend my stay then I may do just that."

"That won't be required. We've got these bastards right where we want them."

Mike was hopeful but not that bullish. "Why do you say that?"

"We haven't heard a thing over the last week. No contact from Planning. They're scared, Mike. They know we have them."

A waiter appeared at the table. Mike asked for a few more minutes.

"They're worried. They've rescheduled the Boca–River game for tomorrow night in case you decide to release your shit bomb. They want to make sure that all eyes are on the football so they can control your fallout. We've got their attention."

"You don't have time for lunch?"

Mike had stood up. "I did when I arrived 45 minutes ago." He smiled to show there was no bad feeling. "I still have to pack. I'll run around like a madman to get to the airport on time only to find the flight delayed by an hour, if I am lucky. Still, I can't let standards slip."

Simon stood and for a second it appeared as if he would move to hug him. Mike had said goodbye enough times to know that there were no good goodbyes. Simon seemed to sense his uneasiness.

"You going to be OK, Mike?"

A good question and one Mike didn't have a ready answer for. There was always the possibility that the government may still come after him, if only to deflect blame from themselves. He would have to see how the pieces fell tomorrow. He hoped that by the time he returned from Montevideo, things might have died down. He had been around long enough to know that things had a habit of dying down in Argentina.

CHAPTER 36

M ike made the mistake of telling the cab driver that he was in a hurry. Rather than take it on board as a general observation, the driver took it as a racing challenge. Mike wasn't sure what the record time was for a trip from central Recoleta to the Jorge Newbery domestic airport but he must have ran it close. He could hear his luggage hurtling across the trunk, thumping left on the right-hand corners before being hurled back right on the left-hand corners, the demented grin of his driver visible in the rear-view mirror. It saved him from conversation, though a seatbelt would have been nice.

They came to an abrupt halt at the entrance to the domestic departures. Mike clambered out, holding the door frame for support. He retrieved his bag from the popped trunk while the driver amused himself hunting the remnants of his last meal in and around his yellowed teeth with a toothpick. Mike closed the trunk and the cab crawled away, honking at a passenger to see if they would like to risk their life with him. Getting no response, the cab screeched off.

Mike extended out the handle of his luggage, hitched his shoulder bag up higher and entered through the large sliding doors that were marked with a green sign, *entrada*.

The departure hall was a convoluted mass of people and strewn baggage, though "hall" seemed a bit too grand a word for the large, shabby open area. Mike stood for a while trying to make sense of the lines of people that were entwined and writhing like balls of mating snakes. Behind him the sliding doors kept opening and bags were dragged across the back of his ankles as travelers threw themselves into the swirling ball of the stressed, anxious, and late.

He located the check-in desk of Austral airlines, and with his head attempted to trace the line backwards to its end. Having identified who he believed was close enough to the last person in the line, he set off through the bodies, with the firmness required when an "excuse me" brought no opening of the path, his luggage trailing behind him.

Finding a place in line he settled into wait. Ahead of him some travelers had laid down, heads resting on their bags, making the most of, if not a bad situation, a common one. Mike cursed his own tardiness. His flight was due to depart in three hours and he knew he should have arrived earlier. Now he would be cutting it fine.

Over the loudspeaker, the one reserved for paging late and lost passengers, a woman apologized for the delays. Mike imagined it must be a full-time job. Austral's baggage handlers had been on strike since Monday. As an affiliate of the now state-owned airline, they felt that a state-sponsored raise was in order. Until a deal was done, only a skeleton crew were manning the shifts.

The line inched forward, travelers awoke, shook their heads clear, slid their baggage forward with a lazy foot and reassumed their slumbering positions. When Mike heard the boarding call for flight AR2382 departing from Buenos Aires to Montevideo he broke ranks with his fellow sufferers and headed for the check-in, excusing himself in loud, tourist English as he went, ignoring the Spanish insults that followed him, knowing that to acknowledge would be to break cover.

At the check-in desk, again the loud tourist English, the confused and worried look, did the trick. Advancing age had its benefits. The pretty girl behind the desk, with her hair slicked back and held tight in a bun, could not have been more accommodating to the *Senor* and he was checked in and ticketed. He dared not look back at the lines behind him and could only imagine what they were thinking at his preferential treatment. Second-class citizens in their own country.

He passed through security, the distracted agents glancing at his identification card and boarding pass with the barest of interest. As his bag passed through the scanner, he noted that the woman monitoring the computer was distracted by a joke with her colleague seated on an adjacent scanner.

He arrived at gate 10 as the last of the passengers on flight AR2382 were heading out a large wooden door marked, *salida*. He handed his ticket to a lady that resembled the lady who had checked him in, then made his way through the door.

On the other side of the door was a flight of metal stairs. He manhandled his luggage down the stairs before coming out into a waiting room of sorts. Through a set of sliding doors, he could see a bus filled with passengers. By the stares levelled in his direction they could only be waiting for one person. He walked onto the bus, pushing some legs and knees out of the way to make room for his baggage. He reached up to grab the metal bar that ran overhead. Thus supported, he waited for the bus to move off.

It didn't and the passengers began to grumble. Mike strained his head to look towards where the driver should have been sitting. There was just an empty chair. A voice called out that there was no driver. An air of dissent and frustration caught like wildfire through the bus. In no time people who had been standing side by side in silence, joined only in their hatred of the late-arriving gringo, struck up heated conversations that started with wondering about the whereabouts of the driver and moved onto the need for complete political renewal if Argentina was ever going to be the country it should be.

There was a real anger and passion in the rhetoric, at one stage Mike had to duck to avoid a stray hand that was making a vehement point. He would not have been surprised if the passengers had commandeered the bus and driven it into the city and through the front doors of the congress. As always, it never got past heated conversation.

The driver appeared, a half-eaten empanada the only indicator that his lateness was culinary not political. He raised an unapologetic hand in apology and took his seat behind the wheel. The bus lurched off, throwing Mike into the passenger behind him who responded with an unimpressed grunt. Mike shrugged.

At the top of the steps of the plane a stewardess greeted Mike and pointed towards seat 4A. He placed his luggage in the overhead compartment and settled into the faux leather window seat. He fastened his seatbelt, pulling it tight against his hips. He produced his phone and checked for messages more out of habit than expectation. He switched it off and returned it to his jacket pocket.

A large man occupied the seat beside him, grey hair slicked back, five o'clock shadow. He had the air of a businessman. They all did when he thought about it. An upward nod of the head and raised eyebrows all the greeting he got. The man then produced a copy of *La Nacion* and tucked it into the seat pocket in front of him.

And then they sat, side by side, waiting for the sound of engines to shake the evening air and signal that they would soon be departing. No signal came, the engines remained silent. Mike looked out the window, a trailer full of bags was sitting unattended under the wing. Other passengers noticed too. The skeleton crew had not got around to flight AR2382 just yet.

Again, the mutinous, conversational wildfire ran through the passengers. The man in 4B, who only minutes ago could not spare a word of greeting to Mike, now launched into a tirade about the complete and absolute hopelessness of Argentina, the corruptibility of its political class, and the need for a return to *mano dura*, dictatorship. His hands banged against the head rest in front of him, striking with each point he made. Mike sat in silence nodding in sympathy rather than agreement.

Argentines could throw themselves into criticism of their country with full abandon, even delight. It was like criticizing family, fine for them to do but they would not abide a bad word from someone outside the family. That was one of the few trespasses that could cause arguments to migrate from words to action.

The turning of the engines put a premature end to the conversations and peace reigned again aboard flight AR2382. Mike fingered the ashtray on his armrest. The flip-up lid had been soldered shut in a token effort to modernize the fleet.

The plane taxied out to the runway and made its headlong dash westwards, gained the air and arced up and north, over the River Plate and towards Uruguay. Mike could see the twinkling lights on the opposite bank of the river, the town of Colonia, he calculated.

He had spent many a pleasant weekend in Colonia. Maybe the move to Sicily wasn't necessary. He could still sell the apartment in Recoleta, and just move across the river. He could manage Buenos Aires in small doses, coming and going as he pleased, dipping in and out, enjoying what he loved and leaving the rest. Hanging out high over the River Plate, banking southwards, Mike knew he was fooling himself, like a man offering up the option of an open relationship to keep an unfaithful wife.

Somehow he drifted off to sleep only to be awoken by the cabin light of his neighbor who had decided that now would be a good time to read his paper. Mike stretched his legs out, one at a time, making use of the limited leg room. The solder on the ashtray had left an indentation on the underside of his forearm. Awake now, he began to read over his neighbor's shoulder, or more accurately his hairy forearm. He read about the release of Paula Saa's son, the investigators having concluded that it was unlikely that he had raped and strangled his mother in a sadistic sex game. Pity, the story could have run for a few more years on that alone.

On page two, uproar that the Boca–River game had been brought forward by two days to a Wednesday night. The rescheduling had caused havoc with the hooligans' plans to sell merchandise, legal and otherwise, scalp fake tickets, and prepare for battle against their opposing fans. Uninterested in another long article on the government's plans to restructure the navy's leadership, Mike waited for his neighbor to turn the page.

On page three, the face of Simon Quinn stared back at him. Mike thought of Governor Castelli seeing the same picture and wondering who he had met that day in Cordoba. The photo didn't show the light, refreshed Simon of that afternoon. It showed the worried, harried face of a man dodging reporters, something to hide, eyes down, planner of atrocities and treason. A photo from the archives. He read the article, which offered nothing new, a recap of the week's events, a well-placed story to keep the government's investigation front of mind or thereabouts.

Mike pointed at the picture and broke cover. "What do you think about this?" he asked his neighbor.

The man turned and stared, surprised at being interrupted. He seemed to consider the question.

"*Que se yo*? What would I know? It's the same bullshit as always. This bloke," he tapped the photo of Simon with the back of his fingers. "Is either trying to steal from the government or the government's trying to steal from him. Who knows? It's all a show that they put on to keep us idiots entertained and here we are reading about it."

"I read that he's going to release some evidence tomorrow. About what the government's been up to."

The man scoffed. He raised his hand, palm upwards, thumb and fingers pinched together to form a small pyramid and shook it back and forth in front of Mike's face.

"He isn't going to release shit. It's all *arreglado.*" Organized, set up, stitched up, fixed. *Arreglado*, the catch-all phrase to say that nothing will change, the decisions have been made, and it is out of our power to influence, decide or even understand.

The man continued. "If he has something that could hurt the government then a deal's been done and we'll never know about it."

"And if he hasn't done a deal?"

The man looked at Mike, with something like pity in his eyes. "With or without a deal they won't let him talk. Like I said, it's all *arreglado*, this shit is just to sell us papers, make us look this way while they rob the country blind." He snapped up the page of the paper, ending the conversation, and Mike's casual reading.

Mike thought about what the man had said. He was right, the government would never let Quinn talk. Mike felt a flush of panic. His neighbor's words begun to echo around the cabin, over the roar of the plane's engines. The government would never let Simon Quinn talk.

He reached for his cell phone. He turned it on and waited. He tried to dial. Of course, no signal. He called the flight attendant.

"How long until we land?"

"Another 40 minutes."

"I need to make a phone call. Now," Mike pleaded.

"That is not possible, sir. Once we land you will be able to use your cell phone." She reached above Mike and turned off the small light that he had used to call her and spotted the lit-up phone display.

"Sir, I have to ask you to turn off your phone, please." Mike obeyed, he had no choice. Strapped into a lounge chair inside a metal tube, travelling at 900km an hour, 30,000 feet above the Argentine coast, even if he were not too late Mike had no way of warning Simon Quinn.

As the plane touched down on the tarmac at the Carrasco International Airport Mike had his cell phone on. He dialed Simon's number. Straight to voice mail. He tried again. Same result. He dialed a third time, no longer expecting an answer. He left a message, all the while imagining the faceless men huddled in a room who might still be listening into Quinn's tapped phone.

Before the plane had come to a stop the passengers, ignoring repeated pleas from the attendants still strapped into their seats at the front of the plane, were standing, pulling luggage from the overhead lockers, preparing for the mad dash to be first off the plane, and devil take the hindmost.

As the last passenger went down the aisle Mike remained seated. The same flight attendant he had spoken to earlier appeared at his side.

"Sir, you can make that call now," she said, smiling her best, brochure smile.

CHAPTER 37

Café Dos Escudos was empty except for the table located in the far, back corner. A lone customer hunched over a free, half-drunk cup of *americano*. When he entered he had asked the waitresses to turn off the small television set.. Mike being a regular, they had obliged. He had been in every morning since returning from Montevideo.

In the Uruguayan capital Mike had spent the morning waiting in the reception area of the British embassy. No, they had no record of his appointment. Yes, they had asked everyone in the office, nobody was expecting him. At the suggestion of the internal security, a gentle palm on his elbow, he had exited the embassy. That afternoon as he waited in the Carrasco International Airport departure lounge he had received a phone call from the British embassy in Buenos Aires. Would he be available to meet with a Mr. Jeremy Nason, our newly arrived Second Secretary? It made no sense but he had agreed to the appointment, tired of casting into the wind.

Mike stared out the window of Café Dos Escudos, a man sitting by the Limay River, watching his thoughts float by, chasing some, letting others continue unimpeded down the rippling waters. The morning held none of the heat of the previous weeks, a false autumn day and like a kiss in a bar it promised things to come but not right now. All in good time. It was one of those days with the perfect mix of sunlight and warmth with a sky so blue it seemed to ache. If you looked up, you couldn't help but wonder just how far on that blue went for. If today was your first day in Buenos Aires, you would want to live there forever.

He had watched the fate of Simon Quinn slide down the pages of the papers, another leaf in the forest of intrigue, that bloomed green, faded, fell from the branches of public interest and was blown away. The story had started life on the front page, under the factual headline, "Multinational Executive Found Dead." It held none of the salaciousness of the Paula Saa case. If Simon had had a habit of frequenting the transvestites that plied their nocturnal trade at the Rosendal or a penchant for young boys, then he may have garnered an extended run.

The first articles carried the bare facts. Simon Quinn had been found on the pavement below his sixth-floor apartment balcony in the stylish suburb of Recoleta. The insertion of the word stylish a small boost for Buenos Aires tourism for when the international press agencies picked up the story. A woman found the body while out walking her greyhound early on the Wednesday morning. No signs of life. The police were called, the time for ambulances having already passed.

The president had felt the need to pronounce on another tragic suicide connected to what now seemed to be an ill-fated project. A tragedy, yes, but let us not forget what brought this young man to take this unpardonable action. He had engaged in unconscionable behavior, corrupt behavior aimed at subverting honest, hard-working Argentines, and when he felt the arm of Argentine justice to be near he had responded with an unjust and criminal ultimatum, one that the Argentine people could never accept.

If he had proof of government interference, of inappropriate government behavior, of corruption, a word that the Yankees like to throw around Latin America, a word never spoken in their own homes, then let him bring it, let him show it, let the courts examine it. His broken body lying on the pavement of Recoleta is the proof of his proofs. When he saw that we would not be intimidated, that we would respond to threats with firmness rather than fear, then he took the coward's way out.

That was Thursday evening. On Friday morning, the *La Nacion* front page carried a story linking the government to the death of Simon Quinn. Nothing factual, just the lightest application of innuendo, like a smear placed at the bottom of a petri dish that under the right conditions would multiply and grow. Cunning journalism that would allow the reader's mind to form the conclusions that great journalism could not. The story was picked up in the senate with the opposition, better informed than *La Nacion*, raining questions upon the government delegates. In response, the government flooded the streets of Buenos Aires with bare-chested sympathizers, faces covered by grimy T-shirts, hands wrapped around pickets and bats, old bottles of Coca-Cola filled with clear liquid, masses bussed in from the humblest neighborhoods of greater Buenos Aires. What could not be won in the senate would be scrapped for in the street. The opposition, sensing blood, raised its own army of support and took to the streets. The country was in crisis. Again.

So, on Friday afternoon, the president stood on the steps of the presidential residency and spoke not of the chaos in the street, not of the families dying of starvation in the northern province of Chaco, not of inflation that was hitting 40 percent, not of the navy who were refusing to recognize their new leadership, but of the murder of Simon Quinn.

"Let us not be fooled by what is happening here. It is easy to look at events and be puzzled. There are people, enemies of the Argentine people, who set out to confuse, to divide, to destroy. We believed that the young executive who was found dead had taken his own life. Today we know that this is not true. He was suicided. Suicided by those who wish to discredit this government. Those who wish to reverse the reforms of this government. Suicided by those who would stop at nothing to eliminate the gains made in the decade that we have won, won from history, won from those who do not believe in Argentina, won from those who wish to see a return to *mano dura,* dictatorship. Sometimes our enemies are not across the oceans, they are not outside our borders. Sometimes our enemies come from within, sometimes our enemies are those that are meant to protect us. We cannot let ourselves become complacent, we cannot delude ourselves. Those that oppose us will not play fair. They will not respect our rights. They will stop at nothing to achieve their nefarious aims."

Mike let go of the memory, letting it swirl and eddy and disappear around the bend. A final thought. Simon

Quinn's body, broken and bent as the papers had showed it, was more flexible in death than ever it was in life.

CHAPTER 38

The third-floor office had the stale feel of bureaucracy. Lampshades wiped down by professional cleaners, carpets shampooed once a month, the picture of Queen Elizabeth hanging square on the wall. Mike Costello stood by a large bookcase that ran the length of the eastern wall opposite the double-plated, soundproof window. His back to the door, he studied the shelves of books, running a distracted finger down the spines, one hand stuffed deep into his trouser pocket. The movement of his finger stopped upon the spine of a light-blue cover. He tilted his head sideways to better read the gold inlaid title printed on the book's spine. As he did so the door to the office opened and he spun to face a short man, pasty complexion, suit and tie, all official bustle, tight-faced with worry.

The man extended his hand to Mike, as if at a funeral. "Jeremy Nason." Mike expected him to say, "My condolences" but he said instead, "Nice to meet you." Mike shook his hand and took a seat at the desk while Jeremy made himself comfortable on the opposite side. Jeremy made a sweeping motion with his hand, taking in the office. "All Alex's stuff. I'm afraid I haven't had time to box it up and get it out of here." He said it as though Alex Harper's belongings were a constant source of annoyance for him. "He of course didn't get a chance. Leaving in such a hurry."

Mike just nodded, unwilling to decide the direction of the conversation just yet, happy to observe the man sent out to replace Alex Harper. Jeremy shuffled some papers that required no shuffling, opened and closed a drawer without removing or depositing anything, then brought his eyes to Mike.

"So, Mr. Costello. Thank you for coming in."

Mike was owed some answers but there was also the question of what Jeremy Nason wanted from Mike.

"I am curious to know how I can help," said Mike.

"No use beating around the bush. Alex's, shall we say, rushed departure, negated the usual handover procedure one could expect to have when coming into a new posting. That makes my job a little more difficult. Places me in an awkward position of not knowing as much as I should. A bit embarrassing, in our line of work." He reached out and shuffled some more papers, all part of the art of appearing nervous. Mike sat sill, refusing to throw the new man a lifeline.

"Your name has appeared quite a lot in Alex's briefing papers. Yet you are not listed among his official contacts. Nor can I see any payments that have been made to you from the fund. So, if I were to ask one question of you, I would like to know what it is you did for Alex?"

"He was a friend. We ate lunch together sometimes."

"Did you provide information to him?"

"Nothing he would not have known already. More than information we discussed events, what was happening, what things meant. I am sure he was much better informed than I. Or at least I hope he was."

Nason ignored the joke. "Did he ever pass information to you?"

"Never anything useful," Mike said. "Sometimes he would recommend I speak to a company who he felt needed some help. That was about it."

Jeremy made some notes on a writing pad. He stopped and re-read his writing, placing a line through a word. "And did Alex ever ask for any compensation for these, shall we call them, leads?"

"No, never. I mean, I paid for lunch sometimes, but that was because he was always complaining about how little he got paid."

"So you bought him lunches?"

"Yes, but not in exchange for anything. As any friend would."

Jeremy scribbled this down as well.

"Did you ever discuss the Falkland's situation with Alex?" He looked up and brought his hands together in front of his face, his pen pointing in Mike's direction across the table.

"He would often mention the Malvinas. He said it was his reason for being here."

"Malvinas? Is that how he referred to the Falklands?" Nason asked, scribbling away before poising to capture Mike's answer.

"Always," said Mike, enjoying the lie that set Nason's pen scribbling.

"What else did he say?"

Mike rubbed the palms of his hands on the tops of his trouser legs as he thought back. He tried to remember.

He had only agreed to meet with Jeremy Nason to get answers as to why Alex Harper had frozen his assets. As he listened to Nason's questions he felt that answering them would bring him closer to answering his own questions.

"He was concerned that British companies might upset the government, which might put the Falklands back in the news."

"What British companies?"

"There was an incident with a ship, the *Polar Mist* and their insurer, Lloyd's of London."

Again Nason bent over his notepad, scribbling away, capturing every word, muttering something about the case sounding familiar.

"What other companies?"

"A client of mine," said Mike, with more caution, feeling like he was now approaching fertile territory for himself and his questioner, as if all previous questions were leading to MinEx.

Nason dug through some papers that were tucked at the back of his notebook. He paused and read through them, flicking back and forth.

"MinEx," he said without a trace of doubt.

Mike's silence served as an affirmative answer.

"Your name pops up quite a lot in relation to MinEx in Alex's notes. Seems like you were quite the expert on them. Would that be fair to say?"

"I wouldn't say expert. They were a client. I advised them."

"And you shared the advice you gave MinEx with Alex?"

"No." Mike thought back on his conversations with Alex. More like Alex advising him. Alex telling him what should be done. Alex telling Mike what he would like Simon to do, what Alex needed Simon to do to not upset the government.

"And no money was ever exchanged between you?"

"Never," Mike reaffirmed.

"I apologize for the questions, Mr. Costello. Just trying to understand the situation that's all. I am sure you understand."

Mike was beginning to understand but he was no longer focused on Jeremy's question. He had come with one question in mind, one that had been percolating in his brain since he had held the Mareva Injunction in his hand and ran his thumb over Alex Harper's signature at the bottom of the page. Why would Alex freeze his assets? Now it was clear. He needed Mike in Argentina. To watch over MinEx. To be Alex's eyes and ears on the ground, guide MinEx's movements, make sure Simon Quinn's actions aligned with the interests of the British government. Preventing Mike from selling his apartment ensured he had someone to do his bidding. Mike had to admit it was well played. The type of cunning trick he struggled to come up with.

"Why was Alex so interested in MinEx?"

"He said he was concerned that they would create a scandal by paying bribes."

"They have a history of that in Africa."

"And I am sure that your government never cared about that. What had Alex so concerned, Jeremy?"

Jeremy closed his notebook and laid his pen on the cover, an act to show that they were going off the record.

"To be honest, I am not sure what Alex was up to here."

"What do you know?"

Nason looked out the window, considering how much to share. "The Argentine government borrowed a hundred and fifty million dollars from the Inter-American Development Bank. We campaigned, behind closed doors of course, for the bank to not make this loan. Alex had developed information that the money was to be used to re-arm the navy. A fully equipped navy presented a legitimate threat to our interests in the Falklands. When the loan was then passed on to MinEx, Alex believed that it would be siphoned back to the government through illegal payments. That will not be happening now." It was the first reference to Simon Quinn's death. Both men let it lie untouched between them, a verbal cadaver, face down.

It was not Simon Quinn's face that was in Mike's mind but the sunburnt face of Alex Harper, adorned with his girlfriend's sunglasses, smiling back at him on Peru Beach. *You've made your home around the edges, Mike, you never see the big picture.* That's what he had said. The replay of Alex's words forced him to reflect. A vision of himself came into sharp relief. As if he had been holding a magnifying glass a little too close to the small print, revealing only blurred outlines and now he had raised his hand an inch or two, and at the correct distance, the full text was brought into sharp and alarming detail. He was tired of giving people the answers piece by piece but never seeing the finished puzzle.

"Jeremy, I need you to lift the Mareva Injunction from my apartment."

Nason nodded, not bothering to deny the injunction or explain why it had been placed. Just another mess of Alex Harper's that he would be forced to clean up.

"I will let you know as soon as it is done."

"One last thing," said Mike, getting to his feet. "I leant Alex a book a while back. I think I saw it on the shelf there when you came in. Do you mind if I take it back? I am sure the bastard never read it."

Jeremy forced his mouth into what passed as a smile, allowing the tension of the interview to diffuse. "Take the lot. You'd be doing me a favor," he said.

Mike stood in front of the bookshelf and located the book with the light-blue cover and gold inlaid print that he had seen when he arrived. He tucked the book into his shoulder bag.

"I look forward to hearing from you soon," he said and left Jeremy Nason to his questions, half-truths and shadows.

Chapter 39

The tea room at the Alvear Hotel began to fill with the aged and infirm of Recoleta. The grey-haired women wore light dresses that hung down over their crepe-paper-thin, sun-blotched skin, with wrists and fingers encrusted by an excess of jewelry that appeared so heavy as to pin their arms to their sides. If not accompanied by women cut from the same expensive cloth, they were led by the arm by slow-moving gentlemen, grey hair swept back and held in place by gel, decked out in three-piece suits. Gentlemen who time had converted into mere human Zimmer frames for the use of their sprightlier better halves.

The polished parquet flooring reflected the light from the chandeliers above them. Noises came from the kitchen. Mike sat at a table near the back of the tea room, cutlery and plates for two people set out before him. He glanced at the book that sat on the chair beside him and then to the doorway. Still not too late to get up and walk out. He looked at the book again. He could walk out now but if he did he would never have anywhere to go.

He had not been seated long before the Doctor walked in, smoothing his hair down as if in apology for interrupting the gossip of the waiters who stood huddled by the buffet table. He sat down opposite Mike.

"A bit fancy for you, Mike," he said, arching his neck to take in the chandelier above him.

"I haven't been here for quite a while. I always thought it belonged to the *Porteños* that thought they were living in Paris. Last time I was here was a job for Lady Safra. I spent a week camped out on the ninth floor. I was never quite sure of the purpose of my detail, whether it was to keep her safe or make sure that she was unaware of the prostitutes that her male relatives were ferrying in and out at all hours of the day. A fantastic tipper though, either way."

"Can I get you another?" The Doctor asked, pointing at Mike's coffee.

"I'm OK."

The Doctor looked around for the waiters who had disappeared into the kitchen.

"Nice obituary, really nice," he said. "I got a sense of who Simon was."

Mike tilted his head to the side. The Doctor was being sincere.

"That's about all we can hope for, isn't it? A nice obituary. That we've left enough of a mark on someone that they would take the time to put pen to paper. And though they could fill books with why we were the worst piece of shit they've ever come across, they ignore that and distil us to the best bits. Like watching the goals on the news at night without having to sit through the whole match."

Mike hoped the Doctor was wrong. He feared he wasn't.

"How are we now?"

"I spoke with Donald Duck. The Planning Minister won't last the week. They're saying the whole government may come down. Donald's confident that this won't go any further for us. Poor old Decoud has now lost political relevance, there'll be no more resources wasted on his death. A new government will have even less interest in pursuing this. That's good. Still, won't hurt to keep our heads down for a while.

"On your client, as we would expect. No footage from the building's security cameras. The electricity had been cut to the building for the previous week. Neighbors thought it was just the usual summer outages. They swapped out the doorman two weeks back. No one had seen the guy before and no one has seen him since. The security company claims not to know anything. I did find one interesting thing though. Appears Simon had a secretary, Cecilia Moya?"

Mike nodded.

"Before MinEx, she worked for Customs, out at the airport. Before that, the Ministry of Planning. Attractive girl from what I've seen. He wasn't sleeping with her, was he?"

Mike shrugged as if to say he didn't know and he didn't care.

"Strange," said the Doctor.

Mike stared out the window, steeling himself.

"I have something for you, Doctor," he said.

The Doctor's face lit up. Mike reached beside him, took hold of the book that he had retrieved from Alex Harper's office and placed it on the table between himself and the Doctor. The title, printed in gold inlaid text on the pale-blue cover read: *A History of British Naval Battles 1785-1805.*

Mike had not known what reaction to expect. He had been trembling in nervous excitement since the Doctor had sat down. It wasn't fear, more like the slight tremble he would feel on a cold morning on the river, before the first cast. It was a tremble more of expectation, of standing on the edge of the unknown. He studied the Doctor's face. A resigned smile, a little forced, spread across his features. He reached out and took the book in his hands, opened it, and flicked through the pages as if seeing it for the first time. He closed the book and placed it back on the table between them. He sat back in his chair and placed his clasped hands on the table in front of him, a gesture of compliance, Mike hoped.

"So you know," he said. Mike sensed relief in his voice. As if he had been going down a trail alone and Mike had at last caught him up. "Where did you get this?"

"I will get to that. But I have some questions of my own first," said Mike.

The Doctor nodded in acceptance.

Mike had a thousand unordered questions and struggled to avoid every question erupting from him at once.

When he had left the office of Jeremy Nason he had sat down at a nearby café and opened the book. Inside he had found the underlining and marking of words as he had seen in the copy of the same book that he had found face down on the Doctor's coffee table. The Doctor was not translating the book for the Naval Museum. Nor was the book a facetious threat from Jeremy Wainwright. The book was their cipher for communicating, a perfect choice that would raise no suspicions if found in the possession of either. The proof that the Doctor was an informant for the British embassy and had been passed on from Jeffrey Wainwright to Alex Harper.

It was unbelievable to Mike. Unbelievable that he had never seen it. Were there any signs that he missed? He couldn't be sure. But didn't it mean something that he had put it together in the end? Or was it just luck? Maybe he had made his own luck. Even knowing that the connection was real, knowing everything he did of the history of his adopted country, it made no sense to Mike that Julian Martinelli, an ex-Argentine navy officer would be willing to help the British government.

Mike raised his coffee to his lips, dousing any emotion that may try to escape. He needed to remain calm.

"Alex Harper used me to manipulate Simon Quinn and MinEx," he started. "As the domestic situation deteriorated, Alex feared that the government would resort to raising the specter of taking back the Falklands. For that to be a credible promise they needed a navy that was armed and operable. Alex had information that the Inter-American Development bank loan was to be laundered through MinEx. The government's objective was to use that money to re-arm the Argentine navy with the purchase of materials from China."

"Very good, Mike."

"And the submarines that were already purchased?"

"Rendered inoperable by our people here once they arrived. Alex was very helpful in that. Just a simple case of disabling the operating software."

"Why would you collaborate with the British to hobble your own navy?"

Laughter echoed around the room as the Doctor rocked back in his chair. He turned his head sideways as if checking to see if anyone else shared in his mirth.

"You are always so close, Mike, aren't you? But that last piece just alludes you. I suppose it can't hurt to share the whole picture with you for once. It will give you something to reflect on when you are on that beach in Sicily."

At the mention of Sicily, Mike realized what should have been obvious from the time he discovered the cipher book. Mike would have been a topic of discussion between Alex and the Doctor. How they must have laughed at him. He felt the humiliation rising in his throat.

"These bastards in government did not want to re-arm the navy for the defense of our nation, so that we can do the job that the constitution entrusts to us. They wanted to re-arm the navy so that they could send us to a war that we could never win, so that they could gain sympathy at home and abroad, so they could consolidate their rotten power, and distract the masses with an act of phony nationalism."

An incredible piece of justification. "So you collaborated with the enemy to stop the funds reaching the government."

"In the beginning, yes. We were once at war with the British but where our interests align then we are allies."

"What do you mean in the beginning?"

"Our initial aim was to stop the IDB money being funneled back to the government. But then the situation changed, bigger opportunities presented themselves."

Mike's mind raced, trying to catch up with the Doctor's words. What bigger opportunities? Images shifted and blurred in his mind, conversations replayed, fast forwarded, analyzed, re-interpreted but through new lenses, one where anything was possible, one where the possibilities were not limited to his own morality or experience.

"You planned this whole fucking thing from the start. You knew how this would play out."

The Doctor smiled. "You give me too much credit, Mike. I reacted to opportunities that presented themselves. That is all."

"You sent me to Cordoba."

"No, I told you to send Simon. You went yourself. You were fortunate that I had asked them to spare Simon's face. I must be going soft."

"There were no Truckers Union thugs. More of Alex Harper's bullshit."

"I prefer to call it misinformation, Mike. Our goal was to stop MinEx providing the government with the money they needed. But then the government made a mistake that I took advantage of."

"When they killed Decoud?"

"The government did not kill Decoud. Decoud killed himself."

"But the nurse said—"

"The nurse said what I paid him to say, Mike." The patience was gone from the Doctor's voice. "Decoud called me before he came to Buenos Aires. He had discovered that the government was inflating the prices of the contract and intending to funnel it back to themselves. I encouraged him to go to the media. The government got wind of it and threatened to expose him as being on their payroll. They had been seeding him for months, small payments into his campaign accounts and he never knew it. It would have been the end of everything he had worked for if that got out. He would have been humiliated. He took the only option left to him."

"And that was the government's mistake? Paying Decoud?"

"No. Claiming that Decoud's death wasn't suicide. Trying to use it to their advantage, trying to pin in it on MinEx."

"You knew that Simon would want to fight them," said Mike, catching up. "And that I would help him."

"And a wonderful job you both did, Mike," said the Doctor. "Once I had the recording of Lopez claiming credit for the murder of Decoud and threatening you with the same, a much larger opportunity presented itself. I just needed you to convince Simon to release the recording."

"The government would never let Simon release the tape, you must have known they would kill him first."

"That did cross my mind," the Doctor said. "The government has history. But that was not our first thought. We hoped that if Simon released the tape it may bring down the government if we could mobilize enough support in the street. A new government may be more amenable to our views."

"Bullshit. You knew they would kill him. You killed him," said Mike. He could have been speaking to himself. "You set him up as the enemy of the government, you enabled him knowing full well what would happen to him."

The old navy intelligence officer paused. The mouth that had held back so many secrets tensed, as if he were about to elaborate. No words came and the moment passed. He said, "You played your part too, remember, Mike."

"And Montevideo. The British embassy."

The Doctor nodded again, seeming to take no pleasure in this deceit. "I did that for you. If you were out of the country the government couldn't accuse you of anything. I am going soft."

A sick feeling spun through Mike's stomach, his fingers, wrapped tight around his coffee cup, his skin itched, irritated at every point of contact with his clothing. The Doctor was right. Mike was culpable. He hadn't seen what was happening and all the while he was leading his client to his death. He was a player, a bit part player on a stage that he never recognized he was on, repeating lines that had been written for him without ever recognizing their meaning or intent. He may as well have thrown Quinn from the balcony himself.

Mike felt the Doctor's eyes on him, he seemed to be reading Mike's mind. "Don't beat yourself up, Mike. How were you to know? Sometimes there is no big picture, no master plan to discover. Life is just a series of moments that exists outside the limits of philosophy and ethics. It is such a small way to live, within the bounds of these concepts, trying to justify every action to satisfy some moral fabric that doesn't even exist. You do not have to be good to do good, Mike. Why should anything be off limits in the pursuit of your own objectives? Do you know why you will never fit in here? Because you refuse to let go of this moral framework that has no place here. You insist on judging yourself by a code that doesn't exist. You limit yourself to the course of action that is justifiable. Imagine the possibilities if nothing needed to be justified? If every option were open? That is freedom. That is power. A certain kind of power that you will never know, Mike."

The Doctor placed his hand on the book that still lay on the table between them. Before he could slide it towards him Mike's hand shot out with a speed that surprised them both and claimed the book.

"Not so fast, Doctor. Your story may play well to yourself. But I wonder how it would play in the press or in front of a court." Mike clicked his tongue. "I am not sure it would do very well." He waggled the book in the air. "I am going to keep this for now. And when I call, you had better fucking pick up, when I have a question you better have the fucking answer, when I need a hole you better have a fucking shovel."

The Doctor stared back at him, his head tilted, unsure if Mike was joking or not. The Doctor appeared a foreigner on the low ground. Deciding that Mike wasn't joking he said, "The book proves nothing. You are out of your depth, Mike. Get on the plane and go. You don't belong here. You never will." He pushed back from the table and stood to leave. He took three steps towards the door before the sound of his own voice stopped him short. He turned back to where Mike still sat, his telephone in hand and coming from the speaker the Doctor's recorded words: *We were once at war with the British but where our interests align then we are allies.*

No more favors. It felt good to do the fucking.

CHAPTER 40

The travel agency was a small affair located on the corner of Posadas and Montevideo. Posters advertising exotic holiday destinations covered the front window. Mike approached from the opposite sidewalk. From a radio on the counter of a laundromat the Intoxicados were singing of the necessity of hating before you could begin to love. A lyric for Buenos Aires and one Mike only now understood. He stopped at the traffic light, waited for the street to fill with cars, then crossed. The little green man was still under suspicion.

Some mornings as he passed by the agency on his way to the Dos Escudos café Mike would stop and examine the fifteen-day options for cruising down the Danube or the six-week odyssey through the Stans—Uzbekistan, Kazakhstan, Turkmenistan, Tajikistan, and Kyrgyzstan. Whenever he thought his job was difficult, he spared a thought for the tourism ministers of the Stans.

How many times had he walked past this door and thought of Sicily?

This morning he pushed through the glass door. A bell tinkled above him alerting the pleasant-faced girl at the desk at the back of the shop. The girl recognized him and waved him in. The agency also represented the Buquebus.

"Good morning, Sr. Costello," she said. "Off to Uruguay, are we?"

"No, no, not Uruguay," he said. "I'd like to look into options to Sicily."

The girl's face went blank. "Here in Argentina?" she asked, her fingers pecking at the keyboard in front of her, the letters worn off the keys.

"Sicily. Italy," Mike clarified. "The island off Italy."

Her brow furrowed as she renewed her attack on the keyboard. "Here we go. We don't get many requests for Sicily," she said in apology of her own ignorance. "Let me bring up some options for you. Just yourself traveling?"

Mike nodded.

"One way or return?"

Forgetting that he had been fired, Finklestein had rung the day before to advise that the Mareva Injunction had been lifted from Mike's apartment. Finklestein was happy to take the credit for it though Mike suspected Jeremy Nason was the real reason. Finklestein also had a potential buyer who was willing to offer, if not Mike's asking price, a reasonable approximation and one that Mike should accept in this current housing market. Mike had no doubt that Finklestein himself was behind the offer. Mike had declined. Argentina hadn't changed, he knew she never would. Wasn't that what he himself had told Quinn? He had refused to hear it himself though. To hope for her to change was madness just as it was madness to think that he could exist at the edge, swim without getting wet, mold her to his own desires. Even to love her as she is without letting go of all he had loved before was impossible.

"Return," Mike said.

He waited as the girl went through the administrative process of the purchase. Half an hour later she printed out the tickets and sealed them in a neat envelope. Mike paid for the tickets in cash and placed the envelope in his jacket pocket.

He walked out of the travel agency and on to the street. A beggar sat against the window of a laundromat, hand outstretched, a look of drugged distance in her eyes. The skin on her exposed legs was scabbed and caked with filth. Mike paused and looked at the pathetic, upturned face.

"At least do something to earn it," he said. "Bang a drum or juggle or whistle." The girl stared back at him, her hand still raised.

"*Una moneda?*" she begged.

"A coin? Sorry, darling, all I have is a wallet full of notes."

He looked up at the sky. By the time he returned from Sicily it would be winter. And in winter Mike Costello could lose himself on the streets of Buenos Aires.

ACKNOWLEDGEMENTS

This story would not be what it is without the time and efforts of so many people. I want to thank Greg Cormack for bringing his unique and insightful sense of story to the manuscript. His structural edits really are a book in themselves and were often far more entertaining than my own efforts. To Lauren Finger, not just for the editing work but for being a guide through the book publishing process. Thank you to my first readers; for your compassionate lies, for not snuffing out my flame of creativity when it was at its most vulnerable. Thank you to my parents for bringing me to live amongst the humans. Finally, thank you to my wonderful wife, Carolina, who lived with half a husband for 12 months, who let me roam the streets of Buenos Aires in my mind, who was constantly woken at 3am as I scrambled to commit an idea to paper; who surfed the depression of a failed plot twist alongside me, who understood, forgave, encouraged, inspired and smiled; who never let me forget that what I was doing was the most important thing in the world and didn't mean a thing.